If I Could Fly

If I Could Fly

Fly

Book two of the Being Me series

by Tricia Copeland

True Bird Publishing LLC

If I Could Fly

Book two of the *Being Me* series
by Tricia Copeland

Copyright © 2015 True Bird Publishing LLC
All rights reserved

ISBN-13: 978-0692555880
ISBN-10: 0692555889

First Edition

License Notes:

Edited by Tia Silverthorne Bach
Proofread by Mollie Turbeville
Interior Formatting by Jo Michaels
all of Indie Books Gone Wild

Cover by Daryl A. McCool of d.a.m. Cool Graphics
Published by True Bird Publishing LLC, Superior, CO

Font: AlbertsthalTypewriter - © Lukas Krakora - Unlimited Commercial Use License Date 21 Oct. 2015 - All rights reserved

acknowledgements

To my dear friends Cheryl, Frances, Sara Elizabeth, Mindy, Danielle, and Amanda, you are truly the wind beneath my wings.

To my editor and dear friend, Tia Bach, you inspire me every day.

To my cover designer, Daryl McCool, thank you for your brilliant eye that perfectly captures my vision.

To my husband, and my kids, especially my daughter, thank you!

Thanks to all my readers, whose excitement for my characters keeps me creating more.

Chapter 1

Slipping into my dorm room, I listened for my roommate's snores. Hearing Elise suck in her breath and release it, I clicked the door closed. Tiptoeing to the bathroom, I turned on the light. I forced myself to brush my teeth and wash my face. My reflection hadn't changed much from when I'd stood here five hours ago. My cheeks were flushed and hair tousled, otherwise I looked the same. But everything was different. In one second, I had flipped my life. Tracing my fingers over my lips, the sensation of Doug's warm kisses pulsed through them.

I didn't want to hear Elise's opinion on my new relationship status and was glad she was already asleep. Doug wasn't a stellar example of a transparent person. Over the course of the last three months, I often pictured him as a tornado, sucking up and spitting out anything in his path. In the end, he was my own personal black hole, with me helpless to escape his gravitational force.

Sliding under my blanket, I shook off the thought and set an alarm on my phone. Then, I scrolled through my messages. The first was from Zack, and the second from Lila, my best friend. Thinking it would be the shortest, I read Zack's first.

JUST CHECKING THAT YOU MADE IT BACK SAFELY.

Ugh! That was way too nice of him. I sent a quick reply. YES, THANKS, AND I'M SORRY.

ME TOO, he sent back immediately.

Next, I braved reading Lila's messages. There were a string of them and the most recent one, now over half an hour old, read, WHERE DID YOU GO? ZACK'S HERE AND YOU'RE NOT. DID YOU LEAVE WITH DOUG?

I sent her a short reply. YES, LEFT WITH DOUG.

EVERYTHING OK? She typed back immediately.

YES. GOOD. VERY GOOD.

SO IT'S DOUG THEN?

YES.

OK.

Okay? Okay wasn't exactly positive. I told myself I didn't care. This was my decision, and it was the right one. No one else knew the depth of our relationship. Unfortunately, given that I'd hidden it from almost everyone, there'd be a fair amount of explanation needed.

Turning my phone over in my hand, I debated whether to call or text my sister, Marissa. With only eleven months between us, we'd always been close, and she and Elise were my only confidants the past few months. It was after one, and I decided to send her a message. I HAVE A NEW BOYFRIEND!

DOUG? She replied back immediately.

:) I sent.

I'M ASSUMING THERE WAS KISSING?

YES.

SO HAPPY FOR U! JUST GETTING IN BED. WANT DETAILS 2MORROW. LUV U, GOODNITE.

LUV U 2!

My pulse still raced as I scrolled through the music on my phone. Lying back, I put my headphones on and started the playlist Doug had created for me. I made the right decision, I repeated to myself. Even though I cared for Zack, being separated from Doug was pure torture. It'd felt like a part of my soul had been stripped away, and living with that pain was almost unbearable.

🕊 🕊 🕊

I bolted up when my alarm went off and hopped out of bed to silence it.

Elise spun her chair to face me. "Wow, what's got you up?"

Heading to the coffee pot, I took a moment to process last night. It wasn't a dream. Doug and I were finally on the same page.

"Rowing with Doug." I abandoned my coffee and popped into the bathroom before she could respond.

🕊 3 🕊

When I finished, she stood at the door, hands on her hips. "So, it's Doug?"

I crossed over to my closet. "Yes, and we have a date."

"At six in the morning?"

"I finally get to go rowing."

Shaking her head, she went back to her computer. The skies were gray and the weather report said it was twenty-four degrees. I dressed in layers and packed my gloves, hat, and mittens in my bag. My phone buzzed, indicating a text message from Doug.

GRABBING BREAKFAST. BE THERE IN 15.

I finished packing my bag and took the stairs down two at a time. It wasn't long before he stopped at the curb. He jumped out, wrapped an arm around me, and kissed me square on the lips.

"Good morning." He smiled, and I melted into him. "Ready for our first date?"

I nodded. "Yes."

"Good." He kissed me again and we walked around the car to the passenger's side.

The car was filled with the aroma of eggs, and my stomach growled. I picked up two Styrofoam boxes that lay in my seat and sat down. Buckling my belt, I opened one of the boxes to peek inside.

"Hey." He pushed the lid down. "Patience."

"But I'm starving." He rolled his eyes. I batted mine and stuck out my bottom lip. "I'll give you a bite."

"Fine," he said, starting the car.

Happy with my small victory, I opened the box, speared a huge bite of the omelet, and held it out to him. I took a bite of the piping hot eggs and shut the lid on the container.

"You talk to anyone?" he asked.

I quickly finished my bite. "Yeah, the usual."

"Zack?"

"I had a message from him. Did you talk to him?"

"Thought I would give him some space."

I nodded my head and tapped my hands on my legs while he wound through the streets near the lake. It was barely ten minutes before we parked in front of what looked like an abandoned warehouse.

"Okay, now what?" I got out of the car and scanned our surroundings while he retrieved a backpack and blanket from the trunk.

He shut the trunk. "Do you have a hat and gloves?"

I recovered them from my bag and showed them to him. "Running gloves, mittens, hat."

"Nice." He took the wool hat and put it on my head.

I waited while he unlocked the warehouse door. I stepped over the metal doorframe and onto a dirt floor. As my eyes adjusted to the low light, I saw rows and rows of boats. I walked to the middle of one aisle and turned back to him. "Can we go boating first?"

"Patience. I thought you were hungry."

I followed him to a small room in the corner. It was barely five by five. He lifted a heater from behind a desk and I backed up, allowing him to pass me. Back in the warehouse, he spread out the blanket and plugged in the heater. I took off the hat, mittens, and coat and sat down next to him.

As we ate, he fired question after question at me, filling in the past six weeks. I admitted I was pretty disappointed with my courses. I'd only gotten to take one introductory international studies course. The rest of my schedule was filled with the chemistry, biology, and calculus courses required for my chemistry double major. He asked about my friends and Dad, and I skirted the topic of how they might feel about our relationship.

When Doug finishing eating, I jumped up and skipped down the aisle between the boats. "Rowing now?"

"You barely touched your food. How old are you again?" He laughed but didn't move.

"What? I'm not allowed to be excited?"

"What's your dad going to think about us? How did he react to Zack?"

"Why does my dad matter? I don't care what he thinks." I tugged at his arm until he followed me. Walking down the aisles, he assessed my height, asked my exact weight, and finally questioned whether I'd actually be able to row with one arm in a sling. With only one week out of the cast, my arm was of little use. He chose a one-person boat and lifted it off the rack.

"We are being completely open now, right?"

I followed him out of the building and to the shore. "I made the right decision. He'll trust me." I didn't want to think about Dad or anything else but being with Doug.

Making sure all the buckles were tightened on my life jacket, he finally got us on the river. The swish of the oars slicing the water and the way we propelled over the surface was like nothing

I'd experienced before. His movements were powerful and elegant at the same time. I was more than content to stare at his beautiful face as he heaved the oars forward and back again and again. When our eyes met, he stopped mid-stroke, letting the oars skim the top of the water, and, leaning forward, kissed me. The gray skies, the damp cold, and the stinging wind on my face didn't matter. I was with him, and I was happy.

When the wind died down, he showed me how to row. Sitting in front of him, I manned the right oar while he manned the left. No matter what we tried, we spun in circles and ended up doubled over, barely able to catch our breaths between laughing fits.

The barrier the water provided from the rest of civilization made the river seem like the most private place in the world. I was in my own heaven, and I never wanted this morning to end.

"You are a horrible rower." He laughed as he helped me out of the boat.

"Yeah, pick on the handicapped girl." I jabbed him in the ribs, and he grabbed my good arm, pulling me in.

"I'm glad I wasn't too late."

I wondered if he could have been too late but then decided yes. Zack and I had just been dating two weeks when Doug had broken up with his girlfriend Zoey and confessed he wanted me. If Doug had waited even two more weeks, I doubt I could have left Zack.

"You're just lucky I can't resist you." I stood on my toes and kissed him.

As he wound his arm around me, his phone chimed. "Yes I am, but we're going to be late." He picked up the boat and walked to the warehouse.

I followed, stowing the heater back in the office and folding the blanket. As he locked the building, I thought about the quarter. Everything seemed to have come full circle, as if Halloween, his ex-girlfriend, and Zack never happened. Even I wasn't naïve enough to convince myself that the decisions we'd made wouldn't have consequences. Could Doug and Zack go back to being friends like nothing happened? Would Zack and I be friends again?

Sliding into the passenger's seat, I tucked those concerns into the back of my mind. I flooded Doug with questions about his courses and family. Back on campus, he drove to the street closest to my building. As he stopped the car and kissed me, I wrapped a hand around his neck. He took my fingers in his hand and pulled them from behind his head. "You're going to be late."

Sighing, I opened the door and stepped onto the curb. My phone alarm sounded, and after a quick wave, I sprinted to my building. In the lecture room, I took two steps at a time down the stairs, thankful that, as usual, my friends saved me a seat in front. I slid in next to Lila and started opening my pack.

"You're almost late." She pointed to the podium where the professor was opening his tablet.

I looked up at the lecture screen and back to her. "Yeah, I know."

Lila grabbed my arm. "OMG, you've been kissing someone. Were you with him all night?"

"No, we went rowing!"

"You were rowing this morning? What time did you get up?"

"Six. It was amazing!"

"Six? You are in so much trouble." She shook her head and focused on the professor as he brought up his first slide.

She was quiet as we walked out of the lecture hall, waiting, I hoped, to accost me until we were alone.

"So," she began, but cut her eyes away. "Never mind."

I followed her gaze. Seeing Doug standing there with a coffee cup and a small brown bag made me smile. I tugged her jacket until she looked me straight in the eyes. I didn't want this day to be tainted with friendly opinions.

"Okay," she said, holding her hands up. "I see that you're tremendously happy, so I'm not going to ruin it for you. He knows he can't screw up again, right?" She grabbed my shoulders and shook me, making me meet her stare.

"I will tell him. I'm sure you're on a long list of people who think that way." I hugged her. "Thank you," I whispered into her ear.

When she stepped back, I turned and walked to Doug, standing on my toes to kiss him. Lila followed slowly behind.

"Hi, Doug," she said as she passed.

"Lila." He nodded.

I took the coffee from him. "Please let this be real coffee." With only four hours of sleep, there was no way the decaf I usually drank was going to get me through two more classes. It'd been nearly two months since the accident in the gym where I'd broken my arm and gotten a concussion. I was on caffeine restriction during my recovery, but fully caffeinated drinks were a must if I was going to make it through finals.

The cup felt warm in my hand, and I shivered. He put his arm around me and guided me to the library. Getting into the elevator in the lobby, he pressed the sixth floor button. I'd never been past the second, and unlike the lower floors, this one was deserted. He led me to a corner, taking my coffee and setting it on a table. I hopped up onto the table, and he stood in front of me.

He peaked his eyebrow. "I figured you wouldn't get a lunch break later." He took a sandwich out of the bag. "I hope you like mozzarella and pesto."

"You don't have to buy me meals." I stuffed the food back into the bag.

"You barely touched breakfast."

I gripped his shirt. "I don't want to waste my time with you eating."

"How was chemistry?"

I kissed him. "I don't know. Someone probably took notes." I didn't want to think about school, although it probably wasn't the best strategy with finals starting in three days. "What did you do with the last hour besides buy me lunch?"

He bent over so we were eye level. "Worked at the house. I actually don't have much time. I have to get back. What are you doing the rest of the day?"

I reviewed my schedule of classes, four tutoring clients, and babysitting for him.

He stared at me, glassy-eyed. "Since when do you do all this?"

I ignored the ping in my chest that reminded me of the night he'd severed our relationship. "I don't know, since November." I tugged at his jacket. He produced a half-crooked smile that usually meant he was happy enough, but something wasn't perfect. "What?" I asked.

"I just wish this would've happened without any issues."

I laced my fingers between his. "Issues, there are issues? I don't want to talk about issues." I wasn't going to let anything burst this bubble.

He smirked. "Umm, my ex-girlfriend, your ex-boyfriend, aka my best friend, all of your friends, probably your dad, and everyone that saw you with Zack last night. Should I go on?"

"Zoey is an issue?"

"She text messages me. If I don't respond, she calls. If I don't answer she leaves a voice message. This happens at least three times a day." His phone rang and he ignored it. "Probably her. She'd be on lunch break about now."

"It could be someone from the fraternity house. Anyway, Lila said she'd be nice, and I'm not answering my phone the rest of the day." I really just wanted him to kiss me for the hundredth time. My phone started playing Zack's "Kryptonite" ringtone.

Doug stepped back, folding his arms over his chest. "Speak of the devil."

I tapped the accept call button. "He's probably looking for you."

"Hey, is Doug there?" Zack said immediately.

"Yes." Smiling, I handed Doug the phone.

He paced between the stacks of books as he talked. I sipped my coffee and waited. Ending the call, he held the phone out to me. "Well, that wasn't awkward."

"What'd he say?"

"All business."

I looked at my shoes and then back up to him, setting the phone on the table beside me. "My friends and Dad can deal." I took his hands and intertwined my fingers with his. I wasn't going to lose this battle on this day. But my phone chimed, and he picked it up.

He shook it in front of my face. "You have class, and I have to get back to the house."

We walked hand in hand to my building, and he kissed me again before we parted. I floated through my lecture and four tutoring sessions, barely caring what was going on around me. Holding tight to my bubble, I was determined no one would invade my personal bliss. I didn't even take my mom's usual after work call.

When Lila met me for dinner, she was composed and civil. "You really like him, don't you? It's different than Zack?"

I nodded.

She accepted my new decision without any other opinion or commentary, save that Mark was sure not to be happy. Mark and I grew up together, and he'd sort of taken on a big brother role at school. Zack and Doug were seniors and the VP and president of their fraternity chapter. During the first week of classes, Mark had cautioned me about dating either of them. But he'd accepted my relationship with Zack. I hoped he'd do the same with Doug.

Finishing our dinner, Lila and I shared a car. She stopped at the house to meet up with her boyfriend Ross, and I continued to my babysitting job. It was after midnight before the parents returned, but Doug was nice enough to give me a ride home. I would have loved to stay up with him all night, but I could barely keep my eyes open. After walking me to the door, he kissed me goodnight and I rode the elevator up to my floor in a zombie state. I fell asleep as soon as my head hit the pillow.

When I awoke the next morning, Elise was already studying at her desk. She spun around as I sat down with my coffee. "So, you and Mr. Taylor are on for real?"

"Mmm, hmm," I nodded, taking my first sip.

"He does know he can't mess up, right?"

"Yes, you're on the list, along with Lila."

She left for the library, and after I freshened up and dressed, Doug and I met for a run and breakfast. I used the run time to listen to the biology lecture from the previous day. At breakfast, however, we were so engrossed in our own world that I forgot about my study group. Fortunately, I had my notifications in my calendar set for fifteen minutes before any event.

Finals, I repeated in my head as he paid the check. I was only five minutes late when he dropped me off at the library. It was hard to focus on biology, but Kate and Jeremy kept us on track. As we finished our study session two hours later, I got a text from Doug. OUTSIDE WAITING FOR YOU IF YOU CAN TAKE A BREAK. I excused myself from the conversation and went to meet him outside.

He wrapped an arm around me and kissed me.

"You don't have to do this."

He took my hand. "What?"

"Meet me every break."

"Would I see you otherwise?"

He was right. My study schedule was tight. I had to do well on my finals to make my scholarship GPA. After being in a fog for weeks after my injury, I'd been playing catch up the rest of the quarter.

I needed to stretch my legs, so we walked around the court-yard hand in hand, talking. When he left for his study group, I returned to the library and reviewed notes from yesterday's chemistry lecture before meeting up with Lila, Kate, and Jeremy for a chemistry study group.

Lila rolled her eyes at me as I approached the table where she and Kate sat. "Okay, it's driving me crazy that I can't tell Mark about Doug. When are you coming clean?"

"Don't tell me you haven't told anyone."

"Just Ross, and it's killing me. How are you going to manage this, especially after you and Zack's little show on Thursday?" At least she'd given me twenty-four hours of not worrying about social drama. "It doesn't make you look good, you know."

I thought about it for a minute. Dating two friends within the span of a week didn't exactly paint me in a favorable light.

"So, what are you going to tell everyone?"

"The truth," I said as I gave her a quick hug. "Can we study now?"

"The truth about what?" Jeremy asked as he sat down.

Lila pointed to me. "Who Manda's dating now."

I shot her a serious look. "Can we talk about this later?"

Over the next two hours, we strictly focused on chemistry. I felt fairly confident I could achieve my GPA goal for chemistry and biology.

As we packed our bags, Jeremy stood and stretched. "I have to know about the new guy."

Kate pointed at him. "Her love life is none of your business."

He turned to Lila. "Well, Lila seems to want to talk."

Stuffing my books in my backpack, I got up. "I'm going."

Lila chucked her books into her bag. "No, this will be good for you. Doug realized he can't live without Amanda. He put his friendship with Zack on the line to profess his feelings for her. As usual with guys like Doug—" she rolled her eyes "—it panned out for him. He got the girl he wanted."

Jeremy pointed at me. "Wait, you were with Zack Thursday night. I thought you guys got back together."

Kate hoisted her backpack on her shoulder. "I'm outta here."

Lila continued. "She was doing Zack a favor by pretending to be his girlfriend still."

"But everyone won't know that. You just look like a slut."

Yes, this was as bad as I thought.

Lila put a hand to one hip and waved the other in the air. "Thank you, Jeremy."

Kate shook her head and walked away.

I picked up my chemistry book. "So, what do I do?"

Jeremy put both hands on the table. "Fortunately for you, it's finals week and no one will be paying attention. Keep your public appearances with Doug minimal, and when you come back after break, it won't be an issue."

Lila slung her bag over her shoulder. "You have to face the music sometime. Better now than later." She hugged me and walked away.

Thankfully, I had a calculus study group as a buffer before seeing Doug. I took the short break before to think about what I should do. The best thing seemed to be talk to Zack first. It wouldn't be comfortable, but it was the fairest thing. Deciding on a plan at least let me clear my mind so I could focus on studying math.

Our session ran over, and Doug found me on the third floor hunched over my notes. After two hours of biology, two hours of chemistry, and over two hours of calculus, I was brain dead. We left the library in silence. Outside I hesitated, torn between needing time to myself and wanting to spend every minute with him. "Mind if we walk?"

The cool air and movement helped me feel re-energized, but my mind kept circling back to the conversation with Jeremy and Lila.

Doug grasped my hand. "You're biting your lip, and I still can't tell if that means you're thinking or worried about something."

"Lila brought up some issues."

I was silent for a few minutes, thinking of how to recite the conversation I'd had with my friends. After explaining to him their opinions and Jeremy's proposed solution, Doug agreed the plan was a prudent one.

"So, what now? Nap, dinner?" he asked as we reached my dorm. "Zack's having a party tonight, so it might be a late one."

A party was the last thing I wanted tonight. I wanted to snuggle up beside him and never return to society.

In the room, he extended my futon while I walked around tidying up. Grabbing me by the legs as I passed, he motioned for me to lie down beside him. With the anxiety over how to save my social reputation, I didn't think I'd be able to fall asleep. But it wasn't long before I was out, and the next thing I knew, I was being kissed on the forehead.

I scanned the room, seeing Elise at her desk.

Doug kissed me. "You have to walk me downstairs."

When I returned, Kate and Elise were applying makeup in the bathroom. Elise leaned through the doorway. "Ready to go out?"

Elise, Kate, and I had planned a girl's night out. Kate was not only a chemistry study buddy, she was also our suitemate. We grabbed some dinner and saw a movie, and I enjoyed that the focus of the conversation wasn't me.

As we drove back to the dorm, I fidgeted with my phone. Elise slapped me on the knee. "Just call him."

I dialed Doug's number from the car, and he answered immediately. "Hi, we were just talking about you. Where are you? I'll come pick you up. Everyone's heading to Zack's."

I'd tried not to think about Zack. Even though we'd broken up two days before, few people knew that. I'd gone with Zack to the club as a favor. What would everyone think when I showed up tonight with Doug? Hadn't we just decided to lay low? Before I could protest, he said he'd be at my dorm in ten minutes and hung up.

Meeting him downstairs, we walked hand in hand to his car. "I had dinner with Zack. We figured out how to fix this little PR issue."

What? He'd talked to Zack, and they had a plan? Without including me?

I yanked my hand from his grip. "What? That's between Zack and me, not you and me." I tried to reel in my tone, but I was livid.

Reaching his car, he stood in front of me. He looked up at the sky and then back at me. Before I could react, his lips were on mine. I mentally tried to fight it for like a nanosecond before I melted into him. When the kiss ended, he smiled down at me.

I shot him the meanest look I could muster. "Don't look so proud of yourself."

He didn't release me. "I am proud. I've wanted to do that since the first time you put these little hands—" he took one hand in each of his "—on your little hips."

"I don't do that."

"Yes you do." He kissed me again. "It used to drive me nuts, because I wanted to kiss you every time you did it." He held my hands up to his chest. "Now I can."

I slid my hands from his. "That doesn't change the issue." Too much my father's daughter, I would not be derailed.

"Wow, you're one tough cookie. That one would have melted a lesser woman's heart."

"I am not a lesser woman."

"Obviously, but will you at least hear the plan?"

I rolled my eyes but listened while he described their plan. I had to admit it wasn't a bad plan, being one, truthful, or as close to imitating the truth as I wanted to go, and two, simple. "Fine." I opened the car door and sat in the passenger's seat.

At Zack's building, I walked ahead of Doug into the apartment. It was crowded, but I picked out a friendly face right away.

Bill crossed the room and wrapped one arm around me. "Hey, long time no see. Zack's in the kitchen." He pointed with his beer.

I managed a smile. "Thanks." Did Bill know about this plan, too? I pushed the thought to the back of my brain. Squeezing his arm, I made my way to the kitchen. I recognized most of the faces, but fortunately nobody felt the need to stop me to talk.

As soon as I entered the kitchen, Zack scooped me up, and swung me around. I wasn't sure how this fit with the plan, but it felt natural for us. As soon as he set me back on my feet, Doug slid in behind me.

Zack looked above my head to Doug. "What took you so long?"

He gestured to me. "She had issues."

Zack looked between us. "Issues?"

"It appears Manda is a very private person."

A huge grin spread across Zack's face. "Could've told you that."

"Yeah, well, guess I have a learning curve." Doug looked at his feet.

Ugh! This thing between Doug, Zack, and me had to stop. It would tonight.

Zack put his hands on my shoulders. "Can we talk?" He cocked his head in the direction of the hallway. I followed his gaze, realizing we had an audience. Anna and a few of her sorority friends stood on the other side of the bar, staring.

"Sure." I followed him down the hall to his bedroom.

Kicking out a couple I didn't recognize, he closed the door. "So, what was your issue?"

"I didn't like that you two were talking about me. This is between you and me."

"Doug likes to fix things."

Yes, fix and protect things, like me. Doug wasn't perfect, this I knew. Still, he was the guy I wanted. Seeing Zack had solidified my decision. I knew the scene in the kitchen was just for show, but I hoped we could go back to being friends.

Zack faked a punch to my arm. "I just want you to be happy."

"Thanks."

It was awkward, but we played basketball with his miniature hoop for a few minutes. Then, we walked out of the room together and into the living room. He held out a fist and bumped it into mine, and then he walked away. I looked to the floor. I assumed we had an audience, and I didn't want to see their reaction. Not sure what to do with myself, I found Lila and Ross sitting on the sofa and squeezed in beside them.

Lila whispered in my ear. "What was with your little show?"

"That was our staged breakup."

"Subtle, but effective. I like more drama myself, but to each his own."

Mark plopped down on the arm of the couch beside me. "Amanda, what's going on? What just happened with Zack? I saw you come in. Did you ride with Doug?"

"Can we talk outside?"

"It's freezing."

"Okay." I grabbed his arm and dragged him down the hall, hoping Zack's bedroom wasn't occupied again.

Mark closed the door behind us. "What's going on? You broke up with Zack, then were with him on Thursday, and now Doug brought you here tonight?"

Succinctly as possible, I explained the situation.

"Really, Manda?" He shook his head.

"I know all of this is not like me, but Doug is who I want to be with."

"Okay, well, I need to talk to him." He turned and walked out.

Shooting out the door, I caught up with him. I wouldn't be treated like a child. "Why?"

"Because, while he's not here, I'm acting for your father."

"Dad wouldn't—"

"Yes, your dad would care."

There was no use fighting him. We walked through the apartment, finding Doug in the kitchen with Zack and Bill.

Mark stood, chest puffed and shoulders back in front of Doug. "Can we talk?"

Doug arched his back, reaching his full six foot three inches, and shrugged. "Sure."

I bit my lip. Zack shrugged, shook his head, and walked away. Spinning on my toes, I made my way into the living room and snuggled in next to Lila again.

It wasn't long before Doug found me. "Ready to go?"

I nodded. He smiled and held out his hand. Taking it, we went to find Zack and Bill to say good-bye. They both hugged me. Zack's smile looked forced and the hug was stiff, and I felt bad again for the way things had gone.

Doug swung our hands between us as we walked to his car. The plan had gone well. Zack and I faked our break up, and I left with Doug just like we'd done many times. In the car, he turned on the music, rolled down the windows, and blasted the heat. "So, where are we going? Do you want to get a coffee or a drink? It would be a shame to waste your outfit. We were barely at Zack's an hour." Happy the hard part of the night was over, I agreed that a coffee sounded good.

He wound through the streets to downtown Evanston and found a parking spot. We walked a couple of blocks to a pub. "How was your talk with Zack?" he asked as we got a spot at the bar.

"Fine, good."

The bartender took our order. "Hmm, again with the privacy thing, eh? You didn't have to be mad earlier, right? Everything was fine."

"I wasn't mad."

"You were."

I turned to face him. "The outcome doesn't really change that I wasn't happy with you talking to Zack like that."

He lifted an eyebrow. "Isn't wasn't happy the same as mad?" I looked at the counter, wondering if we were always going to butt heads. He kissed me on the temple. "I'm sorry."

I let out my breath. "Thank you."

"You're welcome." He took a sip of his beer. "So, are you washing your hair tomorrow?"

"What?"

"I love seeing you dry your hair." He raked his hands through my hair, kissing me on my newly exposed neck. "Remember the night you dried your hair and we got sushi? That was the first night I thought you looked beautiful." He kissed me again.

I poked him in the ribs as the bartender cleared his throat. Doug set his beer on a napkin and looked back to me. "I think Zack had the same reaction to you that night." He lifted his bottle towards me. "You're sure about us, right?"

I spun my barstool to face him. "What?" I studied his face. How could he ask me that? "Yes, I told you. Why would you ask again?"

"Well..." How could he always be so calm? "I wasn't sure how you felt after you talked to Zack and Mark."

"Why are we even talking about this?" I turned back to face the counter.

"Mark doesn't seem to think I'm good for you."

Now I was angry. "Mark doesn't know anything." I started to throw at him how incomplete I'd felt when he'd left me but thought better of it. I took a slow breath and calmed myself. It wouldn't help to fling words at him. I looked him straight in the eyes. "I told you the other night that it's always been you." I traced the lines on his forehead where his brow was furrowed.

"Can we be done talking about this now, please?"

"Yes," He smiled. "I just want you to be sure."

"I am."

Chapter 2

Even with the stress of finals, I floated through the next week. Doug and I were together as much as possible, working out, studying, and eating every meal together. My international studies and English finals were easy, and I felt confident about my grade in those classes. Chemistry and calculus were more challenging, but biology was the test I was really concerned about. Even so, Thursday night, after only an hour of studying, Doug closed the textbook resting on my lap and announced we were going out.

I cut my eyes to Elise who looked up from her book.

"I have a final tomorrow," I whispered, reopening my book.

"You're ready." He closed it again and stood. "As much as you don't want to be a part of this, you have to be. I am president of my fraternity, the Greek council, and student body. I need to be seen. Not that I'm so into the whole social thing, but it reflects on the fraternity, on me, you, and Zack, if people think I'm hiding."

"Why would you be hiding?"

He looked at me with one eyebrow cocked. I'd been so focused on my exams I'd all but forgotten our staged breakup scene at Zack's party. "You want me to come out with you?" No wonder he looked so nice tonight.

"Yes. After all, you are my girlfriend." He spun me around and pushed me toward the closet. "You could wear something sexy."

I looked down at the tank and fitted jeans I was wearing. They were cute, not sexy. I didn't want to seem as if I had to call my sister or Lila for every decision about clothes, so I looked through my closet. I found a grey sleeveless top. It had ruffles that lined a V-neck. I took it out and held it up to him.

"Nice," he smiled.

Discreetly folding a push-up bra into the bundle, I went to the bathroom to change.

As we drove to the club, Doug fiddled with my hand. "I know this really isn't your thing. I'm sorry."

"What? Are you forgetting who you're talking to?"

"Umm, I don't think so. Last I checked, you hated this kind of stuff."

"Do you remember how we met? I've been doing this social scene since I was a baby."

"I'll give you that, but it may be a little different if the room is hostile."

"Who would be hostile?" If there was one thing I learned from my dad, it was to know your enemy. It was sad that I thought this way, but it was ingrained after eighteen years.

"Let's say maybe friends of Zoey, like Anna."

"I don't get it."

"Sorority sisters tend to be very loyal."

"What about your house? Are your brothers mad at you?"

"Probably, and they should be. It was a dick move. But Zack has been cool since the first incident."

"I'm tired of thinking about this." Part of me wanted to put my hands on my hips and say that it didn't matter what anyone thought because they didn't really know anything about us. Yet, the more logical part knew that if I wanted to feel comfortable at this school, I had to walk in there and play the part.

After we parked, he came around the car to meet me. As I closed the door, he wrapped his arms around me, pushing me back against the door. He scanned the parking lot and then kissed me. He rubbed my arms. "You're going to be cold."

"Not for long." I slipped my ID and phone into my back pocket.

"I'm not going to kiss you in there. Let's keep it casual, like we're just hanging out, okay?"

"Sure." I shrugged. We walked across the lot, and as we rounded the corner, I could see a line stretching out past the end of the block. Since the bouncers were Doug's fraternity brothers, we wouldn't be waiting with that crowd. As we got closer, I recognized several kids from my classes. "We're going to walk to the front of that line, aren't we?"

"Sure, we always do. You won't be cold for long."

"It isn't really fair."

He laughed. "Are you turning Democrat on me?"

Maybe I was thinking too critically about every little thing now. I felt like I was in a fish bowl. I wished he hadn't made such a big deal of this outing.

"I know a lot of people in that line."

He stopped. "Okay who do you know? We'll get some of your friends in."

I pointed to Justin.

"The football guy, seriously?"

"You and your thing with football players."

"Several of them got arrested for rape."

"But not Justin, he's a good guy."

"Okay, come on."

As we reached Justin, I introduced him to Doug. They'd already met, but I wasn't sure how else to approach the situation. I could see Doug put on his politician mask as we chatted with Justin and his friends.

"You guys want to grab some girls and head in with us?" Doug asked them.

They followed us to the door. Halfway there Justin caught my arm. "So, you're with him now?"

I nodded. He shook his head and rolled his eyes. I took Doug's hand, refusing to acknowledge whatever judgment Justin had passed.

As we neared the door, Doug greeted his brothers with hand-shakes. "You guys know Amanda, right?"

"Sure, yeah." They nodded. I fidgeted while Doug spoke to one of them.

"Zack's already inside." The other motioned to me and pointed inside. I slid my hand down Doug's arm and took his hand.

Doug rubbed his chin. "Yeah, we're headed in there now. Can Amanda's friends come in with us?" He pointed at Justin.

The brothers looked between one another. "Sure, yeah." One stood and unclipped the rope that hung across the doorway.

Inside, it took a minute to adjust to the low light. Justin thanked us and moved through the crowd ahead of us. "Show-time," Doug whispered in my ear. I followed his gaze to Anna and her friends parked at the end of the bar. This wasn't their regular spot, and I knew it. I forced a smile.

We made our way to the bar, stopping beside Anna. Doug hugged her. "What happened to your table?"

"We get better service here."

He nodded. Anna looked at me and opened her mouth but, instead of talking to me, turned back to Doug. "You headed to your table?"

"Course." He smiled. "Good thing Zack got here early."

Zack approached, gave me a stiff hug, and shook Doug's hand. They stepped up to the bar to order drinks.

Anna grabbed my arm. "What's going on? You broke up with Zack on Saturday, and now Doug brought you out tonight?"

My thoughts raced as I tried to think of an appropriate response. Why hadn't I rehearsed this? I reminded myself she had more than one agenda. She was Zoey's sorority sister and she liked Zack. Before I could speak, Doug held two drinks out to us.

"Hey, Anna, what are you doing for break?"

She rolled her eyes but answered his question. I took the opportunity to down a good portion of the soda I prayed was spiked.

As soon as she'd finished telling him about her trip to Cancun, she turned to me. "So, are you done with finals, Amanda?"

"I have biology left."

"Wow, you must feel really confident."

Doug tipped his head in my direction. "I drug her out. She was studying too much. Rookie mistake."

After giving me an odd stare, Anna's gaze landed on Doug. "Have you talked to Zoey?"

"Not really."

"You should call her. She still seems off."

He squared his shoulders and shook his head. "I think she'll come through okay."

"I don't know—"

"We talked about this before."

"Okay, well, I'll see you guys later, I guess."

"Sounds good."

He wound his arm around my waist.

"Talked about what?" I asked him.

"Zoey is driving her crazy too. She thinks I should go see her."

"Are you going to?"

"No, I think it would just make things worse."

As we made our way through the crowd, we stopped to speak with almost everyone Doug knew. Finally, after an hour, he suggested we join Zack and Bill.

After a few steps towards a set of tables, Doug's huge arm hooked me around the waist and pulled me in the opposite direction. "I'll take that drink now." Doug moved his arm from my waist and put his hand on the small of my back. We pushed through the last of the crowd to our table. Lila caught my eye, and I turned to walk in her direction. Before I could take a step, Doug grabbed my hand. "Can you say hi to Zack and Bill before you talk to your friends?"

I held up a single finger to Lila, signaling that I'd be there in a minute.

Zack lifted his drink. "That took long enough."

Bill took a sip from a bottle of beer and I pointed at him. "Wait. You're twenty-one?"

"Ever since October."

"Where was I?"

They all looked down, and Doug cleared his throat. "It was the week after your accident."

"Oh, well, happy birthday." I clinked my glass to his drink.

After a few minutes of talking with them, I excused myself to find Lila and Mark. I meandered through the crowd to their table. She jumped off her stool and hugged me. "You look great! I didn't get a call about this outfit. Did you call Marissa?"

I spun around in front of her. "No, I picked it out all by myself."

She put a thumb up. "Nice."

Mark pointed at me. "So, you slumming it now? Taking a break from first lady duties?" Lila hit him on the shoulder and he pretended to be hurt. "So, seriously, is this like your dating debut?"

I looked back at Doug's table. "I guess."

Ross lifted his drink to me. "Man, you sure know how to pick them."

Lila pointed her finger at them. "Hey, be nice. You guys like Doug."

"Liking him, and liking him with Amanda, are two different things." Mark took a swig of his drink and set it down on the table. "How's the night going so far?"

"Well, Anna is out of sorts, but that's it."

Lila squeezed my shoulder. "That's good news. You literally talked to everybody that is anybody."

Lila and I chatted about the latest gossip while Ross and Mark rolled their eyes. Mark cut in. "So, you talked to your dad and he's totally okay with this?"

He had me on this one. Of course Marissa knew everything, and I'd told my mom Zack and I broke up, but I hadn't gotten to the part where Doug and I were together yet.

I opened my mouth to speak, but before I could answer, Mark shook his head. "That's what I thought." He turned and gestured to the back wall. "You haven't visited fraternity row yet." I followed his gaze and realized that nearly all their fraternity brothers were there. "Don't worry, they won't say anything to your face."

"How bad is this really?"

Ross piped up. "I think you just want them to not think you sleep around, and for that there's only one solution—time."

The band started, and I texted Doug that Lila and I wanted to dance.

MEET U THERE, he replied.

Lila and I made our way to the band. Doug found us in the crowd and danced with us till the end of the set. After a glass of water back at the table, Lila was ready for more dancing. She pointed to the dance floor, but Doug pointed to his fraternity brothers.

"We've got more people to talk to. You up for round two?"

I hugged Lila. "I'll dance with you more later."

"Okay," she waved and danced away.

I finished the last sip of my water and followed Doug. Zack and Bill joined us and we talked to the brothers gathered there. I'd forgotten how nice they were. There was not an ill one in the bunch except for Mark, and he only annoyed me. To everyone else, he was an angel. The conversations centered mostly on finals and winter break plans. Most of the brothers had ample funds and were headed to amazing places like the Caribbean or Cancun. But none of them could trump Doug's successive trips. I shook off the thought of three weeks away from him while he traveled to Vail, New York City, and Paris.

After about an hour, we rejoined Lila and danced until curfew. Doug took my hand as we made our way to the door. I smiled at him, happy that the night seemed to be a success and that we'd had some fun too. When I refocused on our path to the door, I nearly smacked into Anna.

"Can I talk to you?" she asked.

"Sure," I replied. She titled her head towards the bar, and I followed.

When we reached the end, she turned and faced me. I tried to read her, but her expression gave nothing away. She could have equally slugged me or hugged me. She took a deep breath and raked her hands through her hair.

"Look, I'm sorry about before. I'm not trying to be difficult. It's just hard when I've been such good friends with all of them."

I opened my mouth to speak, unsure what was going to come out, although I knew it was something akin to begging her forgiveness. She held a finger up before I could say anything. "I talked to Zack." She looked over my shoulder to Doug and back to me. "I know this isn't your fault, but Zoey is driving me nuts."

"Doug told me about Zoey. I'm not sure what to say, I feel really bad about the whole situation."

Doug approached us. "This has nothing to do with Amanda."

She glared at Doug. "Well, it does and it doesn't. It's not her fault, but she is involved. Still, I wanted to apologize for before." Returning her attention to me, she continued, "Okay, well, I just needed for us to be clear." She squeezed my arm. "Will I see you at rush next quarter?"

I couldn't keep hedging the question. "No, sorry, I've decided not to rush. I'm saving my pennies."

"No worries," she said. "Have a good break."

"Thanks, you too."

She hugged Doug, and we made our way out of the club to his car. He shook his arms out as we walked. "You did well."

I smiled. "I know."

He jumped in front of me. "This is good. Tonight was fun."

"Yeah, it was." I planted a kiss on his lips.

ᛕ ᛕ ᛕ

I slept well, and on Friday I went to the gym early for a quick run. Afterward, I reviewed my biology notes before the final. Finishing the test, I felt good about my performance, and met Doug at the house. That evening we joined all my friends, Jeremy, Stephen, Kate, Elise, Lila and Ross, as well as Mark, for dinner at a pub in downtown Evanston. Then, Doug dropped me off at the Kemp's house for my babysitting job.

The evening with the kids was quiet. After they were in bed, I had no studying to do and was left with plenty of time to think. Tomorrow I'd pack, and Sunday my parents were supposed to pick me up. Doug and I only had one more day together before winter break. It felt like the planets were misaligned. Doug was traveling to Colorado, New York, and Paris with his brothers and dad the weeks I was home in Champaign. When I went to the Caribbean with my family, Doug was home with his mom. I didn't like the thought of being away from him for a whole month after spending almost every waking moment together for the past week.

On the drive back to my dorm that night, Doug offered to drive me home Sunday so that we could have more time together. I would have jumped at the offer except I hadn't told my parents we were dating. Just two weeks ago, over Thanksgiving break, Zack had visited as my boyfriend. Now I was going to bring Doug home? I knew it wouldn't look good from a parent's perspective. I'd explain and hope they'd understand. It might be uncomfortable, but there was no getting around it. I'd made my choice, and it was a good one.

Doug dropped me off at my dorm. It was late, and I was tired, so I put off calling my parents until the next day. When I got to my room, Elise's boxes were neatly stacked near her bed. I was sad to see them, thinking I'd miss her over the break. I reminded myself I had almost a whole month to spend with my family and enjoy Christmas, our favorite time of year.

The next morning, Doug and I helped Elise load her car. Afterward, I called home.

"What happened with Zack?" my dad asked straight off when I explained that Doug offered to give me a ride home. I hesitated, unsure of how to explain. Dad continued, "Your mother said you and Zack broke up. Is Doug swooping in to rescue you again?" He'd cut to the chase. It left me little room for vagueness. I hadn't planned on telling the whole story over the phone. Standing outside my dorm room door, I moved farther down the hall so Doug wouldn't overhear.

"No, we've been hanging out."

"What does his girlfriend think of this?"

"They broke up."

"Hmm..." There was a long pause. "I'm not sure I'm comfortable with this. Will all your stuff fit in his car? I think I need to come up there and get you right now, or have Ed and

Tia pick you up." He grew more agitated as he spoke. Great, he was playing the older sister card. Tia and her husband, Ed, lived only an hour away.

"Dad, I'm not a child. Everything is fine. I just thought you wouldn't mind skipping a six-hour road trip tomorrow."

"No, I don't mind that part. What I do mind is my daughter throwing herself at guys four years older than her."

His words cut. "It's not like that. Doug and I have always been friends." That part was mostly true. "And we're sort of dating now." I shouldn't have to defend myself. I'd done nothing wrong.

"Well, this is a new development. When did this happen?"

"Last week."

"Now I really think I should have Tia come pick you up. I'm not comfortable with you bringing two different guys home in the span of two weeks." There was a long silence, and I could hear Mom in the background asking him what was wrong.

"I'm riding home with Doug. No one needs to come get me."

"We'll discuss this when you get home." He hung up.

I stared at the wall in front of me. Why had the conversation gone that way? It should've been easy. Walking to my room, I realized I still wasn't sure what the plan was for me getting home. My phone rang and it was Mom. I turned around, paced back the way I came, and answered the call. I reminded Mom that I'd talked to her about seeing Doug and indicated it was a complicated story. She finally got Dad to back down from calling Tia and having her pick me up.

Entering my room, I was embarrassed that I felt the need to ask my parents' permission. I was eighteen and shouldn't need their blessing. I could do whatever I wanted. I cut off my mental debate, not wanting to ruin the last hours Doug and I had together for a month.

Since not all of my things would fit in his car, he volunteered some space at his mom's condo. We sorted what I needed to take home and what could go to his house and then loaded the car. When we were done, we went to his room at the fraternity house so he could pack for his trip to Colorado. I leaned against his desk as he organized his bag. I wished I could stop thinking that we had less than twenty-four hours together.

I realized if we spent the night together, that one, we wouldn't be separated, and two, I wouldn't have to sleep alone in the creepy residence hall. But, I'd never spent a night with a guy before, at least not one I was romantically involved with. Was I totally off the deep end? What kind of person was I that I wanted to stay the night with him? The desire not to be alone in my dorm room trumped all the other apprehensions.

"Doug," is all I got out. He looked at me, and suddenly I was nervous. Maybe it was too fast. Maybe he didn't want to spend the night. I wasn't ready for sex. I just wanted to be with him.

"You're biting your lip." He stood in front of me. "What is it?"

I tucked my hair behind my ear and looked up at him. "I could stay here tonight."

He raised his eyebrows. "What are you saying?"

"It'd be nice not to be alone."

"Okay, but you can't sleep here. You can't ever stay the night at the house. It looks too bad."

"You could stay with me. Nearly everyone's gone, we wouldn't get caught."

His smile was the only answer I needed. "Are you sure?"

"Yes."

He kissed me. "I'd like that too."

We drove to his mom's condo in downtown Chicago and stacked my things in a corner of his room. It was large, probably double my room at home. Decorated in shades of grey, it felt like a place you could sleep forever. Freshening up and changing in the guest room, I joined him, his mom, and Gary, his stepdad. Over cocktails, they retold the story of how they'd met while Doug excused himself to shower.

Gary's first wife was Puerto Rican. They had two daughters and were very active in the Puerto Rican community. His wife lost a battle with cancer when the girls were in grade school. He kept attending community center events and met Paula at one of them. Her sons were all in college when they married two years later. How I felt about love stories was so different than before. Three months ago, I would've been politely interested. Now I was holding back tears. I was becoming a romantic for the first time in my life.

It occurred to me I hadn't gotten *Romeo and Juliet* or *Othello*. I didn't understood how love could move one to such tragedy until now. But I'd lied to my friends and family to protect a relationship with a person I'd met barely three months ago. I'd make amends for my omissions to Lila and Mark. Did I need to tell my parents everything? Wasn't I entitled to some privacy?

When Doug returned from showering, he suggested Mrs. Chen's restaurant for dinner. Having learned a week ago he'd gotten engaged to Zoey there, I was surprised at his choice. Still, he'd taken me to the restaurant the first week we'd met.

Thinking perhaps it held too many hard memories, I questioned him. He took both my hands. "That night was the first time I realized I might really like you."

I didn't need any further coaxing. We walked the couple of blocks to the restaurant. As before, Mrs. Chen stood at the reception desk. "You bring her back." She placed her hands on both sides of my face. "What a beautiful girl. This makes me very happy." My cheeks burned, and I must have blushed a hundred shades of red. "Look, she has color now." Mrs. Chen laughed as she waved us back to our table. She brought wine and a lot of food, and before I knew it, we'd eaten at least four different dishes and drunk the whole bottle of wine.

The drinks had me buzzed, and it hardly bothered me when Mrs. Chen again felt the need to pat my face and compliment me on my hair and skin as we left. Passing a night club on our way back to the car, I pulled him towards the entrance. "Let's go dancing."

"You're not twenty-one, and we have an early morning."

I looked between him and the club, giving him my best pleading look. He whispered in my ear, "I'll dance with you in your room."

Pacified, I let him lead me back to the car.

The dorm was deserted as almost everyone had left for the quarter break. I wondered if I should be nervous about having him stay the night. But my buzz from the wine made it a fleeting thought. Inside my room, we left our shoes by the door. I took his hand instantly and led him over to where stereo equipment had been. He laughed and slipped out his phone, setting it on the desk when he found a ballad.

It felt amazing to be held against his warm chest without any stressors pinging in the back of my mind. Relaxing into him, I realized that I might be the happiest I could ever remember being.

He whispered in my ear, "We should've been doing this every night since Halloween. I wish I'd figured this out sooner."

Not wanting him to dampen the mood, I kissed him on the neck. "Can we just dance?"

He smiled and laughed. "Got it, less regret, more passion." He picked me up and carried me to the futon. Being vertical didn't last long, and I found myself looking up at him.

"See, that wasn't hard," I said when he took a breath.

He shook his head and planted kisses from my neck to my lips. I became lost in the sensation of his touch and slid my hand up his chest, exposing his bare abdomen. His body rested on mine, and his arms wound around me. Kissing his neck, I traced my finger down his chest. He froze and backed away.

"What's wrong?" I sat up, reaching for him.

He kissed me but retreated as soon as the kiss ended.

"Nothing," he began. "But we haven't talked about this yet."

I sat up and raked my hair behind my ear, realizing he meant sex. Sure I was blushing, I slid away from him.

He climbed off the futon to sit in front of me, lifting my chin and forcing me to look at him. "I don't want you to think that I don't want you, but I don't want our first time to be in a dorm room."

"Of course," was all I could think to say. I stood, nervous. I wasn't super comfortable talking about sex. Still a virgin, I wasn't sure I was ready. Before coming to college, and meeting Doug, I'd always thought I'd wait till I was married.

"We should get some sleep." He stood and gave me a quick kiss. We took turns brushing our teeth. When I came out of the bathroom, he had the futon fully extended. Lying next to him, it wasn't easy to fall asleep. He was warm, and my body tingled in places it never had before. But finally, exhaustion won me over.

I awoke to the smell of coffee and was immediately embarrassed I hadn't set an alarm. Two cups of coffee and breakfast sandwiches sat on my desk. When I apologized, he laughed. "You sleep like a rock. I assumed it was the pain meds when I was on invalid duty."

"Invalid duty?" I folded my arms in front of my chest.

"You're the best invalid I've ever been around." He pried my arms from my chest and pointed to the bathroom.

"We should get going if I'm going to get you home and make it back for my flight."

I ducked into the bathroom to freshen up and dress. We packed the car, and the drive seemed to pass more quickly than it ever had before. As we neared Champaign, I grew nervous. Yesterday's conversation with Dad hadn't gone well, and I had no idea what to expect from him.

We pulled into the drive just after eleven. I sighed heavily, and Doug reached over and took my hand. "Nervous?" I tried to smile and look confident, but I must have looked as bad as I felt. "Hmmm," was his only reaction as we got out of the car.

Dad came out the door as we were getting bags from the trunk. He didn't usually come out to meet guests. I hoped his greeting boded well for Doug and me.

He met me halfway across the drive, wrapping one arm around me. "Your mother is just getting into the kitchen to make some brunch. I thought I'd give her some time." Mom was never ill-prepared for anything. If I knew her, she'd showered and dressed and was reheating a casserole she'd prepared the night before.

"Mr. Taylor," he greeted Doug, shaking his hand.

His formality seemed out of place as he'd met Doug a dozen times, although never as my boyfriend.

I stood beside Doug and Dad looked between us, his gaze landing on me. "Your mother could use some help in the kitch-en. We'll join you in a minute."

I couldn't seem to judge his mood, and it made me edgy, but I wasn't going to question his authority. "Okay."

Annoyed at being treated like a child, I went inside. Mom greeted me with a warm hug. As I expected, she was sipping coffee and watching a cooking show while the quiche heated in the oven. "Give him a few minutes and then go rescue Doug."

I opened a cabinet for a coffee mug. "Is there a problem?"

"Being fraternity brothers complicates relationships, but I'm not sure. Your father didn't say much."

Dad was like me. Not saying much usually meant he hadn't made up his mind. When he did, I would know. I hoped that meant he had some questions for Doug, who of course would answer perfectly. I stared out the window, biting my lip and wishing the kitchen faced the front drive. What would I do if Dad didn't approve of my relationship with Doug? It was like anything else having to do with Doug: I was defenseless. He was more than the sum of all other things combined, and I wouldn't give him up.

"I'm sure it'll be fine." Mom squeezed my shoulders and sat back down to watch TV. I didn't know how long I'd stared out the window before my mother bumped me on the hip. "You can go rescue him now." She rolled her eyes. "We won't eat for half an hour, so why don't you guys go for a walk and stretch your legs."

"Thanks." I hugged her.

She rubbed her hands down my arms, taking my hands. "How much do you like this man Amanda? You seem different."

I jostled her hands in mine. "A lot."

She spun around looking out the window, then around to face me again. "Wow, okay then."

I shook my head and raked my hands through my hair, anxious to get outside.

"Go. We'll have plenty of time for details later. With the way Marissa's been walking around like a cat that ate the canary, I know there's got to be a story."

As I walked out the front door, I heard laughter. "What's so funny?" I slipped my arm around Dad.

"Doug says you're going out for the crew team?"

Doug cleared his throat and looked at his feet, smiling.

"I'm getting my arm in shape." I held it up, showcasing my lack of muscle tone for Dad.

"How's breakfast coming along?" he asked.

"Good, Mom says about thirty minutes. How are things out here?" I asked, looking between them.

"Good," Dad answered. I studied his face but couldn't read it.

After excusing ourselves for a short walk, Doug and I headed to the neighborhood trail. Along the way, I pointed out Mark's house two down from ours.

"Almost the girl next door," he commented.

Not being able to contain my curiosity, I asked about his talk with Dad. Doug stopped and faced me.

"At the beginning of the quarter, I did assure him I wasn't interested in you." Defending Dad didn't sit well with me after the accusations he'd flung at me yesterday, but I held my tongue. Doug didn't need to be part of my drama with Dad.

We walked past my elementary school, to the neighborhood coffee shop, and back. It was nice to share a bit of my corner of the world with Doug.

At brunch, my parents were painfully polite. This should've been a hint at what was to come, but I was too caught up in Doug leaving to dwell on it.

After brunch Doug shook hands with my parents, thanked them, and wished everyone a happy holiday. I walked out to the car with him.

"Man, I'm going to miss you," he said, taking my hands. "We'll video chat every day." He kissed me.

"Of course." I put on my best brave face and waved as he drove away.

Chapter 3

Dad came to my room that afternoon just before he left for his flight. "Doug's off to Colorado, eh? It was nice of him to drive you down." He paced my small room. "So, you two are a couple?"

I squared my shoulders and answered, keeping my voice steady. "Yes."

He shrugged and looked at the floor. Looking up, he continued, "Are you drinking? Taking drugs?"

"What? No!" Where had this come from?

"Because this looks like you guys are in one big orgy, trading partners as it pleases you."

Too shocked to speak, I crossed my arms over my chest and tried to come up with a response to such an insane thought.

"What did you say your grades were?" he asked before I could speak.

"My grades are good. I told you, I have a solid three point six."

"Well, we'll see about that."

I threw my hands up, I couldn't form words. "What?"

We'll see about that? What was he thinking? Did he think I was lying? I'd studied hard, really hard, to make up for my less than stellar performance at midterms due to my injury. Okay, so my personal life had gotten a little messy, but I was not doing drugs. No one I knew did drugs. And I wasn't drinking much. Most kids I knew drank way more than me. Two drinks a week did not make me a drunk.

He started towards the door but turned back. "We've raised you girls a certain way. You've always been pretty conservative with a good head on your shoulders. I'm not sure what to think of this. And that Lila is a bad influence." He pointed a finger at me. "She's practically been living with that boyfriend of hers since June."

I was reeling. Conservative? Was he talking about sex? I wasn't going to talk to him about sex, especially since I was still a virgin and hadn't even come close to having sex. More importantly, it was none of his business. I bounced my phone against my leg. It hurt that he was thinking these things about me. And how had he jumped from being upset that I hadn't told them about a new boyfriend to thinking I was doing drugs?

I steadied my breathing, trying to contain my anger. "I'm not doing drugs, I'm not drinking, I'm not sleeping around, and my grades are good. I don't understand where this is coming from."

"Where this is coming from?" he bellowed. "We hear nothing from you for weeks. Then you come home with Zack, and two weeks later you come home with Doug. Suddenly you're training for the crew team. You say your grades are good, but I don't know what to think. We'll see when you get them on Tuesday." He stood, his arms folded on his chest.

I dug my nails into my palms, fighting the tears that threatened to spill. I couldn't look at him anymore. I crossed the room to look out my window and steady my breathing. Getting emotional with my dad never solved anything. How was I supposed to react to such accusations? He was accusing me of lying straight to his face? Did he seriously believe I was so out there? So irresponsible? That I was doing drugs? Drinking? Sleeping around?

When I thought I could speak rationally, I turned to face him again. "I nearly died. I was in a fog for weeks. How can you even think these things?"

"Yes, you nearly died. I should have made you come home. If I'd known this was how things turned out I would have."

"I talked to Mom every day and you a couple times a week."

"Yes, and from what I hear, those conversations were five minutes when you were on the bus going to class. You said nothing about dating Zack or Doug till they were on our door step."

This was totally ludicrous and an exaggeration. I leaned against my desk chair trying to abate the anger growing in my chest. "Dad, I was doing tutoring jobs, and I had a babysitting gig. I volunteered with a campus mentoring organization and went to Latino club meetings. Do you want to look at my calendar, see my bank account, read my emails? I didn't think I needed to give you a minute by minute update on my social life."

"Your social life of clubbing and working out with all the fraternity brothers?"

Clubbing? A laugh escaped, and I clamped my hand over my mouth. I looked him right in the eyes. "Clubbing?"

With his arms still folded over his chest, he lifted a shoulder. "Those dance clubs you guys go to. I know they serve minors."

Did he have spies following me? I was angry beyond words. "Yes, I go out with Mark." I pointed out the window to his house. "Plus, Lila, Ross, and lots of other friends. You can ask Mark. I drink less than everyone else."

"So, you do admit to drinking."

My feet felt like lead at the end of my legs. I was so exasperated I couldn't even move. It was like my nervous system had been temporarily unplugged. I flung my arm in the air and let it fall. "Yes, everyone does. But I've never even been drunk."

"You know you weren't supposed to be drinking after your injury."

I looked to the ceiling and a tear escaped. Wiping it away, I looked back at him. "I didn't, Dad. It was six weeks before I even felt like going out. I can't..." I had no more arguments left in me. I cleared the tears from my cheeks and dried my hands on my pants. I opened my laptop. "I'll forward you my grades on Tuesday when they come in."

He put his hands up, relaxing his stance for the first time in the conversation. "Okay, then. I'll expect them in my inbox on Tuesday. I'll be back Friday, and we can discuss this further then." He spun and walked out the door.

I paced my room, not believing what I had just experienced. I'd never been so angry in my entire life. Since when was I a liar?

I knew exactly when, but my omissions with them had nothing to do with the things he had accused me of. I'd kept the extent of the effects of my injuries secret so I could stay at school. I'd told myself it was just to keep my scholarship, but if I were really honest, it was to be near Doug. My feelings for Doug were the only other thing I'd hidden from them.

Tracing back and forth across my room did nothing to dissipate my anger. I had tutoring sessions tomorrow I needed to prepare for, but I couldn't focus. I was eighteen, an adult, I had a right to have my own private life. They didn't need to know about everything I felt or thought. I'd heard that childhood didn't last from birth to a certain age, but that childhood was the land where no one died. My Bubbe had passed in March, was that when I'd ceased being a child? Was that why Carter's betrayal had barely mattered? Or did I cease being a child when I almost died? Or was it when I decided I knew what was better for me than my parents did? Had that triggered something in them? Were they angry with me for that?

It was all too much to process. I found some workout clothes in my bag and put them on, struggling to keep my cheeks dry of tears. I slipped on my shoes, barely able to see the knots in my laces for the tears pooling in my eyes.

"Sweetie, your dad's heading out, come down and say good-bye," Mom called from downstairs.

His judgments were like stakes piercing my heart. I had no interest in seeing that man and no nice words for him. I closed my eyes, willing the tears to stop. I took a deep breath and opened my door. "Bye," I called.

"Come down and hug your dad," Mom called.

"I said good-bye!" I yelled from the hall.

"Young lady," she said, and I could hear her start up the stairs.

"It's fine," he said. I heard his statement and then his footsteps.

"Bye, sweetie," I heard him say.

"Bye Dad," I heard Marissa's reply.

Then came the sound of the wheels of his bag rolling across the floor and the garage door opening. I stretched, waiting till he left to make my escape.

The garage door closed, and I heard mom's footsteps on the stairs. "Young lady..."

I jogged down the stairs past her.

"Where are you going? It's nearly dark."

"I have to get out." I crossed to the front door, ignoring a wide-eyed Marissa.

Mom caught my hand. "Amanda, what's going on?"

I swung around to face her. "Do you know what he accused me of? What he thinks of me? Do you think I'm on drugs, drinking, and having orgies too?" I swiped away the tears that pooled in my eyes.

"What? Honey, no."

I backed away. "Did you know that's what he thought?"

"Well, he was agitated yesterday after you called. He talked to Tia. She said Doug's ex-girlfriend Zoey is really messed up." She took a step toward me, reaching out a hand.

I balled my hands into fists. "What does Zoey have to do with me?"

"I see that you care about him. But you were on some pretty strong meds, Amanda. That can impair your judgment." She was using the soft, quiet, soothing voice she used on Marissa when trying to placate her. It wasn't going to work on me.

"They gave me a two-week prescription, and I took them for a week. I am not a druggie, and I'm not being manipulated and used by Doug."

"Well, sweetie, what are we supposed to think?"

"You agree with him?" I threw up my hands. "I can't believe this!"

I ran up the stairs, Mom calling after me. I found the bottle of painkillers that'd been prescribed after my accident, still half full. Taking the stairs down two at a time, I stood in front of her, took her hand, and shoved the bottle in it.

"Here's my drug stash from October." Then I turned and walked out, slamming the door behind me.

It was cold out, and I didn't have my gloves. Reaching the street, I forced myself to stop. I blew air into my hands. I had to warm up and stretch or I'd end up with an injury. Tugging my sleeves over my hands, I jogged in place. When I felt looser, I bent over to touch my toes and then stretched out my hamstrings. When I hit the pavement and saw the street stretched out in front of me, I couldn't hold back. I pumped my arms and put everything I had into my legs. Racing past the shadows of tree limbs made by the orange streetlights, all I could think about for a minute was the cold air piercing my lungs. When I got to the dead end, I had to stop. Clutching my chest, I bent over.

Why had I come this way? Now I'd have to pass the house to get anywhere else? I restarted my run at my normal pace, concentrating on evening out my breathing, glaring at my house as

I passed it. Why did they have to ruin my first day back? I ran till my fingers were ice and then turned back. By the end I was numb, but the sight of the front light left on fueled my rage again. Walking in circles on the porch, I texted Lila.

WHAT? R U KIDDING? She responded when I told her what happened.

AND U R A BAD INFLUENCE 2 BTW.

U WOULD B A LONER LOSER WITHOUT ME.

RIGHT, THANKS! I stretched out on the stoop as we messaged back and forth. She said I could come to her place, but I had to prep for my tutoring sessions.

Mom was sitting in the chair in the front room when I came in.

"Sweetie," she said as she started to get up.

I put up my hand to stop her. "I have to prep for my tutoring sessions tomorrow."

I pounded up the stairs to my room, wondering how I would make it through the next four weeks with these people. I knocked on Marissa's door, thinking maybe it would have been a good idea for her to warn me.

"Did you know this was coming?" I asked after telling her about my conversation with Dad.

"Like mom said, he kind of freaked out yesterday with the Doug thing."

I sat on the bed a few minutes still in shock. Heaving myself up, I hugged her and made my way back to my room.

Doug called before he got on the plane to Colorado, and I tried my best to sound upbeat and happy. If nothing else came of the next few weeks, I would convince them I was not a drug addict or alcoholic. I was confident about my grades, so those results would hopefully reassure them that I was also not a slacker.

🕊 🕊 🕊

Still angry, and deciding that avoidance was the best tactic, I waited till Mom left for work the next morning before I went down for coffee. It left me no time for breakfast or to make a lunch, but I grabbed something at the coffee shop in between appointments. After my last tutoring session, I joined Mark for a racquetball game. He pointed out that my avoidance strategy might give them further evidence of the accused behaviors, so I went home, and put on a nice face. I helped Mom cook dinner, and we ate and cleaned up together.

Even though every part of me longed to keep my Doug story private, I summarized the ups and downs of the relationship for her, hoping to explain my behavior. She seemed to appreciate that I was being open, and I felt somewhat optimistic that the situation could be mended.

My grades came in, and my GPA was just as I predicted. I forwarded the report to Dad in an email. His only reply was, BARELY MADE THE CUT ON THAT ONE. CAN YOU SEND ME MARK'S NUMBER?

Frustrated with his curt response, the little hope of resolution I'd formed based on talks with Mom evaporated.

IT'S NOT LIKE I HAD A TRAUMATIC BRAIN INJURY OR ANYTHING, I wrote back with Mark's contact information copied after.

Feeling I was under a microscope, my time at home became grueling. I ate breakfast with Mom, and had Mark, Lila, and

Ross over instead of going out, determined to show them I had nothing to hide. The house became my own private prison.

Thursday night Mom was at her book club, and Marissa was out with her friends. Dad usually came in on Thursdays, but he'd flown to Europe and it took an extra day. I was happy to have silence and space, and I bailed on going out with Mark, Lila, and Ross. I took a long hot shower and washed my hair. I'd started to dry it when my phone buzzed. I picked it up.

"Hey, what's up?" Doug asked.

"Nothing, drying my hair."

"Can you be done in about fifteen minutes?"

"What? Why?"

"I came back from Vail a day early, and I was hoping I could see you."

"What? Like now? Why didn't you say something this morning?"

"I wanted to surprise you. Is that okay?" I jumped off my bed and shuffled through my drawer, trying to find something to wear.

For me, yes. For my parents, maybe not so much, I thought. "Sure," I heard myself say.

"Okay, I'll see you in ten minutes."

I found some jeans, thinking we could meet up with Mark and Lila since Dad would probably be livid if Doug and I stayed at the house alone.

I hated to bother Mom at her book club, so I sent her a short text. DOUG SURPRISED ME WITH VISIT. WE'RE GOING OUT WITH MARK AND LILA. I WILL BE HOME BY 12 OR SO.

If I Could Fly

Is he staying the night?

If that's okay. I guess he could stay with Mark if it's not.

No, I guess it's ok. you'll have to make up the guest bed.

Okay, thanks! I added a blowing kiss graphic at the end.

The doorbell rang, and I ran down to answer it. I'd never been so happy to see someone in my life. I jumped into his arms.

He hugged me tight, picked me up, and walked through the doorway, swinging me around and setting me down just inside. "I missed you."

"I missed you, too." I stood on my tippy toes and kissed him. "Come on." I motioned to the stairs and started to jog up them.

"What's the hurry?" he asked, following me up the stairs.

"I have to finish drying my hair before it's a curly mess. Mark, Lila, and Ross are going out to this local pub, so I thought we could meet up with them."

In my room, I sat on my bed and picked up the blow dryer. He sat beside me sweeping my hair to one side, exposing my neck. He planted kisses from behind my ear down to my shoulder. "Is anyone home? It'd be nice to just be alone."

I ducked away and turned to face him. As good as that sounded, I couldn't have my parents thinking we were having sex while they were away.

"That sounds awesome, but I promised Lila. She was having a bad day." I bit my lip. It wasn't completely a lie as the holidays were always hard with her family issues.

He took my hands. "Is there something else going on?"

"Like what?" I hedged.

"I don't know? You tell me. You're biting your lip."

Dang, that one got me every time.

"My Mom is at her book club, and Marissa is out with her friends. I'm not sure I'm supposed to have guests over." My answer was lame, and I knew it.

"Guests like boyfriend guests?"

"Yes."

"I see." He rocked on his heels.

"Any boyfriend, or me in particular?"

"Any boyfriend, probably." I twirled my hair in my fingers.

He took my hand. "Is everything okay? Should I be concerned?

"Absolutely not." I squeezed his hand and kissed him. "I'm so happy that you came. It's so sweet of you." I kissed him again. "Now I have to dry my hair."

Sitting on my bed with me, he scanned my room while I dried my hair. I didn't take the time to blow it out straight, but it was mostly dry when I stopped. I found a cardigan and slid on my boots. I was so excited to see Doug, and I barely cared I was letting my parents' paranoia dictate our plans.

We drove to the pub and met up with my friends. Mark couldn't help starting in right away. "What's up with your dad? He left me this weird message," he asked as soon as the waitress left with our order.

"You know my dad. He has to be mister private investigator."

Doug rubbed his hand on my leg. "What is there to investigate?"

I shook my head at Doug and turned to Mark. "What did you tell him?"

He lifted his eyebrows and repositioned himself in his chair. "The truth. That you studied more and drank less than the rest of us, but that you made some surprising personal choices."

"Mark!" I said.

Doug leaned forward. "So I'm a surprising personal choice?"

Mark motioned in our direction. "Yeah, I mean Zack, and then you. Amanda's usually pretty conservative when it comes to dating choices."

I pointed my straw at Mark. "That's not fair. Two guys I dated in high school were older than me."

He shook his head. "It's different when the guy is four years older and over drinking age, and you know it."

I took a sip of my soda, thinking I'd love to spray him with a big straw full. This wasn't the way I wanted to spend my twenty-four hours with Doug.

Lila reached both her hands across the table. "Okay, okay, can we just have fun now?"

Ross laughed. "I was having fun. Mark and Amanda haven't had a good fight in a while."

Lila flicked him on the ear. I glared at him and Mark, wishing I could shoot laser beams out of my eyes.

The waitress came with the food, and the conversation drifted to safer topics. I was glad the club had dancing so Doug and I had some time to ourselves.

When a slow song started, I didn't even mind that we were both sweating. I just wanted to be close to him.

"Why didn't you tell me about this thing with your dad?"

"Because he's being unreasonable. His opinions don't even make sense." I traced my fingers in circles on his neck. "You're trying to distract me."

I smiled. "Yes, I am."

"Well, if you want to talk about it. I'll listen."

"Okay, but I don't."

We danced at the pub till eleven thirty. Mark had come with Lila and Ross, but we gave him a lift home. Nothing else was said about Dad, and I let out a sigh of relief when Mark got out of the car.

At home Mom had left a note on the stairs that she'd made the guest bed. He started to walk up the stairs, but I stopped him.

"One more kiss?" I whispered.

"Of course." He kissed me. After a couple of kisses, we decided on the plan for the next day. I had a full tutoring schedule, but we figured most clients wouldn't be opposed to getting a two-for-one deal for the day.

In the morning, Mom was cordial to us. She'd made muffins and had an extra-large pot of coffee brewed when we came down.

"How long are you staying?" she asked Doug as we sat at the table.

"I have to get back tonight. I'll need to head out by six. I'm sorry I'll miss seeing Mr. Avery."

She laughed and patted the table. "You can call him Charlie. I'll give him your apologies. Will you have an early dinner with us?"

"You don't have to do that mom," I said.

"I won't do anything fancy. Maybe just pick up some Italian at the deli around the corner."

"That'd be nice, thanks." I hugged her as I got up. "We'll see you just after five then?"

"Sounds good." She kissed me on the cheek, and I realized that was probably the first time we'd touched since last Saturday morning. At least my relationship with her was better.

The day with Doug was fun. He was animated with the younger kids and perfectly cool with the older tutoring clients. We had good conversation at dinner with Mom and Marissa.

After dinner I walked him out to the car. He wrapped his arms around me. "I wish you could come with me to Paris."

I spoke to him in French. "Yes, that would be amazing." I kissed him.

He squeezed my hands. "I'll call you in the morning before you head out for work."

"Perfect." I kissed him again, and we said good-bye.

Mom, Marissa, and I all stayed in and watched a movie that night.

Everyone except Dad was up early the next morning to start decorating for Christmas. It was normally a fun tradition, but my anxiety over my relationship with Dad hung like a shroud in the back of my mind. He'd gotten in late, so I hadn't seen him the night before. I was a bundle of nerves, wondering what we would say to each other. I was close to hating the man at this point and wishing I could be anywhere but in this house.

He wandered into the living room as we were hanging lights on the tree. "Hey, isn't that my job?"

Marissa put a hand to her hip. "That's what I said, but Mom said to let you sleep."

He grabbed a string of lights, placing them between the branches.

"Good morning, Amanda."

"Morning." I lifted a finger at him as I sipped my coffee.

"So, I hear we had a visit from Mr. Taylor."

"Yep." I nodded.

One of his eyebrows titled up. "Should we expect him again next week?"

"I don't know. He's going to New York after Paris."

"Is that so?"

I stopped unwinding the lights from the package and looked at him. "Yes."

He looked at me over the rims of his glasses. "Okay, well, if you say so."

I stood up. "I'm going to spend New Year's with him in Chicago." It just came out. He'd asked me when we'd said good-bye outside the night before. I had planned on warming them up and asking permission, but his distrustful tone had me infuriated.

He looked to Mom and then me, pushing his glasses up to the bridge of his nose. "We'll have to think about that and talk later."

I was kind of surprised he hadn't forbidden me to go right then. Maybe he'd thought he'd push me too far. In my mind, that line had already been crossed. His accusations were so outrageous I wouldn't listen to anything else he had to say.

"I'm eighteen."

He shook the string of lights at me. "You listen to me, dearie, you would do well to remember who pays for those clothes you're wearing and that coffee you're drinking." He dropped the cords on the floor and stormed out. Mom followed him.

Marissa dropped her lights on the floor as well. "So much for tree decorating, I'll be in my room." She brushed past me.

Ugh! How had I become the disgrace of the family? I went to my room, put in my earbuds, and started some music. Tears flowed from my eyes, and it made me even madder that every time I got angry I cried.

After a few minutes, I heard a knock on the door and Mom peeked in. She held a plate with a sandwich. "We're eating lunch, do you want to come down?"

I took my earbuds out. "No."

She sat down beside me. "I know he seems overbearing right now. We just see you taking a different path than you have before. We don't want you to do something you'll regret or get yourself into a situation that's harmful. Your choices have always been based on a solid foundation of faith and belief." She squeezed my shoulders. "I don't want you to lose sight of those."

I scooted away from her. I'd had it with all of them. "What choices are those exactly?"

"Well, the drinking and these guys you're seeing."

"People drink in college, and I'm seeing one guy." I held up one finger.

She sat up straighter. "But this guy is giving you alcohol."

"You don't know that, and besides, Mark gives us alcohol. He isn't even twenty-one. You let us have drinks sometimes, too."

"Okay, well let's not argue about the drinking." She waved a hand in the air. "Older guys are more experienced, and we feel that maybe you've been pressured into things that you wouldn't normally do. When you think you're in love, it happens sometimes."

I placed my hands on the bed in front of her and looked her right in the eyes. "You had this talk with me every year since I was thirteen. Neither one of them has ever done anything like that. Zack and Doug are good guys. I'm still a virgin. And if I decide not to be, it will be because it is what I want. I can't believe you guys just assumed I was having sex."

She grabbed my hands. "Sweetie, I'm so sorry. That's not what I meant. Tia was just really concerned that these guys were players."

"Players? Mom when have you ever used that word? Do you even hear yourself?" I snatched my hands from her grip. Not what she meant? That was a complete lie. My eyes filled with tears. "Dad said the word orgy, Mom. I think you should go. I want to be alone." I stood up, trying to contain the tears streaming down my face.

She reached out her arms. "Honey..."

I stepped away from her. "Go." I turned my back, and she left.

Marissa came in later to tell me Mom was crying. Good, I thought, I hoped she felt horrible. "Please at least come decorate. You'll see. Everything will blow over."

Not wanting to spoil her holiday, I agreed to go downstairs. We finished decorating the tree and had dinner together, but I didn't talk to them and they didn't try to get me to. Marissa kept up the chatter the whole meal while I pushed my food around the plate. Marissa left to go out with her friends, and I went to my room to mope. I was starving but I waited until my parents went to bed to go down and eat something.

The next morning I got up and had breakfast with them, and then we went to church, same as always. I was going through the motions, doing exactly what I should.

That night I slept at Lila's. It was the perfect diversion. We hadn't had a sleepover in over six months, and it was long overdue. We talked about boyfriends, fashion, hair, and vacations until well past midnight. I was exhausted the next day, but the mental break was worth it.

Dad had taken an extra day off, so his flight didn't leave till Tuesday. Before he left he knocked on my door. "Can we talk?" he asked when I cracked the door open.

I took a step back. He came in, snapping his fingers and clapping his hands together.

"Yes," I prompted.

"So, your mother says you don't seem to be doing drugs and aren't drinking, at least as far as she can tell." I opened my mouth to speak, but he held a finger up. "She thinks you may be exercising a little excessively, but you're eating well enough for the most part. I heard about your talk with her. If Doug wants to visit again, that would be fine with us."

"So, now he's okay? You're giving me your blessing to date him?"

"I didn't say that. I still don't like it, but he is welcome in this house as your guest. I do not like the idea of you spending New Year's with him though. It doesn't look good."

"Dad, they have a guest room, just like we do."

"It still doesn't look good, but as you said, you're eighteen. I can't stop you."

"Fine." I crossed my arms on my chest.

"Just take it easy on your mother, okay? She worries about you."

I teared up. "You guys are the only ones hurting me."

He tousled my hair. "It's called tough love."

"Whatever." I grabbed my phone from the bed, wanting any distraction from the conversation.

He snapped his fingers and clapped his hands together again. "Okay, well I'm off in an hour."

I put my earbuds in my ears. "Okay." I sat down on my bed with my books.

He walked to the door but turned back when he reached it. "Bye, love you."

I forced the words from my lips. "Love you, too."

Doug asked before showing up Friday. He switched his flight so he had forty-eight hours between his Paris and New York trips. I thought he was crazy, but he said it was boring without someone to hang out with. His Dad had a girlfriend with him, and the plan had originally been for Zoey to come along.

My parents were nice enough to Doug when he visited. Still, I packed the twenty-four hours with activities away from our house. We went out to dinner Friday night, and then for a run and ice skating on Saturday. This time I cried after he left. Sick of my family, I wished the next two weeks would evaporate.

Tia and Ed got in Christmas Eve. Her arrival brought on another round of cross-examination. She'd been Dad's right hand man in their Doug-Zoey investigation. She'd acquired abundant knowledge about Zoey and was liberal with judgments on my dating choices. Christmas and the week in the Cancun were pure torture, and I couldn't wait to be away from the lot of them, save Marissa, who was my only sympathizer.

My parents didn't like that I decided to spend New Year's with Doug, but I was beyond caring. At least I told myself I was. Deep inside, their disapproval ate away at my very core. I'd never done anything they'd disagreed with, and a certain amount of shame shrouded the decision. Even when I reminded myself that I was visiting his family, staying in their guest room, the feeling wouldn't go away. I couldn't begin to understand why my relationship with my parents had done such a one-eighty, how everything I did was wrong all of a sudden. Why couldn't they trust that I was making good decisions?

"Now you know what it feels like to be the one always messing up," Marissa told me when I complained to her.

"It's different, and you know it." They'd assumed I was lying to them, deceiving them on purpose. This was way beyond nagging about grades or staying out late.

"I know. Dad is ballistic about Doug."

"Still? What do I do?"

"I have no clue."

Chapter 4

We flew back from Cancun into Chicago on New Year's Eve. Mom, Dad, and Marissa had a connection to Champaign, and Tia and Ed would drive back to Milwaukee. Doug, his dad, and brothers were meeting me in the airport. I felt nervous about having such a big welcoming party. His dad and brothers' flights got in from New York and DC just a half-hour before mine, and Doug's dad insisted we share a car.

In the terminal, I spotted them right away. Amid the brightly dressed families greeting each other, five tall men wearing dark pants and business jackets, faces glued to their phones save one, were hard to miss. Doug saw me and waved.

Even though I was a good two paces ahead of Marissa, the inevitable occurred. Just before Doug reached me, his dad reached out, took Marissa's hand, and kissed her on the cheek.

Doug took my hand and kissed me. He whispered in my ear. "You look amazing! Too bad for my dad your sister is taller than you."

Marissa, with her oozing sex appeal, then proceeded to hug each of the brothers.

"Hi, Dougie." She winked at him, and I fought an eye roll.

The brother standing next to us introduced himself to me first. "Amanda, great to meet you. I'm Michael. You can call me Mike. I'm the doctor. Well, second year med student at Marquette. I may be the shortest but am definitely the best looking." He shook my hand. "Wow, you're much whiter in person. Didn't you just come back from the Mexico?"

I laughed. His humor reminded me of Tia's husband Ed, who took any opportunity to crack a joke at my expense. "I'm doing this reverse tan thing. It's all the craze in California."

Doug's dad stood rattling his change in his pockets until we finished. "Amanda, sorry about that mix-up."

"No worries, Mr. Taylor, Doug should have prepped you. Lots of people make the same mistake."

Marissa tossed her hair behind one shoulder. "Yes, because I'm so much taller, people assume..." She let her words drop off. *Taller, and beautifully built with nice curves and long legs,* I thought.

"Please, call me Christopher." He squeezed my arm and introduced his girlfriend Charlotte.

Doug introduced me to the others. Chris, the oldest brother, worked at his father's law firm in New York. Chris' fiancée Nicole was a lawyer, too. Andrew, the second oldest, lived in DC and was a congressional lobbyist.

We introduced my parents to everyone when they caught up with us. Dad wore a stiff smile, and Mom fiddled with her bracelet. Between them and Doug's dad, who never stopped turning over the change in his pocket, it was tense.

Mom's eyes were watering when I hugged her good-bye. She rubbed my hair and kissed my head. "I love you."

I'm not going to feel guilty I told myself. I wasn't doing anything wrong. "Love you, too, Mom." I squeezed her gently and stepped back. "Bye, Dad." I waved a hand at him.

"Bye."

Marissa gripped my arms, nearly cutting off the circulation. "You're so lucky! I wish I could come out with you!"

"I'll text you at midnight." I hugged her.

"It doesn't have to be right at midnight. But take pictures. I want to see everything."

Doug slid his hand to my back and whispered to me. "In case you haven't noticed my dad is getting antsy."

I nodded at him, gave Marissa another quick hug, and waved good-bye to my parents.

His dad had reserved a limo to take our party to the hotel and then Paula's condo. Doug, Michael, and I waited in the lobby while the others checked in and changed in their rooms.

"Beer or wine?" Michael motioned to me as we down at the hotel bar.

"Diet Coke is fine," I told him.

"Oh, right, sorry, forgot."

They ordered beers, and we sat on the stools talking about holiday trips and school. It took just over an hour for the others to freshen up, and then we took the car to Paula's.

When we arrived at her condo, Paula greeted her sons and Nicole with hugs and kisses. She apologized for speaking in Spanish to Charlotte. "I just get so excited to see all my children in one room that I can't help myself." She smiled and shook Charlotte's hand. Doug and I were in the back of the crowd, and when she saw me, she took my hands. "*Hola, mi bella.*"

My cheeks felt flushed at her compliment, and I hugged her back. "*Hola,* you look amazing. Thank you for having me," I said to her in Spanish.

She squeezed my shoulders with her hands and slid them down my arms. Stepping back, she gripped my hands and held them up. "You were in Mexico for a week?"

Michael gripped his mom's arm and half-whispered in her ear. "She's doing a reverse tan."

Paula laughed and waved us towards the other room. "You have to come meet my other girls."

We walked to the living room where Doug's stepsisters and their dates were gathered with Gary. Both Gabriela and Rosa Maria kissed my cheek and hugged me as they introduced themselves and their dates.

Once everyone had met, Paula served drinks and appetizers. After having a bit to eat, Doug and I excused ourselves to freshen up. Finding my room at the end of the hall, he opened the door and motioned me in. He closed the door behind him, and as I spun to face him, his arms wound round me and he kissed me.

"I have been waiting for three hours to do that," he said when he ended the kiss.

I raked my hand through his hair as he held me against his chest. "I missed you."

He slid his hands from the top of my head down my back and to my hips. "Two weeks is too long." He kissed me again, backing me into the bed as his hands traced from my hips to my waist.

I pried his arms from around me. "What time is dinner? I need to shower and do my hair and makeup.

He picked up a section of my hair. "You're beautiful just like this."

"I looked up the restaurant and club. It's really fancy."

He kissed me again, and I couldn't resist melting into him. The phone in his pocket buzzed. He backed away and took it out. I sat on the bed and peeled my sweater off.

He tapped on his phone screen and then looked up. "Zack and Bill and their dates will be here in a half-hour."

I jumped up. "What?"

He held a hand up to me. "It's okay, we don't have to leave for the restaurant for an hour." I sat back down on the bed. He leaned down so that we were face to face and took my hands. I kissed him. "Okay, so maybe we need to get ready now. I'm just down the hall when you finish," he said, backing away.

"Got it." I got up to retrieve my suitcase.

I showered quickly and put my hair up curls and all. My dress was white with rhinestones lining the two front panels crossed over my chest. It was more Marissa's style than mine. She'd picked it out, but I'd went with it wanting to look a little sexier tonight.

I left my bag and shoes on the floor just inside the door and padded down to Doug's room. The door was cracked a bit, but I knocked anyway. He called from the bathroom to me.

When I came in he put down his razor and looked at me. "You look amazing!" He kissed me and stepped back. "But how does one spend an entire week in Cancun and not get a tan?"

I grabbed a pillow from the bed and threw it at him.

When we joined his family in the living room, Zack and Bill had already been introduced to everyone. I met their dates, and Doug got a beer for himself and a club soda for me. After everyone had a drink, we took two limos to the restaurant. Zack, Bill, and their dates—as well as Michael, Paula, and Gary—rode with us. Doug's dad, brothers, Charlotte, Nicole, and stepsisters took a second car.

We were shown to one long table at the restaurant, and his dad ordered a round of champagne. I'd only drunk champagne once before when Lila had stolen some from her mom's alcohol refrigerator. I was sure it was the cheap grocery kind as it tasted like bitter sour grapes. This champagne was crisp and smooth.

In the beginning, we sat near Gabriela and Rosa Maria, whose dates also spoke Spanish. Before dessert, Doug's dad had us switch places.

"To mix it up," he said.

Doug whispered in my ear, "Dad's Spanish must be rusty."

I hit him lightly on the arm, thinking perhaps I had a bit of a buzz from the champagne. "Be nice."

"Oh, that was," he took another swig of his wine and stood up. We traded with Paula, Gary, Andrew, and Michael to sit across from Zack and Bill and their dates. I paced myself, having only a few sips to drink and taking only a few bites each course, because they served us five courses bringing us a different glass of wine with each. After dinner we rode in the limos to a club. Paula and Gary weren't joining us for that part of the evening, so they took a cab home. Doug suggested I invite Lila, Ross, Mark, and Holli, and they were meeting us.

When we got to the club, we waited in line a few minutes and then were ushered into a large bar area. I was texting Lila, trying to find her, when Doug placed his hands on my shoulders and turned me in the direction of the bar. Lila stood on a stool, waving a hand in the air.

Lila squealed and threw her arms around me when we reached her. "You look amazing! I can't believe you're here! I can't believe your dad let you come."

I forced a thin smile, hoping she would see my attempt at shushing her. Hugging her, I whispered in her ear, "Dad didn't like it, but he didn't expressly forbid it."

She backed away, pretending to pat my hair and fluff my dress. "You did good. I'm proud of you. Finally taking a page from my book and spreading those wings." She swung my arms out to the side.

Lila's parents were polar opposites of mine, never seeming to care where she was or what she did. I always felt my family balanced out the absence of hers, and she balanced me out. Without her coaxing ever since middle school, I probably would have been studying Middle Eastern history tonight.

We ordered drinks at the bar and then moved into the lounge area and eventually to the dance floor. The night was perfect. As we counted down to midnight, Doug wound his arms around me. I tried to kiss him, but he pulled away, sticking his fingers in front of my face. "Three, two, one."

He kissed me, picked me up, and spun me around. Lila was right beside us, and she grabbed me and hugged me. Mark, and the rest of us, took turns wishing one another a happy New Year. My phone buzzed, and I answered a text from Marissa with New Year's greetings.

As I was texting, "Viva la Vida" by Coldplay started, and Doug slid his arms around me from behind. He kissed me on the neck. "It's our song."

I turned around, slipped my phone into my bag, and wrapped my arms around him.

He whispered in my ear as we danced, "Last year got really bad there for a while. Meeting you changed that. I'm so excited to spend this year with you."

I looked up at him, grinning from ear to ear. "Me too."

After finishing the champagne from the toast, everyone got a second wind and we stayed at the club until well past two. Outside I hugged Lila and Mark good-bye, and Doug and I shared a cab back to his mom's with Michael. By the time we got back to the condo, I was fighting to keep my eyes open.

In the elevator, Doug pointed at the ceiling. "Want to go to the roof?"

"Yes," I nodded. Michael got out on his floor and we rode up to the top. Outside, we sat looking out over the lake in the quiet, snuggled against one another. Eventually the wind got to me, and I shivered.

"Bed time?" Doug asked.

I turned to face him. "I don't want to sleep."

"You don't want to sleep or be alone?"

"Be alone."

"I'll see you tomorrow, and the next day, and the next day." He tucked a stray strand of hair behind my ear.

"Okay." I took his hand. We walked back to the elevator and rode to his floor. Inside we took off our shoes and tiptoed down to our rooms. We slipped inside my room, and he held me to him and kissed me. "I could stay with you."

"What about Michael, your mom, and Gary?"

He waved a hand in the air. "Other side of the condo."

I smiled and slid my arms around him. "Okay," I pointed to the bathroom. "I just want to brush my teeth and change." I grabbed my pajamas and closed the door behind me. When I came out, he was sitting and resting his back against the head-board, legs crossed out in front of him with just a T-shirt and soft pants on.

I walked around the other side and slid under covers. He slid under the covers and over to me, kissing me on the neck. "I'm so tired."

"Me too." I turned my head to kiss him.

"Goodnight," he whispered. He brushed my hair out of my face and kissed me softly on the lips.

I snuggled into him and was asleep within minutes.

🕊 🕊 🕊

The next thing I knew his lips were kissing my forehead. I opened my eyes and sat up. "What time is it?" With my ten-hour sleep inclination, it could be noon and a house full of guests could be waiting on me.

"Don't worry, I woke you in plenty of time to be presentable."

I lay back, relieved. "What time is that exactly?"

"Eleven."

"I only need half an hour to get ready." I covered my head with the pillow. He jerked it away. "Hey!" I retrieved another from behind my head and swatted it at him. He batted it away and launched another pillow at me.

"Yes, but then I won't be able to enjoy being with you. I have to be at the house early tomorrow. We only have the whole day today."

"Okay, I'm awake." I jumped up and went into the bathroom. I brushed my teeth and snuggled back beside him. We talked a little, but the conversation led to kissing, and before I knew it, I was completely lost in warmth of his lips on mine.

At the end of a kiss he cleared his throat. "Now you should get ready."

I propped myself up on my elbows as he stood and put on his shirt. "Does your mom know you slept here?"

"No. I got you coffee." He pointed to the desk. "I told her I was waking you."

"Ooh, thanks!" I jumped up and picked up the cup. After several gulps, I hurried into the bathroom to shower. As I did my hair and makeup, I sent a short text to Marissa and Lila. HAPPY NEW YEAR AGAIN!

Marissa replied first. HOW WAS YOUR NITE? DETAILS NOW!

SUPER FUN. GOTTA GET DRESSED. LUV U.

I NEED DEETS ASAP. LUV U 2.

I had no clue what I was supposed to wear for brunch and sent Doug out to see what his mom was wearing. "She says casual," he told me when he poked his head in the bathroom. He stood behind me and hooked his fingers the loops of the robe as I applied my makeup.

"I don't know why you wear that stuff. You are so beautiful." He scooped my hair back and kissed me on the neck. All my muscles melted and I turned to face him.

"You really shouldn't do that. I need to get dressed."

He left me to change, and I opted for New York casual. One step above my idea of casual, the outfit included black pants, a white top, and a long grey cardigan. Elegant but comfy is how Marissa described it when she put it in my bag. Checking my hair and makeup one last time, I put on some black ankle boots and made my way out of the room. Hearing noise at the end of the hall, I walked to the kitchen.

I found Doug at the end of the counter, sampling food from the dishes in front of him. He smiled and wound an arm around me when I approached. "More coffee?" He held up one of the two mugs that sat in front of him.

"Morning, Amanda." His mom stopped her prep work and hugged me. "Could you be a dear and get this boy away from my food?" She pointed at Doug. "Go find Michael and make sure he's awake and can be appropriately dressed in fifteen minutes."

I shoved Doug off the stool and took his place. After a few sips of coffee, I offered my help to his mom. She had me carting dishes to the table in the dining room within seconds.

His stepsisters, father, Charlotte, Chris, and Nicole were right on time. Charlotte looked even more pained than she had the previous night, perhaps due to some over-indulgence in alcohol. His father and brothers seemed like they recovered well enough though.

I was seated between Doug and his father, and inevitably, the conversation turned to me. "So, how did you meet Doug?" his father started.

I was caught off guard as this was the only thing he'd said to me since our awkward greeting in the airport. Before I could answer, Michael interjected. "Haven't you heard the story?" He projected his voice down the table. My face warmed, and I could feel the blood rushing to my cheeks. "Doug smashed her into the gym floor during a volleyball game. She ended up with an internal brain hemorrhage, in a coma for six hours, and screws and plates in her arm." He motioned to me. "Hey, do you have your X-rays and CT scan images? I would like to see those." He stuffed a bite of pancake in his mouth.

My eyes scanned the room. Everyone had stopped mid-bite and their eyes were locked on me. His mom got up and set a new pitcher of water on the table. "Michael, we're eating. I don't think people want to hear about medical stuff at the table."

Mr. Taylor pointed at Doug. "Oh, this is the girl you were telling me about at Thanksgiving."

Doug squeezed my leg under the table. "Yes."

His father pointed a fork at Doug. "When Michael said 'smashed her into the floor,' what exactly did he mean?"

I stepped in quickly. "It really was more of a mutual crashing to be precise."

"Mutual crashing? Doug, you didn't tell me any of this. There aren't liability and insurance issues, are there? Do you need a lawyer?"

He punched Michael. "No, I cleared it with the chapter lawyers. Her dad is an alumni brother. We're all good."

"So, how did this mutual crashing occur exactly?" Chris asked. "No offense, but you don't look like the volleyball type."

"Yeah, and you should tell them about the other ER visit while you're at it," Michael said, shoving another bite in his mouth. He swallowed. "You should've heard Doug telling me about her. This girl knows five languages. Then the next night he says, 'This girl—'"

"Okay, they get the picture," Doug said. I squeezed Doug's hand under the table.

Michael pointed his glass at Doug. "I'm just glad she finally has a name."

"So what was the other ER visit?" Chris directed his question at me.

"I'm kinda clumsy," I started, sure that my face was blood red. "My friend roped me into playing flag football. Since I didn't have cleats, I slipped on the turf."

"Slipped is an understatement, but you were fine until you saw the blood," Doug said.

"People are eating," their mom scolded.

"We just want more dirt on Doug," Michael said.

I rolled my eyes. "Yeah, I got nothing." Fortunately, the conversation moved to other topics. After the meal, we moved into the entertainment room to play pool and darts. His dad and brothers left just before three to catch their flights home.

Doug's sisters left soon after, and the rest of the afternoon we spent with Michael. Doug and Michael played games virtual games and I refereed their arguments. Gary came in later to announce they were going to Mass.

Doug whispered to me. "We don't have to go."

"Don't you usually go?"

"I'm sure Mom sent Gary so you wouldn't feel pressured into going. The service is in Spanish, and all of mom's Puerto Rican friends will be there."

This was like a dream come true for me. The excitement must have shown in my eyes. "Of course you want to go." He rubbed his hand alongside his pants. "I'm going to be the only one embarrassed here. Just please don't sound better than me."

"Now I really want to go." I said in Spanish using my best Puerto Rican accent.

Michael pointed at me. "Your Puerto Rican accent is good."

Doug stood, too. "Mom even complimented her."

Michael stretched. "Count me in."

I walked down the hall to my room, with Doug trailing behind. I scrubbed my teeth, swooshed some mouthwash, and ran a brush through my hair. Grabbing my boots, I made my way to the foyer.

"Oh, Amanda, you're so sweet. You don't need to come," his mother said as I approached them.

"Amanda takes any opportunity to use her Spanish," Doug said to them in her native tongue.

We walked the few blocks to the church. Anxious, I fidgeted with my sweater as we found a pew and knelt. We sat down, and Doug put his hand on my leg and looked around. "Okay, so maybe you stand out a little."

I poked him in the ribs.

I'd never been to a Spanish service before, and it was more beautiful and moving than I could have imagined. Grateful to have Doug and Paula in my life, I found myself fighting back tears.

After the service, I was introduced, in English, to many of Paula's friends. They all spoke to each other in Spanish but always addressed me in English. I caught the woman next to me whispering in Spanish to her neighbor, "Why did they bring her here if she understands nothing?"

I answered her using my best Puerto Rican accent. "It's no problem for me. I understand perfectly."

The crowd around us grew quiet. I glanced at his mother, and she was beaming. After that, I was encircled by her friends, each of whom seemed to have a hundred questions for me.

On the walk home, we trailed behind his mom and Gary. "Thanks a lot, man." Michael hit Doug on the back. "You've set a really high bar for all of our girlfriends."

"Just keeping' it real," Doug said, kissing my hand.

We had dinner with Paula, Gary, and Michael. Michael packed and left for Milwaukee and then Paula brought out all the old picture albums from Doug's childhood. It was hard to imagine him and his brothers ever being little.

The night came too fast. I was tired before I wanted to be. The next day Doug would help me move into my dorm early and then spend the afternoon at the fraternity house helping his brothers get their things in. Lila was meeting her mom in the city and my Sunday seemed to stretch out in front of me like an empty void. I berated myself, wondering when I had become anxious about being alone.

Doug slept with me in the guest room again. It felt so wonderful to be lying next to him, and I couldn't imagine sleeping any other way.

"Are you just going to be in your room alone all day?" Doug's mom asked over breakfast. "We could go shopping."

"Mom, she's okay. I don't think Amanda wants to shop," Doug said.

"Oh, okay." The corners of her mouth turned down.

I chimed in right away. "Actually, that sounds fun."

She smiled at him "See, she does want to go shopping with me."

The four of us drove to my dorm and unloaded my things. Afterwards, we dropped Doug off at the house, and then Gary dropped Paula and me off near the Magnificent Mile shopping district. I was in way over my head, but Paula's warmth and energy made her easy to be with. Anything beat staring at my four dorm walls all day. Complaining that she never got to pick out girl's clothes, she insisted on buying me something.

"Gabriella and Rosa Maria used to pick the opposite of what I chose just to spite me." She laughed. She had good taste and wouldn't let me talk her out of paying for a whole outfit, including a beautiful pair of brown boots. She found several outfits for herself as we walked through at least ten other stores. Fortunately, just when I was running out of steam, she stopped at a coffee shop. We were just walking out when Doug called.

"Tell him I'll put you in a cab to the fraternity house. But first ask him if he's feeding you," Paula said loudly enough for Doug to hear.

"You're still with my mom? Are you okay?"

"Of course." I laughed at him. The shopping trip drained me, but I felt recharged after my coffee. I took a cab to the fraternity house and we picked up sushi and ate it in my room. Doug offered to help me unpack, and we had my room re-organized in under an hour. I surveyed the space, thinking it felt different. Perhaps it was too quiet without Elise bouncing around, complaining about something.

"Are you excited to finally sleep in your bunk?" He pointed up to my loft. I actually wasn't as happy to be back here as I thought I might be—happy to be back at Northwestern with Doug, away from my parents, definitely, but being on campus already had me stressed about classes.

Since when was I worried about grades? Where was the anxiety coming from? The apprehension about my courses had started with Dad's badgering. His lack of confidence in me was affecting mine. Thinking this, I realized I missed my parents more now than at the beginning of fall quarter. No, I missed the relationship I used to have with them, I corrected myself. That's why I didn't want to be alone today. I shook off the thoughts, determined to enjoy my last few days before classes started.

As we folded the boxes and stored them under the futon, the exhaustion hit. I plopped down and lay back on the pillow. Doug stretched out beside me. "I am exhausted," he told me, sliding his fingers through mine. We extended the futon and lay down and watched a movie. Before I knew it, I was awoken by him nudging me.

"Hey, I should go."

"No," I tugged at his arm, still in a haze.

"It's past curfew. I have to go."

"Can I come with you?" I pushed myself up on my elbow. Rush started tomorrow, and I'd barely see him till the weekend.

"No, we talked about that. I'll see you tomorrow. We could have breakfast if you want." He kissed me.

No! I screamed inside my head. Partly at him, and partly at myself for being clingy. What was my deal?

"You could stay then." I planted kisses across the back of his neck.

"That's not fair."

"No one's here, and it's spooky." I continued placing the kisses down his neck to his chest.

"Spooky? You are very, umm..." He cleared his throat. "You're safe here. I really shouldn't."

I looked him straight in the eyes. "Come on, I have an extra toothbrush?" I smiled at him and put on my most pleading face, lacing my fingers in his. I had no idea if he would give in or not. We'd always been butting heads, digging in our heels. "It's not really any different than the last time." My argument was sound. There was precedent. Happy with my play, I thought maybe I should be a lawyer.

"Okay, I'll stay."

"You won't be sorry." I pressed my lips to his.

"That's not why I stayed." That was what he said, but he answered my kisses, backing me into the wall. His lips traced down my neck to my shoulder and onto my chest. "We should get some sleep though. I need to be at the house by seven."

Happy, I jumped up and grabbed a toothbrush and toothpaste. I let him use the bathroom first while I changed into a tank and pajama shorts.

"Are these new?" He asked when I joined him on my futon.

"You're too hot." I fanned myself.

"That was lame." He scooped me up. "Maybe you should sleep up in your bunk, and I'll sleep down here."

I wound my arms around his neck and leaned in so I was only an inch from his face. "You wouldn't do that."

"You're right," he set me on the futon, placing his arms on either side of me. "But I do need sleep." He rolled over and lay beside me.

I turned around to face him, balancing on my elbow. "Thanks for staying."

"Are you awake now?"

"Yes, why?"

"I have something for you." He sat up and reached for his backpack.

"What?" I sat up and bundled my hair behind me. "Why?"

"It's a late Christmas present." He unzipped his bag, reached inside and took out a small envelope.

"But you already got me the picture." I reached over to my desk and held it up for him. It'd been taken of us on Halloween night. We'd exchanged gifts the weekend before Christmas. I wasn't sure if he'd get me a present, but I'd gotten him a photo album he could put his trip pictures in. I'd been nervous to give it to him because it was sort of a geeky present. But I'd found it already full of photos and sitting on his bedside table when we were transferring my boxes to his car.

"Well, this is the present you were supposed to have for Christmas. I had these ordered, but they just came." He turned over the envelope and two silver chains fell into his hand. One had the fraternity letters and the second had a Chinese symbol dangling from it. "You don't have to wear my letters if you don't want."

"Are you kidding? These are great. Will you put them on?" I turned around and lifted my hair up so he could clasp them around my neck. I walked into the bathroom to look in the mirror, and he followed me. The necklaces had short chains and the charms rested right on my collarbone.

I studied the Chinese symbol.

"It means strong, mighty, powerful," he said.

"You're kidding, right?"

He spun me around, "No, it's perfect for you." I looked back in the mirror and touched the charm, thinking I didn't feel that way anymore. I'd definitely come to school last quarter with the sense that I could achieve anything. But my parent's criticism had deflated me. Would I let their judgments affect my confidence? No, that would be crazy, I was strong and capable.

Doug gathered my hair in his hands. "What are you thinking?"

"They're awesome. Thank you." I hugged him.

"Okay, so sleep now?" He kissed the top of my head. We turned off the light and lay down. I fell asleep with my head resting on his arm and woke to his hands running through my hair.

"You don't have to get up yet," Doug said when I opened my eyes. He was fully dressed with his shoes on and his backpack on his shoulder.

"Are you leaving?"

"You don't have coffee."

I groaned. This was not a good thing. "Sorry, I forgot."

"It's okay. I have coffee at the house."

I covered my head with the pillow but then sat up and shoved it behind me. "I can get up." I pushed myself up and went into the bathroom and brushed my teeth. I saw my necklaces in the mirror, and they made me happy. When I came back, he was sitting on the futon tapping on his phone. I slid in beside him and rested my chin on his shoulder.

He bumped me with his shoulder. "What are you doing today?"

"Gym, run, maybe the bookstore. Elise and Lila will get in this afternoon."

"I'll miss you. Want to have dinner tonight?"

I played with his hair, thinking I'd miss him but also wanted to spend time with Elise. "I'll text you. Maybe we could do something later. Can you wait two minutes? I'll walk down with you."

"Sure." I kissed him. He squeezed my hand. "Focus."

"Got it." Grabbing my gym clothes, I changed in the bathroom. My water bottle was still in my gym bag, so I rinsed it out and slipped on my shoes.

I opened the door to the hall, peeking out to make sure no one was around. Doug wasn't supposed to be there, and I prayed we didn't run into a resident assistant. We took the elevator down, and as we entered the common area, he gripped my hand. I froze. Someone entered the room from the guy's dorm side. Recognizing Stephen, I exhaled.

Adjusting his headphones, he stopped mid-stride when he saw us. "Oh, hi, you're here already? And heading for the gym?" He pointed at me. "Guess we're back to our routine." He rocked on his heels.

"Yeah, I guess so."

"Okay, well I'll see you there." He started towards the doors.

We followed him out. "Okay, I'll meet you there." I called as he turned in the direction of the gym.

He nodded and waved his hand, without even acknowledging Doug.

Doug took my hand. "I'm not sure he wanted to see that."

"What?"

"Never mind." He kissed me. "Good thing he wasn't a resident assistant. They could've kicked you out of the dorm."

"It would've been your fault."

"You begged me to stay." He picked me up and spun me in a circle. "I'll call you."

"Okay." I gave him a peck on the cheek. "I'm going to catch up with Stephen."

When I turned the corner, I found Stephen pacing in a circle. "You didn't have to wait. I said I would meet you at the gym."

He shrugged his shoulders and fell in beside me as I caught up to him. "So, that was awkward."

"I'm so glad you weren't a resident assistant," I said as I kicked a pebble out of my way.

"So, you and Doug?"

"Yeah, we started seeing each other at the end of last quarter."

"Sure, just seems fast, that's all."

"You knew we were dating."

We crossed the street to the next block in silence. "You really aren't a morning person, are you?"

"Haven't we covered that before?"

"Yes, that one we covered." He hesitated, "So, Doug…"

"You won't tell, will you? Those dorms are like a ghost town, and I didn't want to stay there alone."

"It's none of my business." He shrugged, stuffing his hands in his pockets. "I just had you pegged as a different type. But you were with Zack, I guess."

He'd lost me. "Different type?"

"Wow, you really aren't a morning person, are you?" The words were comical, but there was no hint of amusement on his face.

We finally reached the gym doors, and I stopped. "What are you talking about?"

"You and Doug and the dorm thing. Really, it's none of my business."

"Oh, yeah, I know I shouldn't break the rules that way, but weren't you at all freaked out with no one in the dorm last night?"

All I got was a blank stare for a few seconds. "We aren't talking about the same thing," he said.

"Okay, I'm lost. Yes, Doug and I broke the rules. A guy stayed in my room overnight."

"Never mind." He waved a hand and walked up the stairs towards the treadmills.

I started up after him. Now my adrenaline was going. "I feel like you're mad, and I don't get why."

"Like I said, it's none of my business."

"What's none of your business?"

"You and Doug." He turned around to face me.

"What, that we're going out? That he's my boyfriend?" I still had no idea where this conversation was going. Stephen and I were friends, or at least I thought we were. Sure, Lila and Mark had tried to set me up with Stephen last quarter. We'd enjoyed being running partners, and we'd hung out several times. I hadn't expected to have to defend myself to him though.

"I just thought you were a different person," he repeated, and I waited. "With the Catholic, small town thing, and all..."

Catholic, small town thing. Was he giving me a clue? Someone who was Catholic would ... then it came to me. My face immediately blazed. He thought I'd had sex with Doug? That was what Doug meant about it being awkward. It wasn't any of Stephan's business whether Doug and I had sex or not. Who was Stephen to judge me? He thought I was a different person, more like him? Maybe he had liked me more than I thought. Maybe he was just being protective like Mark. Mark wouldn't approve if he thought I was sleeping with Doug either. But right now I was talking to Stephen, and I was livid.

I stopped in front of the treadmills and looked at him. "I haven't ever had sex, have you?"

"Wow," he held his hands up, "well, yeah. Guess I read that wrong. I'm so sorry."

His sudden retreat threw me. Mark wouldn't have backed off. He would have defended his right to his opinion and told me that it didn't matter that Doug and I hadn't had sex. The fact that it looked like we had sex would have been incriminating enough.

I was still mortified. "Can we pretend this conversation never happened?"

"That's great with me." He stepped onto the treadmill and started setting a program. I did the same on a machine beside him. He turned to me. "I wasn't surprised when you guys got together. You'd have to be blind not to see—whatever it is—you have between you. He is just so much older, you know." He pushed the start button, and we started jogging.

"I've gotten enough criticism from my family about that to last a lifetime."

"Sorry."

"Thanks." We continued our programs, getting in a good hour's run.

After a shower back in my room, I met him in the lobby of the residence hall. We got brunch and then went to the bookstore. Thankfully, he only brought up sex once more.

In the English literature section, he tapped my shoulder and whispered to me. "I want to apologize for before, again. You really are the perfect girl."

I wasn't sure how to respond to his comment, but I was glad I was honest with him. Maybe he had more respect for me than he would have. He seemed like a good person.

I really didn't have many books to buy. My chemistry, biology, and math books were the same as first quarter, so all I needed were books for my literature course. Somehow I lost Stephen, so I browsed the foreign languages section. My phone buzzed as I was leafing through a Japanese culture book.

"Hi, where are you?" came Doug's voice.

"At the bookstore," I whispered, looking around to see if anyone was close enough to be annoyed by the phone conversation.

"What are you doing there?"

"Buying books."

"Anything good?"

"Chinese lit. I'm actually browsing through the language section now."

"I guess that would be better than math but not chemistry." I rolled my eyes as he went into a long dissertation on chemistry and its application to attraction between people. It wasn't like him, but it was amusing.

"Where are you?" I asked.

"I'm at the sandwich shop. Do you want anything?"

"No, I just had breakfast. How's everything at the house?"

"Fine. Hold on just a minute. There is this really beautiful girl here..."

I heard the words through my phone and behind me at the same time. I spun around, and he planted a kiss on my lips. "You're here."

"I only have fifteen minutes." He examined the books I had in my hands and we looked through the foreign section together. Within minutes I had a stack of books he thought I needed to read.

Stephen found us before Doug made my pile higher than my credit limit. Doug offered to pay for the books that were optional reading material. It was a nice offer, but I put them back on the shelf. My scholarship only covered books for my courses. I was watching my pennies, saving up to live off campus next year.

After we paid for our books, Doug headed back to the house, and Stephen and I took the shuttle back to the dorm. In my room, I got in a solid hour nap before Elise arrived.

"Hello," she said as she came through the door, rolling her suitcase behind her, "Did you miss me?"

I hugged her as she approached.

"What was that for?" she asked.

"I missed you."

"You never hugged me before."

"I haven't? Oh, sorry."

"I'm not complaining, but I'm just wondering if an alien took over my roommate's body."

I helped her unload the rest of her things from the car and organize them in the room. We plugged in the fridge and went to the market to get some food. She absolutely had to know everything about my break. I described my holiday, including the dilemma with my parents.

"You had to know that was coming. Unless you're like twenty-five, no parent is going to like you dating someone who is four years older," she told me as we drove home.

"I guess. I just don't get how they jumped to all the other stuff."

"Maybe it just freaked them out to see you all grown up."

Even after brainstorming for an hour, we had no good solutions for solving the issues between me and my parents.

In the next few days before classes started, Doug and I spent the few hours of free time he had between rush events, grabbing lunches, or watching late night movies together. Lila and I helped out with some of the parties, but many were for just guys or by invite only.

Once classes started, I was able to form a routine. Doug and I worked out with Zack and Bill on Monday, Wednesday, and Friday mornings. Tuesdays, Thursdays, and Saturday mornings were blocked out for rowing. Zack was fully invested in training me to be a coxswain. I had tutoring sessions a couple of afternoons and continued babysitting on Friday nights.

Mark wasn't super thrilled with the idea of Doug and I being glued at the hip, as he described it. I kept up our Tuesday and Thursday racquetball sessions, though, and that made him happy. Doug and I studied together most evenings, but Wednesday nights I reserved for time with Lila. She resumed her role as social director, making sure everyone was out on Thursday nights. I saved Friday and Sunday dinners for time with Elise and Kate. This was how I imagined college life to be, and Doug was icing on my slice of life.

Chapter 5

Thursday night, two weeks into the quarter, I walked over to the house, looking forward to a well-deserved night out with friends. It was nine when I arrived, a little later than I'd hoped after tennis with Lila and a shower. As soon as I stepped out of the stairwell on the second floor, I knew something was wrong. It was too quiet. Already feeling disconnected because Doug hadn't texted me after class, a knot started to form in the pit of my stomach.

I found Bill, Mark, Ross, and Lila, textbooks on their in laps, seated in front of the muted TV. Not one of them was dressed for going out, not even Lila. I checked the time on my phone and scanned the room. Each of them met my gaze separately as I plopped my backpack on the floor and sat down on the arm of the sofa next to Mark. It was Thursday night. There should be banter over who would win the basketball game or discussion of the club choice. Each of them had their eyes glued to their study materials. I checked my phone again for a message from Doug.

Bill spoke first. "Did Doug call you?"

"No." I looked between all of them, panic growing in my chest. "What happened?" I sprung up, planning to sprint to his room. Bill jumped up and blocked my path with his arm. He motioned for me to follow him. I looked back to Lila for reassurance, but she only shrugged.

Bill walked down the hall in the opposite direction from Doug's room. "He didn't text or call after class. I texted him, but he didn't text me back," I started. "He usually calls or at least texts. You guys would call me if something happened, right?"

Bill wiped his chin. "Everyone is okay," he began. That never boded well.

"Bill—"

He held his hand up, and I stopped and took a breath, letting him proceed. He explained that Doug had been on his phone when he got to the house and went straight to his room. He'd gone downstairs for dinner, was social, talking with the pledges and a few brothers for half an hour, and then returned to his room without eating. Around seven he'd come out to the common area and motioned for Zack. "They've been in his room ever since," he finished.

I walked a few steps away and then back to Bill, and repeated the movement. "How can you say everyone is okay? Obviously he's not."

"Well, physically."

"Okay, fine. What should I do?" I knew I could trust Bill to give me good advice on Doug.

He grabbed my wrist. "Pacing like a hamster on a wheel isn't going to help. Just hang out with us." He pointed at the sofa.

I went back and sat down, taking a seat between Mark and Bill. Eventually Mark, Ross, and Lila retired to their room, claiming they needed a quieter area to study. Bill and I sat there pretending to watch TV, with me flipping my phone over and over in my hand until he snatched it from me. It was over an hour before Zack and Doug emerged from his room.

I heard the door open and watched Doug walk down the hall. He didn't look up until he reached the common area. When he did, his eyes were vacant, as if he'd been stripped of his will to live. His eyes met mine for a few seconds, and then he looked down and back up at me. He lifted his chin and tilted his head back towards his room. "Can we talk?" He put out his hand.

I cut my eyes to Zack for reassurance. He only nodded. I swallowed hard, forcing myself to get up and follow Doug down the hall. He waited in his doorway, taking my backpack as I caught up with him.

He motioned for me to enter, and I stepped past him. Deciding that sitting might be premature, I leaned against the desk. He placed my backpack beside me and then sat down on his futon, dropping his head into his hands. In the silence that followed, I was glad I hadn't eaten. The knot in my stomach churned uncontrollably, and my chest felt like it was locked in an ever-tightening vice. I clenched my arms around my stomach, unable to take my eyes off him. He finally looked up at me and, in one fluid motion, crossed over to me and gathered me in his arms.

With his warm arms around me, I started to relax. Taking in his smell, the knot in my stomach loosened, and my breathing slowed. I wanted to ask what was wrong but was afraid to hear the answer. I buried my face in his chest and let him hold me.

It was a long time before he moved. He grasped a section of my hair and held it up to his face. "You washed your hair."

I couldn't be silent any longer. "Is everyone..." I couldn't finish my sentence. "Your family?"

"I'm so sorry." My mind raced. Sorry? For what? "I didn't know you were waiting. I meant to call and tell you not to come. You shouldn't have had to witness this." He stepped back and walked from one end of the room to the other.

I bit my lip to keep from flinging a zillion questions at him. Whatever it was, I was resolved to let him tell me on his own time. Obviously this wasn't about me.

With his hands stuffed in his pockets, he stopped for a few seconds but then resumed pacing. He came back to stand in front of me, and placed his palms flat on the desk on either side of me, his arms trapping me in my spot. "You have to know, I..." He shook his head. "You are important to me. I don't want ..." He brushed his fingers along my cheek.

He pushed himself away from the desk, hesitating, but started pacing again. My empathy for his pain quickly turned to panic as my mind raced through the various scenarios that would prompt him to make such a statement.

He hands raked through his hair as he continued to circle around the room. "I can't believe it, just when I thought we ... I just got cleared."

Cleared? What did that mean?

"We could finally…" He stopped for a second and looked at me, but then shook his head and started pacing again. "It happened before you and I got together. I wasn't drunk. She brought wine, and I had few sips to try and placate her. She was determined to get me back. She wouldn't stop. The way she came at me, it caught me off guard. It happened so fast, and we didn't use anything." He stopped pacing and stood directly in front of me. "She's pregnant."

The air felt like it was trapped in my lungs. I scanned the room, unable to look him in the face. Zoey, my brain tried to register, pregnant? Doug's going to be a father, a father to Zoey's child?

He took my hands forcing me to look at him. "I'm so sorry."

Did he think I would be mad? I didn't like thinking about him being with her like that, but he'd told me they had a very physical relationship. "You told me you were with her," was all I could think to say.

His pacing resumed as if he hadn't even heard me. Suddenly I just wanted to be away from him, to think, to process.

"She seems unstable, and I don't know what she'll do." He took my hands and stood before me, his face just a foot from mine. "I am so sorry. I just got all the tests back. I'm clean. I was thinking we could…"

He let his words trail off and just stared at me. I wasn't following, I wasn't getting something.

He shook his head and my hands. "You haven't…you don't know what I'm talking about."

I couldn't tell whether he was phrasing a question or statement. I studied his face.

He let my hands drop and turned his back to me forming his hands into fists. "You haven't before…" He shook his fists in the air. "I should have known. We should have talked about this by now." His walked to the far wall and stood looking at his photos. "Zack probably knew, and that's why you guys didn't. I should've given him more credit."

Sex, this was about sex. He was ready for us to have sex. As I realized what he was talking about, my heart felt like it was going to beat out of my chest. Suddenly I was too warm and couldn't breathe. Sweat formed on my forehead. I put my hand on his back. "Doug."

He twisted around to face me. "You should go."

I kicked into full panic mode, reaching out to him. "Doug…"

"You need to go." He picked up my backpack and held it up to me. He opened the door. "Zack!" he yelled down the hall. Zack seemed to materialize out of nowhere. "Will you take her home? She probably hasn't eaten, so make sure she gets something."

He handed me my backpack and closed the door.

Zack closed the distance between us. "What did you say to him? He's even worse than before."

Angry, hurt, and on the verge of tears, I brushed past him. That was a thousand miles from how I'd wanted my first talk about sex with Doug to go. I flung the exit door open and started down the stairwell. "You don't have to drive me. I can take the bus."

He was faster than me, catching my arm before I could get past the first landing. "Hey, let me take you. We can talk. Plus, Doug will be even madder if…"

I jerked away from him. "If what?"

"I don't know. What'd you say to him?"

My arms and legs were shaking so hard I couldn't stand any longer. I sat down on the cold concrete. "You don't want to know Zack."

He sat down beside me. "Okay, that sounds bad and you look like you're about to faint or puke, or both. Let me drive you back to the residence hall. We can get some dinner on the way."

All I wanted to do was go back to my room and curl up in my bed alone. I reached for the railing and stood up. "Fine, I just want to be away from here." I rubbed my cheek on my sleeve, trying to erase the tear that escaped my eye.

He took my backpack and carried it to the car, opening the passenger's door for me. He drummed his fingers on the steering wheel as he drove.

"He's only telling you and me. If you want to talk to someone, I'm it. There's no one else."

"This is wrong."

"We've talked about sex before."

"He didn't know that I hadn't..." I waved my hand in the air and brushed it across both cheeks to catch the tears running down them.

"You're kidding. You guys never talked about that. And he was planning..."

"I know, I get it, and to make things worse, he assumed correctly that you knew."

"No wonder he was upset, or more upset." There was a moment of silence. "Everything will be fine. Doug always does the right thing."

Thinking this was meant to console me, I realized he didn't know what Doug would think the right thing was. Doug and I were cut from the same Catholic stock. I believed Doug was a father of a baby, not a ten-week old fetus—a baby. I was sure Doug perceived the situation similarly. There wasn't room for me in that equation. Focusing on harboring that fear somewhere it couldn't be accessed, I didn't voice these thoughts. I let Zack think he was helping.

"Okay, dinner?" He tapped his fingers on the wheel again.

"I have food in my room."

"Promise me you'll eat?"

"Yes," I lied.

There was silence, and Zack turned on the radio. It was loud and he hummed along. I shut him out, turning over every word Doug had said, trying to figure out what he was going to do. I turned the music down.

"He said she didn't seem stable. What does he think she'll do?"

"That is a complete understatement. She's been harassing him for weeks, trying to get him to go back to her, and then she comes out with this."

"What do you mean?"

"I think she could've made it up."

"Did you tell Doug?"

"That's the first thing I told him."

"And?"

"He wouldn't even consider it. To him, the hormones explain her crazy behavior. Not that I blame him. I wouldn't want to think someone I dated would do something like that either."

Now I had crazy on top of crazy. Zoey was depressed or bipolar, or something clinical. But was she crazy enough to fake a pregnancy to get Doug back? Doug didn't believe she was. Was he not able to look at the situation objectively? I had no idea what to think or believe.

Zack dropped me at my dorm, and I ducked past the students in the lobby and took the stairs. In my room, I shed my heels and club outfit. Slipping on a tank and leggings, I curled up under my blanket on my top bunk. I pulled my phone and books out of my backpack. My phone displayed four text messages from Lila. I answered them with an explanation that Doug had a family situation and that I'd realized I forgot to finish some work.

At least I could get some studying in. It really wasn't worth thinking about Doug. He was mad, but not at me. There was nothing I could do or say to make it better. Desperate for a distraction, I picked calculus, the subject that needed the most concentration. To work through the problems, I'd have to focus, so there was less chance my mind would wander. It worked for a while. I had most of the problems for next day's lesson done when my stomach began to demand attention.

I went to the kitchen and melted some cheese on a bagel. Back in my room, I set my plate up on my bed and climbed up. My bunk was my private haven. It was sort of an unspoken rule between Elise and me that our bunks were our private space. If we were in them, we wanted privacy.

I started reading chemistry next, trying to focus on the material. As it got later, I grew more anxious, checking my phone every few minutes. I didn't think I'd be able to sleep without hearing from Doug. Thankfully, just after eleven, I got a text from him.

SORRY BOUT B4. R U AROUND? CAN WE TALK?

SURE, I replied.

K, BE THERE IN 15.

I finished the chemistry chapter and walked downstairs to the lobby. Not in the mood to talk to anyone, I tried my best to avoid eye contact. Fortunately, it was only a few minutes before I saw him. He had his hands stuffed in his pockets as he walked towards the building.

I met him halfway, and his arms enveloped me into a vice-like hug. We stood like that, motionless, for what seemed like minutes. Releasing me, he brushed my hair from my face. "Sorry about before." He squeezed my hand and released it. We walked up to my room in silence.

Inside, he surveyed my room. "Studying?" I nodded. He picked up the plate I'd left on the futon. "You ate." I nodded again. He stuffed his hands in his pockets. "Come here." He reached out with one arm, gripped me to him, and stroked my hair. When I looked up at him, I could see the panic lurking just below the surface of his calm façade.

He sat down on my futon, and I followed. "I'm sorry I lost it before. It just put me over the edge."

I didn't know what to say to him, so I just sat there.

"You talk to anyone?"

I shook my head. "Just Zack."

He scrunched his eyebrows together. "No one else? Your mom? Your sisters? Lila? Elise?" I shook my head at each question.

"I'm not going to tell anyone. This isn't about me."

"I'm driving up to see her tomorrow. I'll leave after my last class and stay with Michael till Sunday if needed." He shook his head, and turned to look at me finally. "I meant what I said before. You are..." He wrapped his hands around mine. "I don't want to lose you. What happened that night will never happen again."

He was going to see her? This was happening too fast. The question of the future of our relationship had been on the fringe of my thoughts all night. The miraculous sequence of events needed to keep us together hadn't quite formed in my mind yet. Still, I clung to the idea that a positive outcome was possible. It was a coping mechanism, but I needed it. Thinking of the other scenario was too much to handle after what I'd already been through with him.

I could hear Tia's voice in my head. "*Girlfriend, you've got to be kidding. You are so screwed. You need to dump him like a hot potato.*" This was exactly where she would have predicted this relationship would lead. But I trusted Doug, and I knew he cared about me. He would be honest. Maybe I wouldn't know the details of the back and forth between Zoey and him, but I would know where I stood.

I couldn't think about it anymore. "Good, so you're helping me with my English paper, right?"

"Was I doing that tonight?"

"Yes." I jumped up to grab my laptop from my desk. I sat beside him, letting him read what I'd written so far. It'd developed into our usual studying routine, and it felt good to be doing something familiar. I ignored that he was about as animated as a doorknob. He stayed until nearly one. I hated to see him go, especially since it seemed like there was a possibility we may never be together again.

"I'll call you in the morning," he told me when I walked him downstairs. He squeezed my hand and walked away. I watched him go. He didn't look back.

As exhausted as I was from the turmoil of the evening, I couldn't relax. I heard Elise come in after two and pretended to be asleep. Finally, exhaustion won and my brain shut down.

My phone's vibration under the pillow woke me. The display read six forty. I swiped the screen to read the text message.

GOING TO MASS AND BREAKFAST WITH FATHER. CALL YOU LATER, Doug wrote.

OK, THX. I wrote back.

WHY R U UP?

FELL ASLEEP WITH PHONE.

SORRY.

NO WORRIES.

K. CALL U LATER.

This was exactly what I was afraid of, not seeing him. Fridays were our mornings. Most of our time together was taken up with workouts, studying, or socializing, but Friday we'd set aside for just us. Of course today would have been our two-week anniversary of this tradition. I saw how silly it was for me to miss it already. But, it wasn't just the Friday morning. It was the thought that I'd lose him. We were so happy. I was so happy. It couldn't be the end of that. It just wasn't fair.

Elise stopped mid-bite when I heaved myself over the edge of my bunk. "What are you doing up so early? Some sadistic rowing initiation?"

"No, couldn't sleep."

"Everything okay? I thought you guys were coming out last night."

It took me a minute to figure out how to phrase it. I grabbed a mug from the shelf. "Doug had a family issue come up, so..." I'd already decided I would be proactive about telling people at least this partial bit of information. I figured it would explain his behavior without arousing too much curiosity.

She studied me. "Bad?"

"Pretty." I poured a cup of coffee and took a sip.

"Sorry. He's not coming then?"

I shook my head. "I'm going running."

"Sure, exercise more to make us all look even worse."

"It's just my thing." I set my coffee on my desk and changed quickly into my workout clothes. Stephen was running on the treadmills when I got to the gym. I was glad to have company. What I wasn't prepared for was to see Zack and Bill. With Stephen I could pretend like nothing was wrong, but Zack and Bill were a different story.

"Hey, you're not supposed to be here." Zack popped me with a towel. He had me on a strict training regimen, and Friday was my day off. He looked between Stephen and me and motioned for me to stop my run. He put his head close to mine. "You okay? Did you talk to him?"

"He came over last night."

"So, all's well, right?" He snapped the towel in my direction. "What are you doing here?"

"I wouldn't say that. He's at Mass now, but he's going to see her tonight."

He scrunched his face into a pained look. "Okay, well, I'll let this one slide."

"Thanks, I need the distraction."

Zack started the treadmill beside me. "Distraction complements of Zack, Bill... and Stephen."

"And Stephen what?"

I shook my head at Stephen, and he seemed to get that he didn't need to respond as he nodded and put his headphones back on.

After our first mile warm-up, Stephen and I ran five miles in forty minutes. I was happy with how I felt. A little extra adrenaline in the system never hurt anyone.

I showered quickly, thinking Doug might call anytime. He didn't. I read chemistry and biology, thinking he would call any minute. He didn't. At ten thirty, Kate knocked on my door, and we walked to class together. I tried really hard to pay attention to the conversation, but nothing was sinking in. I hoped it wasn't too obvious.

Finally, just as we were nearing the chemistry building, I caught a glimpse of a figure running across the courtyard towards us. It was Doug. My chest expanded and I took in a full breath.

I put on my most convincing smile. "You could text."

"I know." He hugged me tight. "Sorry, I got caught up," he said into my ear and then stepped back, taking my hand. "What have you been up to?"

"Studying."

"Anything else?"

"Not really."

"Nothing like a seven o'clock run or anything?"

"Maybe something like that."

"Friday is supposed to be your day off."

"I was bored."

"Bored?" he cocked an eyebrow. "Okay, well, we're both going to be late. I'll meet you after class." He squeezed my hand and walked away. As I had last night, I watched him. At least I would see him again before he left for Milwaukee.

Lila, Kate, and Jeremy saved me a seat as usual, and I slipped into it just ahead of the professor reaching the podium. Lila wrote U OK? on the side of a piece of paper and shoved it at me. I hadn't lied to her, I told myself. Doug did have a family issue. A huge family issue! I was studying. But, now I had secret number two of our ten-year friendship to keep from her. It wasn't my story to tell. I shouldn't feel guilty. So why did I?

Sure. I wrote back on a corner of the paper.

The end of class couldn't come fast enough. "Coming to the house?" Lila asked as we walked out of the lecture hall.

"Doug said he'd meet me."

"Okay. See you later." She waved and walked away.

I headed in the direction I knew Doug would be coming from.

Walking to his building, I found him with his phone to his ear, pacing. When I approached, he motioned for me to wait. Watching him talk seemed like eavesdropping, so I meandered back the way I came. Just as I turned around to retrace my steps, I saw him, hands stuffed in pockets, making his way towards me. As I neared him, he stopped and held out his hand to me. His expression didn't change from the scowl he'd worn as he approached, but I put my hand in his hoping it comforted him. All I felt was a limp, rough hand in mine.

We walked to the house in silence. "I need to be at lunch," he told me as we reached the front door.

"I'll be upstairs."

"Okay." He squeezed my hand, letting go to hold the door open for me.

I found Lila upstairs, eating her lunch. I'd only had a banana all day, and it occurred to me that I should be hungrier after my run. Hunger wasn't a sensation that registered with me today. I listened to Lila ramble about the schedule of events for the weekend and nodded appropriately. Slow deep breaths kept me from panicking about the wide expanse of a weekend I had to fill with waiting for an outcome I couldn't control. I entered the plans in my calendar, knowing I'd never remember scheduling tennis and brunch with her.

As I fought clumsily with my calendar app, she grabbed the phone from my hand. "Are you more spacey than usual or what today?"

Refocusing, I apologized for my lack of attentiveness and hoped she didn't notice my anxiety. Fortunately, she blamed my ineptness on my technology-challenged brain.

After Doug finished lunch, we walked to class. I felt like the earth had shifted and a chasm twenty feet wide stood between us. It was none of my business and all of my business at the same time. The mental anguish he seemed to be in tugged at my heart, and I wished I could do something, say something, to make it better.

He stopped in front of my building, finally facing me. He made eye contact briefly but then looked down and kicked the sidewalk. "I'll call you tomorrow, if not before."

I reached for his hand, but he formed a fist. Trying to look unfazed, I fiddled with my jacket. "Be careful on the drive."

He looked away again. "Zack will pick you up for rowing to-morrow. What are you doing tonight?" He rubbed his forehead.

"Babysitting."

"Good, okay, so should I have Zack pick you up after?"

"No, and he doesn't need to pick me up for rowing either." There was no way I was going to tear Zack away from whatever he was doing late on a Friday night.

"Okay, then, tomorrow." He hesitated. "Take care," he told me more seriously. "Call my mom if you need anything."

"Sure."

"Okay, we're late." He motioned to the doors. "Bye." He reached out and squeezed my hand. "I don't know if you want me to kiss you. I feel like you should hate me right now."

"I don't hate you, and I do want a kiss." If this was to be the last day we had together, I definitely wanted a kiss. Even if I had no clue what part of crazy to believe in this situation, I still wanted him. I probably shouldn't have, but there was no way I could make that decision with him standing right in front of me. Maybe when he was gone I could convince myself that I'd be better off without him. Maybe, but I doubted it.

His lips pressed hard against mine, and he folded his fingers around my neck. I gripped his wrist, not wanting him to stop. His phone buzzed and he pried my hand from his arm.

He stepped back. "I'll call you." He waved, turned, and ran towards his lecture hall.

Even though my phone alarm buzzed in my pocket, I watched him go. The air seemed to thicken in my lungs the farther and farther away he got until I had to force it out. I wiped the tears from my cheeks and forced myself to walk into the building.

I sat in the back row of the lecture hall and took meticulous notes. Afterward, I changed at the gym and played racquetball with Mark. I paid attention and responded, forcing myself to be present. With just enough time for a quick shower, Elise and I met up for an early dinner before my babysitting gig. That night, although exhausted from my charade of being fine, and meager food intake, the worry in the pit of my stomach kept me up well past one. Watching *Top Gun* for the hundredth time allowed me drift off.

After my late night, my early wake up alarm was not a welcome sound. My only consolation was that Doug said he would call by today. Even though I'd said a ride from Zack was unnecessary, within minutes of being up, I received a text from him.

BE THERE AT QUARTER TILL. CAN YOU MAKE ME A COFFEE? I RAN OUT.

It was better than taking the bus or walking in the cold, so I started a large pot of coffee and put on my workout clothes. Stuffing all my gear in a bag, I made my way down to the curb with two steaming cups. It wasn't long before I saw Zack's SUV pull up.

He stopped and rolled down the window. He reached for one of the coffee cups when I held it out. "You look like hell. Guess you talked to Doug, eh?"

I froze mid-handoff. "What? No. You talked to him? Is everything okay?" I backed away from the car instinctively.

He stuck his hand further out the window. "Where are you going?"

"I don't know. To call Doug."

Zack motioned to me. "Get in the car. It's freezing."

"What do you know?" I hoped he could see that my eyes were burning a hole through his head, and that if he didn't spill what he knew, I was going to explode.

"Just get in so we can get to practice."

Every fiber of my being wanted to go find Doug, but I complied, realizing I had no clue where he was.

"He didn't call you?" He asked as he put the car in drive. It was only half a question, really more of a statement. Obviously Zack was under the impression that whatever he knew I knew. "He showed up at my place around two last night."

"He came back?" My hand went to the door latch. I had the door half open, ready to jump out, when Zack's huge arm pinned me to the seat. He slammed on the brakes. My head was spinning. He said he'd call by today. Why wouldn't he call me if he came home early?

"Jumping out of a moving car isn't going to help anything!" We sat there silent for a minute, me, shocked at my reaction, and him, breathing heavily. Then he laughed. "Well, actually, ER visits have served you well in the past where Doug is concerned. Knock yourself out." He reached over and re-opened the door for me. "I haven't got any better ideas."

"Funny." I closed the door. He returned his hands to the wheel, and I re-buckled my seat belt. "So, how bad is it?"

"He said he wouldn't be too late for rowing."

"That's all you're going to tell me. Were you supposed to tell me he was back or coming?"

He shrugged and lifted his hands from the wheel. "I don't know."

"You don't know what happened, or you don't know if you're supposed to tell me? He told me he'd call me."

"You need to focus. I need you today."

He wasn't going to tell me anything. "Fine."

"That's my girl!" He patted my leg, and I swiped his hand away.

We pulled into the athletic gym lot, the only busy place on campus this morning. The basketball players, baseball players, and rowers walked in clusters into the building. I took a deep breath and put on my game face. Bill was waiting for us at the door. I wondered if he knew anything. If he did, he didn't let on.

Inside, I tried to focus, but I couldn't help but watch the door. I could count and watch at the same time. The counting made the waiting bearable at least. Zack was right. We hadn't been there ten minutes when Doug walked in. He scanned the room, making his way to Zack first. They talked for a minute, and then he started over to me. Zack grabbed Doug's arm before he got one step away and whispered something in his ear. Whatever it was, Doug shook his head in agreement. He dropped his bag on a bench and started to stretch out.

Zack had me working with the other team, and I still had to keep pace. Doug watched from the wall, waiting till we finished our sequence to approach me. He greeted the other guys and crouched down beside me.

"Sorry I didn't call. It was late."

"You said you would call me."

The other guys started heckling him and he shook his head. "We'll talk after." He stood and walked over to join his team.

My emotions vacillated between anger and hurt, but either way they spawned adrenaline. I concentrated on keeping pace, and poured myself into the training session. Zack found me at the end to compliment me on the workout.

"See, Mini-Girl." He used his nickname for me for the first time since we'd broken up. "Passion is good."

I felt like punching his face. I pointed at him. "Never mind."

"That's what I thought." He shoved me into the girl's locker room. After showering, I dried off and changed as quickly as I could. But even with my hurrying, Doug, Zack, and Bill were waiting in the lobby for me.

"Everyone's going to breakfast. Do you want to come?" Doug asked, keeping a solid two feet between us.

I didn't want to go to brunch. I wanted to know what had happened with Zoey, and why he came back at two in the morning without calling me.

"Come on, Mini-Girl." Zack rolled his arm in the air. "Everyone's going. It's a team thing."

I just stared at Doug. "Sure."

Bill and I followed Doug to his car. Once we arrived at the restaurant, I sat between Doug and Zack. Doug didn't say much to anyone, and Zack and Bill kept me entertained by divulging funny facts about each of the other teammates. Each of these was followed by that person retelling something embarrassing about Zack or Bill.

After brunch Bill said he'd catch a ride back to the house with Zack. When Doug and I reached his car, he stopped. "We need to talk. Where do you want to go?"

My stomach turned immediately, and I regretted eating the small amount I had. I was at a loss. I didn't know where I wanted to be when he left me for the third time. It certainly wasn't in a diner again. I clenched my stomach, realizing I'd finally acknowledged the real fear clawing at my heart.

"Do you want to go to my mom's? We could get some studying done." His mom's? Studying? I exhaled, thinking that at least this destination was probably not a venue where he intended to break up with me. On the other hand, it'd mean I'd be a captive audience.

"Elise is out for the day. Can we go to my room?"

He nodded his head. "I guess." We stopped by the fraternity house, and he picked up his computer and books. We drove to my dorm in silence, my anxiety growing by the minute. When we entered my room, he set his backpack on the floor and slipped off his shoes.

"Do you mind?" He pointed to the futon.

"No." I took off my shoes, put away my workout clothes, and excused myself to brush my teeth.

Back in the room, I leaned against my closet door. "You look tired." The words came out too sharp as my nerves were frayed.

"You do, too." He patted the space beside him. I sat next to him, and he reclined onto the back cushion.

I turned and folded my legs under each other. "Was it bad?"

He looked at the ceiling "Yeah." He didn't say anything else, so I waited. "She wants me back. I thought we were having a rational conversation, but then she just threw herself at me like before. I had to get out of there. I couldn't stay. I still don't know what we're going to do, or how this is going to work. She's called me ten times since I left."

My mind screamed that he should just cut her off, do anything to sever contact.

He covered his eyes with his hands. "If it were just me, there would be no issue. But I can't ... I have to try and protect this life." He sat up and looked at me, his eyes wet with tears. "You get that, right?"

I placed my hands on his leg. "Yeah, I do."

"Okay." He shook his head back and forth and stood, shaking out his arms and legs. "I need a nap. Do you mind?"

"No, I need one to." We got up and extended the futon all the way out. Lying next to him, breathing in his scent, relaxed me, despite the tension of the situation. I drifted off into a fitful sleep with dreams of wicked stepmothers and evil stepsisters. I woke to the sound of Elise and Kate's voices. They were just inside the door and stopped short when they noticed us. I got up, apologized to Elise, and started rubbing Doug's back to wake him.

He woke easily. Elise went to take a shower, so we had a few minutes alone. "I was thinking of joining Mom for Mass and then having dinner with her and Gary. Do you want to come?"

Knowing this was the only time I would get alone with him, I agreed. We met Paula and Gary at the church. It was a good choice for me, as the service calmed my panic, even if only for an hour. After dinner with his mom and Gary, we studied in his room. I wouldn't have chosen that activity for a Saturday night, but he took his books out and I followed suit. If something good could come out of this, it was that I'd be better prepared for my lectures.

He closed his computer just after eleven. "I should get you back."

I didn't know what I had expected. Being separated from him was not what I wanted. But, I packed my computer and books, thinking he may need time alone.

Doug led us past the family room where Paula and Gary were watching a movie. "I'm taking Amanda home," he said to them.

His mom shot up off the couch. "What? No, it's late. You should both stay. I don't want you out driving this late."

"It's not late. We need to get back to campus, and she doesn't have any clothes." This wasn't true as I'd folded pajamas and an outfit for tomorrow in my backpack.

"I was planning brunch for everyone. Michael is driving down."

"Michael?" Doug questioned her. He turned to me. "Amanda, do you mind?"

"I'll wait in the foyer." I went into the other room and checked my phone for messages. There were several from Lila, Marissa, and Mom I'd ignored before, so I replied to those.

Doug came and found me about fifteen minutes later. "I'll take you home, and then I'll drive back tonight or either first thing in the morning."

"I can get a car or a taxi."

"I am not putting you in a car. Plus I'd like more time with you."

"I have clothes, so I could sleep in the guest room. It's a lot of driving." I held up my backpack.

"You don't have to stay."

I looked him straight in the eyes. "What do you want?"

"I want to be with you." Of course that was more than enough for me.

"Then I'll stay."

He smiled and kissed me.

We crossed back into the family room where Paula and Gary sat. "We're going to stay. We're turning in. We'll see you in the morning."

Paula got up, hugged Doug, and then me.

Doug shook his head. "Goodnight," he said to her and Gary.

Doug left me in the guest room to change and freshen up. When I was finished, I made my way to his room. The door was half open, and he was lying on the bed channel surfing. He'd taken out his contacts and had his glasses on. I knocked quietly. He motioned for me to come in and switched off the TV. "I was just seeing what was on."

Still standing at the door, I motioned to my room. "I can turn in."

"What are you doing over there? Come here." He got up and met me halfway. "Will you sleep in here with me? Or do you want to sleep alone?" He held my hands.

"Here with you works," I told him, thinking I was probably masochistic.

"Good." He stripped off his shirt and held up the covers as we slid in bed. "We should get some sleep. Michael will be here at nine."

For today, I was grateful just to be with him, but my body tingled lying beside him, and it was hard to relax. His breathing slowed and evened out within minutes. I thought of how different this night was from last week. It was unsettling to me that maybe this time next week we wouldn't even be together. I pushed that thought away as soon as it entered my mind. He'd said he wanted to be with me, and I had to focus on that.

Sleep finally came, although it was again filled with odd dreams that were forgotten as soon as I opened my eyes. He sat next to me, his legs touching my back, and held a cup of coffee. "Morning." He smiled, smoothing my hair with his free hand.

"Hi. What time is it?"

"Just after seven." He handed me the mug as I sat up. Setting it down on the table next to the bed, I excused myself to brush my teeth. When I came back, I snuggled in beside him again. He bumped his knee against my leg.

"Want to run?" I asked.

"Can you read my mind?"

"Your leg is bouncing a mile a minute."

"Oh, sorry." He got up. We changed and rode the elevator down to the gym on the second floor. When we finished an hour's run, I showered and dressed for brunch. Michael got in just after nine and we had the meal together with his mom and Gary in their dining room. Afterward, I retired to my room to give Doug time to be with his brother and Mom. After almost two hours, Doug and his brother invited me to join them for a game of pool. We hung out and played darts, foosball, and ping pong until the late afternoon.

I didn't want to go back to campus and to interact with my friends in a normal way. I'd hoped by today there would've been some resolution, some outcome I could deal with. Instead, I found myself in a place reminiscent of November. Again, I had a secret. But now, the secret wasn't mine.

"Will you come to dinner tonight?" I asked as he walked me to my building.

He shook his head. "I've got lots to do." I expected as much. Still I would miss him. "I'll call you later tonight."

As much as I wanted to, I couldn't watch him walk away this time. I willed myself to turn and go. Like yanking off a Band-Aid, I knew it'd hurt less if I did it quickly.

Elise had left a note that she'd be studying till late and suggested we order take out for dinner. I gathered my laundry and started a load in the basement. I cleaned the bathroom, showered, and washed my hair. I didn't have the patience to dry and brush it straight. It would be curly, but I didn't care. I made the obligatory calls to Lila, my mom, and sisters. I sat down with my computer to study. At least Dad would get his stellar GPA out of this quarter.

Elise got back just after seven. I'd already picked up our take out from the delivery guy downstairs as she'd texted me her approximate arrival time. As always, she was in a perky mood, and I put on my game face. It was amazing to me that she could come home from a day out with friends and still want to be with more friends.

Bill and Zack were the first to join us, followed by Mark, Lila, and Ross. Zack sidled up next to me and whispered in my ear. "Is he coming?"

I shook my head.

"Okay, well, nice curls." He looped his finger through one of my curls, and I dodged the descent of his hand on my head. "Did he talk to her again?"

Mark approached, catching the last bit of our conversation. "Talk to who? Where is that boyfriend of yours anyway?" He poked me in the ribs.

I looked at Zack. "We visited his mom last night." I said, hoping that answered Mark's queries.

"So Doug says she adores you," Zack said.

"Wonderful, you guys might as well be married, already." Mark rolled his eyes and walked away. I wondered what his problem was now. Mark would tell me sooner or later, so I wasn't going to fret about yet another issue.

Chapter 6

Perhaps to everyone else Doug seemed no different than he'd been the past two weeks. But he didn't smile. He was distracted, easily frustrated, and very often not mentally present. He sat beside me, wrapping his arm around me. He held my hand briefly but never kissed me. He didn't share his problems with Zoey with me. I tried to remain upbeat, but it was hard. Maybe he was trying to spare me the daily drama or maybe he had no clue how the situation would be resolved, but he didn't talk to me about it. I knew she called and they talked, but I didn't know about what or how often.

In all honesty, part of me didn't want to know. I didn't want to picture them together, especially knowing how crazy she was now. I started to worry about the guy I was dating. What type of person dated a girl like that? Proposed to them? I finally got up the courage to ask Zack during one of our workouts. "Did you ever think Zoey was crazy before?"

He stopped our workout. "She was always very driven. She always got her way. But that's looking back. At the time I just thought she worked hard and was blessed with good genes." I decided I wasn't dating a psycho, and that alleviated some of my tension.

As for my interactions with Doug, I followed his lead. I pretended everything was the same and hoped it looked that way. He went to Mass every morning and joined us for workouts after. He met me between classes, and we studied together in the evenings. Mark or Lila asked me every day how Doug was, how his family was, and I answered the same each time. They were getting through.

Thursday my anxiety ramped up. The weekend was coming, and with it the opportunity for Doug to see Zoey again. Arriving at the house after nine, I couldn't help but feel a sense of déjà vu. Zack caught my eye and cocked his head back towards Doug's room. I tried to read Zack's expression, but it told me nothing. Doug's door was cracked, but I knocked anyway.

He waved me in, and I stepped just inside. He paced, phone in hand, raking his other one through his hair. Instantly anxious, I froze. His tortured look pained me, and I fought the urge to comfort him. As the week ticked by, he had grown more and more distant, even recoiling when I reached out to him. I waited and he finally stopped and looked at me.

"I have to go see her again tomorrow morning and try to figure this out." He wrapped a hand around the back of my neck and rested his forehead on mine.

"Okay." I lifted my gaze to his. He looked exhausted. The thought I'd been skirting all week demanded attention. Our relationship complicated this problem. As much as I loved him, neither of us were benefitting from this torture.

I gathered all my will and spoke. "Doug, this may be easier for you if I'm not in the picture. You don't owe me anything."

As I spoke, he started shaking his head. "I want to be with you, I just need to figure this out. We'll figure out something." He hugged me to him. I wasn't sure what the definition of we was. I had plenty of confidence in the Doug part of that equation, but not so much in a Zoey part.

He smoothed my hair with his hand. "Zack's going to take you out tonight."

I backed away. "I don't want to go out with Zack. I want to stay here."

"You should go out and have fun. All work and no play isn't good for..." He hesitated, and then continued, "young people."

"Young people like me? What about you?"

"Yes, young people like you. I have studying and fraternity business to catch up on." He scraped a finger down my nose. "It's all arranged. Zack is thrilled!"

"And what if I refuse."

"You should go out and have some fun." Going out without Zack didn't sound like fun. It sounded miserable. "He's taking you to Nine Twenty Six."

"What's that?"

"A night club downtown."

"Why?"

"Please, just do this for me?"

I looked at him. He looked horrible, tormented. Contemplating his request, it occurred to me that this could be the last night we had together. Yet, he was sending me away.

"Will I see you tomorrow?"

"I could bring you coffee and breakfast if you want."

"If I'm going to be out late with Zack, you better be bringing me coffee, fully caffeinated, and breakfast." I pointed a finger at him. Comedy was a great distraction. Really it was either laugh or cry at this point. I hated crying.

He picked up on my tone. "And what time exactly will you need this coffee?" He crossed the room again and picked up his phone, opening his calendar app.

"Hmm, nine-thirty."

"Then nine-thirty it shall be. Does this mean you're going out with Zack?"

"If I don't get coffee hand delivered by nine-thirty, I'm going to be really mad."

"I'll be there." He kissed me on the forehead. It was all I could do not to melt into him.

"Okay." I wasn't happy about the night's plans. It was probably some sort of social, be-seen thing. He, and his need to keep up appearances, could be so annoying.

"Good." He took out his phone and texted Zack.

Within seconds he was at the door. "So, we're going out? I have to change, and you'll have to change. At least you washed your hair." He looked me up and down and gestured to the door. I liked this even less than I did before.

Walking down the back stairwell, he started giving me dress code orders. I couldn't stomach it. All I wanted to do was curl up in my bed. "Look, Zack, I don't really feel like going out."

"It doesn't matter. We're going out. Doug's orders."

I stopped, putting my hand to my hips. "You can't make me go."

Reaching his car, he turned to face me. "Just do this for Doug, okay?"

"Fine." I climbed in the passenger's side without another word.

He cranked up the car and backed up. "Don't worry. Doug will do the right thing." This was a repeat of the speech he'd given last week, believing he was reassuring me, and again I ignored him. When we got to my dorm, he had me change into a black cocktail dress and high boots. Touching up my makeup, I twisted a few strands of my hair around the curling rod, and we were back outside within twenty minutes.

At his apartment, Zack changed to dark pants, a silk shirt, and a blazer.

It was a half hour drive to the club. He distracted me with talk about rowing and intramurals. Missing Doug already, I hoped I wasn't supposed to be paying attention. As we drove into the parking lot, I saw the line for the club. It stretched to the end of the block, and I was glad I'd brought my coat. Zack stopped at the valet station.

"I don't mind walking."

"I don't want my car stolen." He got out and met me on the sidewalk. "You've got to get your game face on." He rubbed my shoulders.

"Okay." My back relaxed, but my psyche was still ablaze.

He continued massaging the muscles in my back. "Things will be fine. Doug will do the right thing. You'll see." He took my hand and started towards the door.

I snapped my hand from his grip. "Stop saying that."

Hands out, he spun around to face me. "What's the problem? I'm just trying to help." He backed me against the wall.

"What do you think the right thing is? What do you think Doug thinks is the right thing?" I felt bad about yelling at Zack, but I couldn't stop it. It was like a bottle of soda had been shaken, and the cap popped off. "For someone like Doug, what is the right thing? Do you know what Catholics believe about life? They believe in the sanctity of life from conception. Forty years ago, he would have already married her. Making sure this baby is taken care of is what Doug thinks the right thing is. I doubt that's what you were thinking." I folded my arms over my chest.

"Shit." He looked up at the sky and then back to me. "Okay, no, that's not what I was thinking. I just figured. I'm sorry." He grabbed both of my hands and swung them between us. He leaned down so our faces were barely an inch apart. "You still like me better than that Stephen guy, right?"

I hit him on the shoulder. "What? Zack seriously!"

He laughed but didn't release my hands. "Just making sure I'm still in the running." He took a step back. "Okay, now that that's out, game face." He jiggled my hands between us.

"Fine." I turned to walk toward the end of the line. Within a stride, he was ahead of me. He circled around to face me, blocking my path. "So, you good?"

"Who are you talking to?" I put my hands on my hips.

"Ice woman, obviously." He swatted his hand at my face.

I ducked out of his reach. "Hey, makeup."

Fortunately he knew the bouncers, so we didn't have to wait. He talked with them for a few minutes and then motioned for me to join him. Zack scanned the line and found the friends he was looking for. They looked familiar, but I couldn't place them. I assumed they were seniors.

"Hey, we thought you stiffed us," the one in front said as he approached Zack.

"Sorry, we had issues." He motioned to me.

"Women usually do. This your girl?"

"No, Doug's."

"Amanda, right?" another one of the other guys offered me his hand. "Kyle, we met at the end of last quarter."

"Right." I nodded to him. The other two introduced themselves as Andrew, who had asked if I was Zack's girl, and Justin. They, like Zack and Doug, were tall and handsome and had that confident air about them.

"So, is Doug coming?" Justin asked.

"He had stuff to do," Zack told them, rolling his eyes nonchalantly. There was some conversation about how lucky Doug was to be at the top of his business class and have the language advantage.

Kyle nodded at the door. "So, we doing this?"

"We need a few girls to come in with us." They strutted down the line, found a group of four girls, and asked them to come in with us. The girls were more than agreeable, although as soon as we were inside they split.

We wound our way through the sea of people on the dance floor, looking for a table.

"So why is she here?" Justin asked after they ordered their first round of drinks.

"Wingman." Zack poked me in the ribs.

"That work? You sure this isn't something else?" I was starting not to like him.

"Man, you see the necklace." Andrew hit Justin. "The letters and the symbol? Just like Doug's tattoo, right?" he asked me.

I nodded. The symbol wasn't the same but I didn't feel like explaining. I didn't want to think about my relationship with Doug.

"Where do you go? Like U of C or something? I don't see you around," Justin said.

"No, I go to Northwestern."

Zack lifted his drink to me. "She's only a freshman but a language genius. Good as Doug, maybe better." He winked at me. "And the wingman thing, like bees to honey. Who are you?" he asked, turning to me.

"Hmm, your sister visiting from Champaign?" We had the same light coloring, so it didn't seem that far-fetched.

The conversation turned to other subjects like rush, induction, hazing, and alcohol rules. I only half paid attention. Looking around the table, I realized these guys were the presidents of all the biggest fraternities on campus. I was at an offline Greek Council meeting.

Mistakenly, I let my mind wander back to Doug. He needed a night alone. I could see that. He also thought I might need a night out, which it turns out wasn't a half-bad idea. There wouldn't be anyone else I would be more comfortable with right now than Zack, so he had also been right on that count.

I thought back to my conversation with Zack. I felt bad for freaking out on him. But if Doug decided to be with Zoey, or even just not with me, then this could have been our last night together, except we weren't together. Suddenly I felt nauseous. Scanning our table, the faces seemed to float, and beyond them, the sea of bodies swayed in the low light.

I felt a warm arm around my back and turned to find Zack's chest inches from me. "You okay?" he whispered in my ear.

"Hey, you okay?" Justin rang in more loudly. "You look pale, well paler than before."

"I must have locked my knees."

Zack hailed a waitress and grabbed a chair from the other table. "Coke, a real one," he said when the waitress appeared. My soda seemed to come amazingly fast. Maybe it was a low blood sugar, time-warp thing. Between the sitting and the Coke, I felt better in minutes and forced myself back into the conversation.

They finished their business topics, and then the conversation wandered to me. There was the obligatory question about how Doug and I met, which led to the crash incident. Zack was more than willing to spin that topic.

The number of girls they talked to and danced with that night was staggering. They didn't need me at all. Girls were drawn to them like moths to a flame. At least with Justin it seemed like it might be an appropriate analogy, but maybe I was judging him prematurely.

Zack slid me a drink after my soda, and I finally relaxed. Letting go and just being into the music felt good. Ignoring curfew, we danced until after one.

Outside, the cold night air brought me back to reality more quickly than I would have liked.

"Hey, you're quiet. You okay?" Zack asked as we waited for his car.

"Just tired. Tonight was good, so thanks. Did you have a good time?"

"Course, I always do when I'm with you." A small ping of guilt played at the edge of my thoughts, but I pushed it away, glad we had re-formed our friendship.

The car came, and we piled in. Justin and Andrew had hooked up with a couple of girls and stayed inside, but Kyle rode with us. As we drove, he looked like he was asleep in the backseat. With the music playing, I assumed he couldn't really hear our conversation.

"You don't regret bringing me?"

"You kidding? Look at my arm." He pushed up his sleeve and turned his arm over. "I wouldn't have had any more room for numbers on here if I wanted them."

I laughed. "I guess not. You could have stayed. I could have taken a cab."

"Yeah, and I enjoy being punched by Doug."

I wished he hadn't mentioned Doug. I was barely able to keep from thinking of him on my own. I winced and glanced to the backseat. Zack squeezed my hand. Until then, I hadn't noticed he was holding it.

He dropped Kyle off first, and approaching my dorm, he started to turn into the parking lot.

"You can just drop me off."

"You sure you'll be okay?"

"Course."

"You seeing him tomorrow before..."

"He is supposed to have coffee and breakfast for me by nine thirty."

"Good, okay then, sweet dreams. Don't let the bed bugs bite, and all that nonsense." He reached over me and opened my door.

The dorm was busier than I thought. Ducking my head, I slinked to the elevator, not wanting to have to talk to anyone. Inside my room, I turned on my phone. A string of texts waited for me, but none were from Doug. He hadn't called either. Not even to say goodnight. He always called or texted before he went to sleep. This couldn't be good. I sent a text to let him know I was home, but there was no reply.

Answering all the other messages, I tried not to think about him. But staring at the ceiling, there was no distraction. Putting my earphones in, I blocked out the sounds from the hall. For the first time in a week, I let myself cry. I had worried that if I started I wouldn't be able to stop, and I'd been right. It was just so unfair. I'd fought so hard for him, we'd been through so much, and now we'd only been given two weeks to be happy together. Was there something I'd done to deserve the first guy I'd ever loved being stripped from me? What was the saying? Bad luck comes in threes. There was my first accident on the soccer field, the second one on the volleyball court, and now this.

Hoping the bad luck was the issue and not the outcome of the issue, I tried to console myself. Everyone had a first love, and everyone suffered at least one broken heart. I imagined ninety-nine percent of them recovered. But my chest felt as if it were cracking in two. I couldn't imagine walking through campus without him.

Maybe Mark had been right. We'd become too serious too fast. But really the outward signs that Mark saw as us being too serious were just that. I'd fallen in love with Doug the first night I met him. He'd broken off our relationship before and that ache echoed in my chest as if it were yesterday. This time would be worse. Before I hadn't even kissed him, hadn't spent every waking hour with him.

Scolding myself, I wiped the tears from my eyes and cracked the window to get some air. I was tired and being overly dramatic. What did you think would happen? The voice asked. Really? You've known him for four months, it continued. This course of thinking wasn't productive either. I tried to control my breathing so that I didn't wake Elise. It wouldn't do for anyone to see me like this. I focused on taking even slow breaths. Everything would seem better in the morning.

Finally, fatigue won over, and I fell into a pained sleep. In my dreams I was trapped in a dark crevice, cold and alone. The loneliness covered me like hard rock, cold and unyielding.

⚶ ⚶ ⚶

"Are you crazy? This room is like an iceberg."

I sat up quickly, trying to figure out why Elise was screaming at me. The sun poured into our room through an open window.

Had I done that? Yes, I thought back. The heat had been pouring from the vent, and I'd felt as though I would suffocate. I looked over the edge of my bunk.

"Sorry."

"Oh, were you sleeping? Or trying to freeze us to death? And maybe you could stop that phone buzzing, I had a late night." Phone buzzing? Thrusting the covers about, I searched for my phone.

I found it. "Sorry about the window. It was hot when I came in." I squinted at the screen through puffy eyes.

The text was from Doug. OFF 2 MASS. TXT ME WHEN U WAKE UP. CAN COME BY EARLIER IF U WANT.

I looked at the time received and checked the time now. Just five minutes ago. Still, he'd already be in the service. I would text him after eight. Maybe have him come at eight thirty instead, if I could recover my face. If there was some decision, I wanted to hear it sooner rather than later.

"What time was that exactly?"

"Just after two."

"You should go back to sleep."

My heart was racing from being startled awake, and I would never get back to sleep now. Besides, if my face looked anywhere near how it felt, I'd need an hour to be presentable.

I climbed down and sat on my futon, texting Lila, Marissa, and my mom till Elise finished in the bathroom. I still hadn't looked in the mirror, so I didn't look up at her.

"What'd you do last night? Nobody knew where you were. That makes two weeks in a row that you ditched us."

"I went with Zack to some club in the city."

She lifted an eyebrow. "Zack? Not Doug?"

"Doug had all these projects, so Zack and I went." I tried to sound nonchalant.

She shrugged. "That sounds dangerous. You have fun?"

"Yeah, it was good."

I went to the bathroom and saw my face wasn't too puffy. There was time for a relatively long shower, as long as I felt I could take in the dorm. After, I soaked my face in cool water and then added lots of moisturizer and some anti-puff cream. It almost looked as if I'd had eight hours of sleep. My hair was a little tussled, but it was nothing a good brushing and some product couldn't tame.

Returning to my room to dress, I sent Doug a text. UP EARLY IF U WANT 2 COME BY. ANYTIME IS GOOD.

He replied instantly. B THERE IN 20 WITH COFFEE!

Feeling like wearing something soft and comfortable, I scanned my closet and found a pair of soft jeans and a sweater.

Then, I waited. I turned on the TV, but it was annoying. Pulling out my computer, I reviewed my chemistry notes. It wasn't like I needed to study, since I'd done plenty in the past week. When Doug phoned, his voice sounded light and almost happy.

Meeting him downstairs, I thought he looked well rested and calm, definitely better than he'd looked last night. "You didn't get enough sleep." He handed me the coffee and wrapped his free arm around me. It felt good to be near him. His smell and voice were soothing to me.

"You look good." I rubbed his arm as we walked to the elevator.

I took a long sip of the coffee, letting it warm me.

"How was last night?" he asked as we entered my room.

"Okay."

"Just okay?"

I rolled my eyes. "I ended up having fun, but I missed you." I set my cup down and reached for his hand.

He backed away. "See, you needed to get out."

I wondered whether I should tell him about my conversation with Zack. It sort of broke our code of not discussing Zoey though, so I decided not to. We talked about classes, my plans for the weekend, studied for a bit, and then walked to class with Kate. As we neared our building, she walked ahead of us.

He hugged me with one arm and kissed me on the temple. I wished I could tell that it didn't matter what happened, because I would always love him. But I wasn't brave enough. "Be careful driving."

"I will." He walked away.

Jeremy caught me, watching his retreating figure, and dragged me into class. "I hate people who have significant others." He made a few more cracks about being in love, but I blocked him out. He usually stopped when he didn't get a reaction, and fortunately this time was no different.

I made it through biology and chemistry by concentrating on the lecture. Unable to settle my mind, I opted for a racquetball game instead of a nap that afternoon. I had a late night of babysitting ahead of me, but I figured I could load up with caffeine.

That evening, once the kids were in bed, I needed activity to keep my mind off Doug. I washed the dishes, cleaned the kitchen, and moved to the family room. I didn't want to run the vacuum, so I dusted and mopped. These activities got me to eleven. Since I still had two hours to go, I started a load of the kid's laundry.

Although I felt like a crazy person, it got me through the evening, and I'd exhausted myself in the process. Sleep came easily, and I was well rested for rowing the next morning.

Zack was punctual as always, his SUV arriving at the curb at exactly seven thirty. At the gym, we were a few minutes early, so we warmed up together. I hopped on a rowing machine, while he went to lift weights. Remembering last week, I'd convinced myself not to worry about a call from Doug till this afternoon.

Bill came in and scanned the room. I expected him to head for Zack, but his gaze stopped on me instead. He came over and squatted down next to me. "Hey, you okay?"

"Yeah, why?" Zack's approaching form caught my eye. He was shaking his head but stopped when he saw that I noticed him. His lips formed thin lines and his temple wrinkled. I looked back to Bill whose eyes were now as big as saucers. "What's going on?"

"You didn't talk to him?"

Zack reached us. "Bill, hey, glad you're early. Come help me with the line-up for today." He tugged on Bill's arm.

I pushed myself between them. Figuring Bill would cave first, I faced him. "Didn't talk to who? Doug?"

Bill stepped away from me. "I'm going to start my workout now." He hurried towards the weight area.

I spun around to Zack. "What's going on?"

He motioned for me to follow him. In the lobby, he stopped. "He got in last night." He looked at the floor. My breath caught in my lungs. "He went to his mom's." He scanned the room before he spoke again. "Everything will be fine."

"What does that mean? What happened?"

He leaned in so his face was inches from mine. "He will get through this. You guys will be fine. You need to focus. Go finish your warm up."

My mind raced. Doug was back in Chicago. He'd gotten back last night but hadn't called me, again. This was unacceptable. I'd been clear last week that I didn't appreciate being left out. Was it so hard to text someone? He wasn't coming to the workout. It probably meant that whatever happened was bad. But Zack was right, I needed to focus. Doug hadn't contacted me, so it was none of my business. I only had one more thought. "You better not be lying to me Zack Walters."

"Everything will be okay. You're with the other team again." He pointed to where another group had started their workout.

Focusing on my breathing, I tried to block out the thoughts swirling through my head. I was just collateral damage. Had I convinced myself of that? He said he wanted us—wanted me. But how much weight did that carry against another life, a son or daughter? I convinced myself that now the wait was over, and Doug would have some resolution.

Skipping a shower, I slipped some pants over my shorts after the workout. Zack and Bill were waiting for me in the lobby. Making our way out to Zack's car, no one spoke until we exited the parking lot.

"You coming to brunch with us?" Zack asked.

"No, I have study group and need a shower." My study groups didn't start till one, but I wanted to be alone.

At my dorm, Zack jumped out of the car and walked me to the front door. "Sorry about before."

"It's okay. It's not your fault."

"Don't you have study groups to get to, or was that a lie?"

I don't lie, I thought. But I corrected myself, thinking I lied sometimes, or a lot, but only about one topic. Doug.

"No, I have biology and chemistry tests this week."

"Okay, call me later. Everyone's hanging out at my place."

I took the stairs to my floor, thinking maybe I would go to Zack's later. First, I had to think about whether to contact Doug or not. It took me fifteen minutes to decide, and another fifteen to figure out text versus email. I'd ruled out a call immediately. I took me another half hour to craft a message that was short, simple, and conveyed concern without sounding desperate.

BILL SAID YOU WERE BACK. I'M AROUND IF YOU WANT TO TALK, I finally texted him.

I got in the shower. By the time I entered the library for study group an hour later, Doug still hadn't replied. Glad to have four straight hours of diversion, I turned off my phone. When the sessions ended, Kate and I walked back to our dorm. Elise, Kate, and I had planned a girls' night in, and we ordered pizza and watched a movie. It was fun for a while, but they chose a sappy romantic comedy and I got antsy. I wasn't sure how long I could keep up my charade, so I ended up calling for a car to take me to Zack's.

At his place, I was able to wedge myself between Mark and Lila and nod when appropriate, with no questions asked. At the end of the evening, I served as the designated driver, using Zack's SUV to drop off Bill, Mark, Lila, and Ross off at the fraternity. It was after two when I parked the car in the dorm lot, but I still hadn't gotten any communication from Doug. Maybe he needed space, but at least he could've texted. Did he just figure information from Zack and Bill was good enough?

The next morning I ended up at the gym with Stephen as was beginning to be my weekend routine. I couldn't help but think of Zack's comment about him being higher on my list than Stephen. Without Doug, I couldn't imagine feeling anything. I tried to literally run those thoughts out of my brain as my feet pounded the deck of the treadmill.

"Manda." I removed my earbuds and stopped the machine. "Are you going to stop anytime? I'm about to hyperventilate. Are you trying to kill me or just yourself?"

Looking at the readout, I realized I'd run seven miles in fifty-eight minutes. Not bad, I thought. "Just myself. Sorry."

He rolled his eyes at me. "You're a maniac."

We cooled down, stretched, and then bundled up for the walk back to the dorm. Back in my room, I was glad to find Elise had gone out to brunch with some friends. Feeling worried about Doug, I wanted nothing but to snuggle up with Mom or Marissa and have some tea. A phone call would have to suffice, and in the shower, I sorted out what I could tell them. Doug was having family issues. They already knew those details. He was away for the second weekend in a row. I missed him and was worried about him. This was what I could share.

Heating up some soup, I snuggled under a blanket to call home. I opted out of sharing my story with Mom, realizing it might only give her more cause to dislike Doug. But even I disliked Doug right then. I talked to Marissa, Mom, and Dad, and by the time Elise got back, I was ready to ditch my pity party. We did laundry and the cleaning together and then went to the grocery store.

Even with my lack of ability to concentrate, we created a decent Indian dinner. Our company distracted me for most of the evening. I avoided Zack and Bill, not wanting to know if they'd heard anything from Doug. As it got later, my anxiety grew. Thinking he'd come back to campus by tonight, I'd expected at least a text. As I was washing dishes after everyone left, I received a text message from Zack.

YOU HEAR FROM DOUG?

NO, YOU?

NO. NOT BILL EITHER.

I'M WORRIED ABOUT HIM.

YOU'RE GOOD YOU KNOW. JUST LIKE NOVEMBER. NO ONE WOULD EVER KNOW YOU WERE FREAKED OUT.

That evening, I finished my English paper and pre-read for all my other subjects. Reading biology did me in, and the next thing I knew there was music playing in my ear. I woke up enough to realize it was Zack's ring tone. I checked the time. My screen read seven thirty.

"Yes," I whispered into the phone, wishing I didn't have to leave my bed all day.

"Umm, do you want me to pick you up for our workout?" My heart sank. The absence of Doug was everywhere. There was no escape.

"Sure," I told Zack.

"Okay, I'll see you in fifteen."

Changing quickly, I brushed my teeth and poured myself coffee from the pot Elise had started. In the elevator, I flipped my phone over and over in my hand, trying to decide if I should text Doug.

At the curb, Bill emerged from the front seat, holding the door open for me to jump in.

"So?" I asked them.

"Nothing," Zack said, shaking his head.

Bill stuck his head between us. "He didn't come back to the house last night."

Zack raked his hand over my face. "You look like hell."

"Thanks, Tom Cat." I hit him on the bicep.

"Tom Cat?"

"Yeah." I taunted him. It was a coping mechanism. The other option was full out crying, which I was not up for right now. I'd save that for after chemistry lab when I could crawl into my bed and hide till tomorrow.

"I kind of like it, scruffy, yet loveable."

We kept up our banter as we walked through the gym to the treadmills. It helped distract me. We found the group of rowers who were the usual Monday through Wednesday workout crew. After short runs, we made our way to the weight room.

"Just make sure she keeps breathing," Zack told Bill, pairing up with another teammate.

I found he was right. I wasn't breathing, not really. To breathe, really breathe, in and out, I would have to relax. To relax would mean that reality would descend. Reality wasn't a world I wanted to live in.

Bill was more animated than usual, probably trying to distract me. He was such a quiet and serious guy, and I wondered if I ever would feel like I knew him. We'd gotten closer last quarter, but there seemed some kind of distance between us now. It was probably the same distance Zack and I flirted around the edges of. They were Doug's friends, not mine, but I was glad they included me. Whatever was going on with Doug, I hoped he would let them help him.

Zack drove me back to my dorm after our workout.

"Make sure you get a good breakfast," he called to me as I got out of the car.

I waved good-bye to him and didn't look back.

It was worse than the weekend. I hadn't expected him to be there on Saturday and Sunday. But by Monday, I had thought I'd see him or hear something. Plus, I had to answer questions I wasn't prepared to answer.

Lila knew he hadn't come back to the house. "So, what's going on with Doug? Is everything okay?" She asked as we walked out of our chemistry lecture.

"I think so," I hedged, the tightness in my chest ratcheting up. "He had some things to take care of."

She crinkled her eyes at me. "Okay, are you coming to the house for lunch?"

I shook my head and looked back over my shoulder. "I think I'll catch up with Kate. I'll see you in lab." If he wasn't there, I wouldn't be able to hold it together. If he was back, I didn't want to see him. I checked my phone again. The status of the text I'd sent was just the same, delivered but not read. I knew he probably saw the message unless he wasn't even looking at his phone. At this point, I was just angry. How hard was it to tap a screen?

I found a corner of the library and read biology until it was time for class. I tried not to look for him, but I couldn't help it. Angry and worried, it was hard to focus during the lecture. Afterward, I had chemistry lab with Lila, Jeremy, and Kate. Jeremy and Kate were always cracking jokes and served as a good distraction.

Because of their antics, the lab took the whole three hours. I realized I didn't want to leave, didn't want to face unstructured time. After we cleaned up, I hurried out the door, biting my lip. I took the back staircase down, hoping to lose Lila. The pressure of my teeth on my lip was the only thing holding back the tears. I stopped on a landing and paced, trying to dissipate the pent up emotions. It helped, and I continued down the stairs.

The cold air felt good on my face. I slid off the tie around my ponytail and shook out my hair. It was nearly dark, and I made my way to the bus stop. Halfway there, I noticed a figure jogging towards me. Doug stopped a few feet from me. He adjusted his ball cap and stuffed his hands in his pockets.

He was smart to keep his distance, because I felt like punching him right then. I flexed my hands, unsure of what to do next.

He stretched out his hand. "Can we talk?"

I ignored the hand hanging in the air. "I was getting the bus. I need to get dinner." With my anxiety, I'd only had a muffin and coffee all day. If I had to deal with any more emotions, I'd never get a meal in. My desire to touch him, to feel his warm skin, smell his cologne, be wrapped in his strong arms, angered me. I couldn't look at him. Taking a step sideways, I started to walk around him.

He caught my sleeve. "I'm sorry."

"No," I snapped my arm away.

He held up his hands. "Will you just listen?"

I threw up my arms. "There are phones and computers, how hard would it have been to just tap a screen or push a couple of keys."

"Anything I sent wouldn't have been enough."

"Yes, it would have."

"Do you even want to know what happened? Because if we're done, I'll just leave you alone."

"You're not going to be with her?"

He held his palms out. "Are you crazy?"

"Yes, crazy for staying with you."

His shoulders slumped, and he adjusted his cap. "You're right. But I'm here. That situation was really messed up, and now I'm pretty messed up. But I still care about you." He caught my hand. "You can hit me if you want. Or take some time. I'll wait."

Again, I slid away from his grip. "This won't happen again?"

"No, not ever."

"You'll tell me everything right now?"

"Right now?"

I pointed to the ground. "Right now."

"Okay," he rubbed his arms. He took a deep breath and looked at the ground. "I was selfish. I didn't want to lose you. I thought I could work something out with her. I should've realized there would be no compromise. She's not the person she used to be or I thought she was. I had no idea..."

His looked up at the sky. "She did it Thursday, didn't even give me a chance to talk her out of it. She said I didn't love her, didn't want her." The street light beside us flickered and slowly brightened. He stuffed his hands in his pockets and looked at me. I hadn't ever seen someone look so lost. Not even Dad after his mom's death. The sick feeling that I'd had in the pit of my stomach exploded. The baby was gone.

I reached out for him, but he backed away. "It's my fault."

My mind reeled. He felt responsible for the death of his child. How was one supposed to recover from that?

I slid my hands down his arms and gripped his hands.

He looked away. "Zack thought maybe it was a hoax, a ploy to get me back. I saw the paperwork. She said she couldn't do it, raise the baby alone. I'd told her I would help. I'd called and scheduled an appointment at the Catholic services center. That's why I drove up Friday morning."

He'd done everything right, but it wasn't enough. She'd made the decision without consulting him, and he felt responsible for the ending of a life, his child's life. I didn't know what to say, so I just stood there holding his hands.

He eventually looked at me. "You're shivering. I'll walk you to the bus or back to your dorm." He squeezed my hands and dropped them.

I picked them up and held them between us. "I'm so sorry. I understand if you want to be alone. But I care about you, and I want to be here for you."

"Thanks." He gathered me in a hug, and I slipped my arms around his waist. We stood like that, his head resting on my shoulder and mine tucked in his chest, till we heard the bus.

He pointed at the bus. "Are you getting on?"

"I wouldn't mind walking with you if you want to walk."

"Yeah, I do." He took my hand, and we started down the sidewalk towards my building. I looked at him and he met my gaze, but we walked in silence most of the way.

We stopped just outside my building. "Do you want to come up? I can make you dinner?"

He shook his head. "No, I'm going to go."

"Okay, well..." I let the words trail off, unsure of where we went from here.

"Should I pick you up for rowing tomorrow?"

"That would be nice."

"Okay," he nodded his head and smiled for the first time that evening. He looked at the ground, back at me, and then took my hand. "Thanks."

"You're welcome."

"Okay, tomorrow, yeah." He swung my hand between us. I looked at his face, and all I could think about was how his lips felt on mine. It felt wrong to want that right now. My mind and body craved reassurance that things could be like they were before, that he would recover from this, that we would be happy again.

I dropped his hand and stepped back. "Goodnight." I used all my willpower to turn and walk into the building. Taking the stairs, my eyes teared up and prayed I could sneak into the room without being seen. By the time I reached the floor, my face was soaked.

Chapter 7

If I'd thought waiting for Doug to contact me that weekend had been grueling, I didn't know anything about mental anguish. To an outsider, things probably didn't look much different. He sat beside me, put his arm around me, held my hand, and walked me to my classes. We studied together and hung out with our friends just like before. But he wasn't there. He didn't smile, or joke, or tease me. He didn't really talk at all unless it was absolutely necessary.

In the beginning he'd told me I wasn't the person that could or should be his confidant. He said he didn't want to burden me. I understood that. But it was hard to sit there and see his pain day in and day out. Still I was happier when I was with him than when I wasn't. I worried about my sanity and how much of a codependent person I was becoming. Sometimes he seemed more agitated than others. He never talked about it, and I didn't ask.

Having been briefed by Michael on the situation, his dad visited the next weekend. Doug wasn't happy to see his father, although he did appreciate that for once his dad didn't bring a girlfriend. Doug included me each time he saw his dad and Michael, and I was fairly sure I was being used as a buffer.

Still, his dad had come to talk to Doug and wouldn't be swayed. At brunch on Sunday, just before his flight, his dad, normally so collected, tapped his finger on the table. "I came all this way because I was worried about you. Michael said you were taking this hard. Do you want me to help you or not?"

Doug exploded. "So, what are you proposing? What legal document do you have to fix things?"

His father stood quietly, started down the hall, and motioned for Doug and his brother to follow. They walked into the study together, closing the door behind them. They talked inside for over an hour, sometimes in hushed tones, but much of the time in a loud verbal debate.

His mom tried to make conversation with me to cover their discussion. "How are you holding up? You know he adores you. We all do. All we can do is be there for him."

Trying to concentrate on deciphering the discussion in the other room, I smiled and attempted to exchange some pleasantries without being rude.

When they came out of the study, Doug's father thanked his mom for a wonderful brunch, apologized to me for his rudeness, and left.

Doug and Michael played a game of pool while I helped his mother and Gary clean up the dining room and kitchen. I hoped Doug would forgive Michael for telling his father. Doug needed Michael. He was one of the few people who knew the situation.

Rowing and Zack were the only things that kept me sane. Zack would check in on me every day, always with a similar phrase. "Hey there, pip squeak, you doing okay?" Each time he managed to come up with a new term that alluded to my small stature. There was little bit, shrimp, pixie, and sweet pea. His banter didn't bother me. I had pretty good comebacks for most of his nicknames. My proudest moments were when I commented, "Fine, of course, Jolly Green" and "Why wouldn't I be Mega-man?"

I worried about Doug, and how he was dealing with his guilt. Of course not knowing what precisely to worry about kept me anxious twenty-four hours a day. Finally, the second week, I broke down and asked Zack.

"He talks to you, right?"

He cocked an eyebrow at me. "What do you mean?"

I put a hand to my hip. Did I have to spell this out for him? "Look, I don't need to know details. I just need to know that he talks to someone."

"Yeah, he talks to me, and the priest, his brother, too, I think." He bumped into me. "We need to swim tomorrow."

"Swim?" I asked. "Why?" I got that it was good for a whole body workout, but I had already lost what little tan I had from my Caribbean vacation. Putting on a bathing suit wasn't high on the list of things I wanted to do.

He rubbed the sweat off his abs and swatted the hand at my face. I jumped away just in time to miss getting slathered. "Because rowing in boats is on the water, and if you want to be on the team, you have to pass a swim test."

"I'm on the team if I pass a swim test?" It was the only good thing I'd heard in a month.

"Talked to coach this morning. You have something other than a bikini, right?"

"Yes," I lied. I'd have to go to the sporting goods store. I prayed they would have a decent color in my size.

"Okay, meet me at the pool at eight sharp."

"Here?" I questioned. I'd seen the pool in the athletic building. All the workout floors had glass walls overlooking it. There wouldn't be anyone in the building that couldn't see my blinding white skin.

"Where else?" It wasn't worth discussing with Zack. He'd just have more fuel for teasing.

When I asked Elise to come shopping to find a bathing suit that afternoon, she laughed. With her glowing bronze skin, she wasn't any help in the empathy department, but she drove me to the store anyway. I ended up needing a girl's size fourteen. They had a teal one piece, it had light pink piping but it was well-lined. I just had to hope the pool was heated.

The next morning Zack and Bill were waiting for me outside the athletic department building when I got there. I clutched my backpack straps as my heart seemed to miss its rhythm. I looked between them. "Where's Doug?"

"He's late," Zack said. "Come on."

"Why?" I asked, not moving. I studied Bill's face. Like me, he could rarely hide if something was wrong. He didn't look overly shaken, though, and slowly a smile formed on his face.

"There were plumbing issues at the house. He'll be here in a minute."

I pointed a finger in both their faces. "I'm going to be mad if you're lying."

Once inside, we wound down the hall to the pool. About ten other guys from the rowing team were there, including the team I usually trained with. They nodded in my direction. Everyone took their shoes off and left them on the benches, so I followed suit. The coach walked in and was talking with some of the other team members.

"So, are you ready?" Zack asked me, stretching out.

"Sure." I'd already been warming up, stretching out my arm especially. I hadn't swum much since the accident, and I didn't want to over extend anything. Suddenly he scooped me up, lifted me chest high, and threw me into the water.

My shrill cry was silenced by the water. Darn that Zack Walters. What was the deal? I still had my exercise pants and a jacket on. Thanks goodness my phone was in my backpack.

"What was that for?" I asked, coming to the surface. All the guys were standing on the deck laughing.

"You have to jump in fully clothed and tread water for twenty minutes. Didn't you read the team manual?" Zack said, shaking it in the air at me. Standing behind him, the coach rolled his eyes.

"Fine!" I yelled at him, pulling my pants off, leg by leg. I hurled them as hard as I could at him.

They landed in the water a few feet shy of the crowd that had gathered, but at least the splash got a couple of them before they jumped back. Zack, looking his smuggest, didn't flinch. *Fine, I still have my jacket*, I thought. It was smaller and lighter, and he didn't even try to dodge it so I hit my target. He just laughed.

After a few minutes, I got tired of them watching, waiting for me to drown. "Are you wimps just going to stand there for twenty minutes, or are you swimming?"

The coach nodded, shrugged, and walked away. The guys started stripping down to their suits and doing cannonballs over my head.

Zack was the only one left on the deck when Doug came in. There were several football players behind him. I had forgotten about the audience on the second floor. I looked up to see the windows lined with athletes. When I turned back to Doug, he was actually smiling.

"I heard you tried to drown my girlfriend," he said, shoving Zack in the pool.

Doug stripped his pants and shirt off to reveal his swim trunks underneath. I never seemed to get used to his perfect physique, and it always caught me off guard. Even more amazing, he was smiling. It wasn't the half smile that never reach his eyes, but a full on smile.

Doug cannonballed into the water, and they finished the twenty minutes of treading with me, splashing and razzing each other the whole time. After the tread test, there was a four hundred meter distance test. A head's up on that would have been helpful also as I was winded by the end. But I did it, slow and steady, with Doug swimming beside me the whole way.

Someone found a ball and we formed teams, popping the ball back and forth over the lane rope. The game devolved into a chicken match with me on Doug's shoulders and Bill on Zack's. It wasn't much of a competition as I ended up in the water each time. There was a cannonball competition, which I also showed poorly at. Then they decided that the best game was seeing how far they could throw me. I put a stop to that when guys we didn't know started getting in line. The coach called us out just before ten. I was exhausted, but I wouldn't have traded those two hours for the world. For the first time in a month, we were having fun.

"Showers, and then a meeting in five," Coach yelled as we got out of the water.

"You might want to make it ten for girly here," Zack said, pointing at me.

"Fine, ten then." The coach smiled and winked at me.

Doug helped me out of the water, slipping his arm around my waist. I was surprised when he slid his fingers through mine. He scanned the pool, and I followed suit. Everyone seemed to be concentrating on getting to the showers.

"You are amazing!" he said, wrapping an arm around me.

"I think that may be stretching things a bit."

"I am so proud of you, especially the way you've come back from your accident."

"Thanks." Suddenly I sensed someone behind me. I heard a snapping sound, and Doug swung me out of the way just in time to avoid Zack's towel that popped in the air.

"Hey, Coach said showers." He pointed at us. "And that's just gross guys."

"Fine." Doug released me. In the shower, I stood under the warm water for a few minutes, and shampooed and conditioned my hair. After I dried off, I ran a comb and some product through my hair. It would be curly after air-drying, but there was nothing to be done about it. I went back out onto the swim deck where all the guys were already gathered.

I had no idea what was going on, but everyone seemed to be looking at me. Before I reached the crew, the coach approached me. "Come talk to me in my office afterward." He nodded to the group and walked back towards his office. I looked between Doug and Zack.

Zack called everyone to attention and motioned to Bill who handed Zack a clothing box. "So, we're not much on making things pretty—" Zack handed the box to me "—but welcome to the team, Mini-Girl."

I didn't like being in the spotlight, and I nervously opened the box and held up the team jacket that lay inside. My cheeks were warm, and I was sure my face was redder than a beet. Fortunately, there weren't any speeches, and the group broke up quickly.

"Coach wanted to talk to me," I told Doug as we turned to leave.

"I'll wait."

At the end of the hall, I knocked on the coach's door.

"Amanda, sit down." He pushed a chair up beside his desk. "Welcome to the team."

"Thanks."

"Zack seems to think very highly of you, and I've been watching you. So far, I'm impressed." I folded my hands in my lap, waiting. "I have concerns about your relationship with Doug."

He hesitated perhaps to let that sink in. "We need a good coxswain. Doug's probably our best rower, but drama doesn't make for good rowing." He passed some papers to me over the desk. "Here's all the paperwork. Bring it back when you've had a chance to think about it. We need team members we can count on."

I'd gotten his message loud and clear. His concern brought my fears about the stability of my relationship with Doug front and center. Not a thought I generally liked to entertain for very long. But now I had to.

Doug was outside, leaning up against a wall with his head pressed against the bricks, his phone dangling in his hand. He didn't notice me until I was right in front of him. "Hi, you ready?"

"Sure."

He didn't look at me. "We should get something to eat. What did Coach want?"

"Just had some paperwork for me," I heard myself say. I had become a coward. Three months ago, I would have come right out with it. Back then I had nothing to lose. Now, I had everything to lose. He'd said he wanted to be with me, and I loved him. But the depression that seemed to envelope him worried me. I wasn't sure when he would come out of it.

We walked to a breakfast place just off campus. It was the first time we'd been alone in a long time. If we were studying, it was usually in my room with Elise or at the library. That's all we had done besides workout for the past four weeks. We chatted about rowing, fraternity issues, and my tutoring clients. After the meal we ran out of topics, and Doug became lost in his silent world again. He always seemed to be in that state.

Maybe I should try to push him out, I thought. Maybe he needed a kick in the ass. That was definitely what Marissa or Lila would do to me, probably even Elise.

"That was fun," I told him when we got to my building.

He smiled and squeezed my hand. "It was. We should go out more often."

"Definitely." I smiled at him.

After we parted, I texted Zack and lured him to my room with promises of hot coffee and brownies, which I purchased from the coffee shop just off campus.

He ran his fingers over my face when he met me outside my dorm. I ducked away. "That's so annoying."

"You look horrible."

"It's the hair. Air-drying doesn't equal my best look."

"No, you know I like your hair that way. You just look beat. Did the swim totally wipe you out?"

"Yes, but no," I said, tripping over my words.

All the time he'd put into training me had come down to a question of whether I'd be able to hold it together in the event that Doug broke up with me. If I could hold it together and stay on the team, would I be a distraction to Doug?

In my room, I handed Zack the brownies and started to pace.

"Hey, if you're going to be mad, be mad at someone you're really mad at, like Doug or Zoey."

"I'm not mad."

"You totally are. What's going on?"

"I should go for a run. You want to come with me?" I had to clear my mind, get rid of all the feelings swirling around in my head.

"No, I don't, and you don't need to run either. You did plenty working out this morning, and you have to row tomorrow."

I stopped in front of him. "Do you know what Coach wanted to talk to me about? My relationship with Doug and if it was a good thing for me to be on the team. What happens if we break up? Either you're out a coxswain, or things are really tense."

"Okay, how much coffee did you have?" A grin spread across his face. "No, this is what happens. I make a play for you, Doug punches me, I punch him back, and then we'd be all one big happy family again.

"Ugh!" I slapped my hand to my forehead and walked to the other side of the room.

"Did you talk to Doug?"

"No."

"Why not?"

"And look like the insecure whiny girlfriend?"

"Isn't that how girlfriends are?"

"He's not happy as it is?"

"And you think he would be happier if he were planning a shotgun wedding?" He pointed a finger gun at his head and pulled the trigger.

"I don't know, but this is hell."

"I can't argue with you on that one."

"Do you think I should just do something, you know, give him a kick in the ass?"

"Did you just say ass? Ha, well, if someone's going to do it'd have to be you. He adores you."

I sat down beside him. "You don't know that."

"You're right." My heart sank. "It's only a hunch. But I'd probably take the odds."

"So should I stick with rowing?"

"Hell yes. Rowing has nothing to do with Doug. It's about you and me baby, and you kick ass. I didn't spend all this time on you for you to quit now."

I didn't feel quite as confident as he sounded, but I decided it was good enough for me. Besides, I'd worked really hard and was this far in. Why not "buy the farm" as my Bubbe would say?

"So, we're good, right? You're not backing out on me?"

I took in a huge breath and released it. "No."

"Good, okay," he said, standing. "And this—" he pointed between us "—never happened."

Just then, Elise walked in. "What never happened?"

"Hey guys. What's going on?"

"We're having a brownie party to celebrate Manda joining the rowing team."

"Are these special brownies? Did she eat any? Because that girl could use some lightening up." Elise set her backpack on her desk.

"No, they're clean. Are you kidding? Drugs kill brain and muscle cells." He flexed his left bicep. "She hasn't had any yet, so you should see to that." Zack handed her the package, moving to the door. I walked him downstairs, thanking him profusely for getting me through my paranoid insanity.

"Actually, we should talk like this at least once a week, brownies and ass we could call it."

"Yeah, right." I waved good-bye as he walked out the door.

*   *   *

I'd hoped the swimming event had broken the cycle, but Doug didn't seem better. Mid-February, and the associated holiday, loomed like a gauntlet over my head. It was Monday, and as usual, Doug and I were studying in my room.

Marissa called to highlight her latest dramas. I was trying to get some real studying in, so I made it short. "I'll see you Friday. I love you."

Doug looked up from his book. "You're going to Champaign this weekend?"

"It's my mom's fiftieth birthday."

My dad had been very clear on only one point about the weekend. I was not allowed to bring Doug. It was a family only event, so I hadn't mentioned it to him. Really, I was living day to day and rarely thought about much a week out, so it'd snuck up on me.

"We're throwing a big party."

"That sounds like fun. I'm excited for you." I eyed him suspiciously. Who was this person, and what had he done with Doug? Had he actually used the words fun and excited? I wished he had used them in a context of something we might do together.

When the topic of the fraternity formal came up at the house on Wednesday, it put me on edge again. When we went back to his room, he didn't speak, so I took out my computer like always.

After a few minutes, he tapped me on the leg. "I'd like you to come to the formal with me. Do you want to go and get a room?"

Would I be comfortable going to formal with him? Would it be weird if we got a room together? Our relationship seemed almost platonic at this point. "Doug, I'm not sure—"

"What do you mean?"

I got up and stood in front of him, deciding to try my kick in the ass approach. He could decide whether he wanted to be in or out. "You don't have to invite me. I can't even drink with the rest of your friends."

"What are you talking about? Who else would I take?" He stood up and then bent down so we were face to face, and moving a strand of hair from my face. "Of course I want you to come with me. My mom's already got a shopping trip planned, and I reserved a big suite. You'll come, right?"

"Sure."

His straightened his back. "Sure?"

"Yes." Gathering all my courage I pushed myself up on my toes and kissed him on the mouth.

He answered my kiss with his own. I pressed into him but he lost balance and backed away.

"That was nice."

"It was." He smiled and took my hands. "You're biting your lip. Is everything okay?"

"You don't talk much lately. I just need more from you."

"Okay, well I can work on that."

🕊 🕊 🕊

The rest of that week he did seem more present. And on Friday, when Tia and Ed picked me up at my dorm to the drive to Champaign, Doug was there to see me off.

He flexed my hand back and forth in his as their car approached. I turned to look at him, and for the first time in a long time, he was actually looking into my eyes. "I'm going to miss you."

"Me too," I said, but I wondered if I actually would. I was essentially alone most of the time I was with him anyway.

Then he leaned in and kissed me. He pressed his lips against mine and slid a hand under my jacket up my back. I let my bag drop and clutched his arm. His other hand wound around my neck. His kisses continued until I had to breathe. He looked at me again and gave me another short kiss.

Then, he put his forehead to mine. "I really am going to miss you." The hand around my neck caressed the scar from my volleyball injury.

Now I was going to miss the feel of his lips, the calluses on his hands, and the warmth of his body. "I'll be back in two days."

"Good." He smiled and locked his lips on mine again.

"Hello!" Tia's voice brought me out of my paradise, and I turned to see her body half out of the window. "We can't park here forever. You see your boyfriend every day. This is forty-eight hours."

I looked at Doug, and he smiled at me. "That was long over-due." He kissed me again. "I'll text you."

I nodded, barely able to believe what had just transpired.

Doug opened the car door for me. "See you Sunday." He waved as he closed the door. I watched him watch us drive away till we turned the corner.

Ed looked at me in the rearview mirror. "I guess that answers the question of how is Doug. So how long has it been since you've been home? I am most impressed with your ability to maintain existence after six weeks of separation from your family."

"If we don't get there soon, I may turn into a vampire or something much more sinister."

"What do you mean? Someone like your older sister?"

Tia hit him on the head. "So what's new with you? Did Doug get his family thing resolved?"

"I think they're starting to come through the other side," I said. It was my latest stock answer, but after that kiss, I was hoping it might be true. I'd been seeing flickers of sunlight filtering through Doug's wall of darkness, and that kiss was like what my Aunt Clara would call a Jesus beam.

"Those necklaces are new."

I put my hand to my neck instinctively and realized I hadn't felt very strong this quarter. Making the rowing team was a positive, but my personal life had been a disaster. I was happy that I'd finally nudged Doug a little. No, it wasn't a kick in the ass, but my small request for more seemed to have gotten through to him. "Doug got them for me for Christmas. It's the Chinese symbol for strength."

"And the Fraternity letters? Do Mom and Dad know about this?"

"I made the rowing team."

"Yeah, Mom told me that. Don't they have meets like every weekend in the spring?"

"Yep."

Tia shook her head back and forth.

"What?" I asked.

"It's going to impact your grades."

"You're just like Dad. I'm not allowed to have a life?"

"So, are you putting me to shame this weekend in our arm wrestling tournament?" Ed asked.

"I'm just a coxswain, so no promises. Zack seems to think I might make the girls' team."

Tia turned around to look at me. "How does the whole Doug-Zack thing work anyway? You guys just hook up as it pleases you?"

What the hell? My face flooded with heat. "It's not like that. Doug is my boyfriend, and Zack and I are friends."

I didn't say anything else to them the rest of the drive. Doug texted me as promised, and we talked more via text in that three-hour drive than we had the whole quarter.

As we turned into our neighborhood, Tia said, "I hope your grades are good, Amanda. Dad has you on a short leash."

I wished I could shoot laser beams at her.

It was great to see Marissa and Mom. Tia had been right about Dad. At least her comment had prepared me for the onslaught of his inquisition. We picked up just were we'd left off Christmas break. He grilled me about every minute detail of my life. He didn't like that I was on the rowing team or that Doug had given me a piece of jewelry. He didn't have much ammunition though when I told him my GPA was a 3.8. All he had left to criticize was that my only B was in my major.

Thanks to the tension with Dad, Sunday couldn't come soon enough. Getting up, I slipped on some jeans and a sweatshirt and crept quietly downstairs. In the kitchen, Mom gave me a half hug, squeezing my shoulders and whispering good morning in my ear. Dad lifted his cup my way. I poured myself a full cup of black coffee. Marissa had kept me up till two, and it was just after eight. If I was going to be awake at all, I'd need at least two cups. I sat down at the bar beside Mom.

"So what about formal? When's Doug's?" Tia spoke up when I was only two sips in.

"Umm, in a couple of weeks," I told her, trying to mentally kick start my brain.

"You didn't tell us about any formal." Mom put one hand to her hip.

"Yeah, well it just came up this week. It's not a big deal." Out of the corner of my eye, I saw Dad look over his paper.

Tia set her cup on the table. "Not a big deal? It's only the social occasion of the season, and it's Doug's senior year. Did he ask you?"

I scanned the faces and considered lying to them. *I'm an adult!* I screamed in my head. "Yes."

Mom set her coffee down and peered at me over her reading glasses. "Why didn't you tell us? Don't you need a dress?"

"Doug's mom offered to take me shopping next weekend. There wasn't time this weekend anyway."

"That's nice, but I don't—"

Dad slammed his paper on the table. "This is not acceptable. You shouldn't be accepting gifts from his family. And you should not be going to any formal. I know what happens at those things with everyone getting hotel rooms and staying overnight."

I stood up, ready to bolt from the room. Mom put a hand on my arm. "You guys haven't dated that long. It seems like you're limiting yourself, especially since he's graduating in May."

I scanned the room. All eyes were glued on me except Ed, who was doing his best to look invisible behind his paper. Full defense mode kicked in. I took a deep breath, trying not to react.

Tia started again. "You know, Manda, we saw Zoey a couple of weeks ago. She's still pretty messed up. Word is she's calling Doug all the time. I saw her dial his number and leave him a message. Did you know about that?"

I could feel all the blood running to my cheeks. My heart felt like it was going to beat out of my chest, so I put my hand on the island to steady myself before turning to face her.

Dad stood. "There are just too many issues with this boy, Amanda. And a formal is out of the question. It's completely inappropriate."

I pointed at Tia. "Tia went with Ed her freshman year. They got a room."

Ed got up, and Tia grabbed his arm. He tugged it away and walked out of the room. She looked back to me. "It was a group thing."

"Doug is getting a suite. Everyone is staying there."

Mom crossed back over to the counter, continuing her breakfast pep. "I'm not sure I'm comfortable with his mom taking you shopping. You have lots of dresses Marissa got you. You could wear one of those."

I looked down at the counter, taking deep breaths, and tried to focus. Had Tia clued Mom and Dad into Zoey already? Was this another planned intervention? I scanned the room, meeting each person's gaze. "So, what you're saying is I'm not supposed to go to formal or have a relationship with Doug?" I looked squarely at Dad.

"As I said, it's completely inappropriate."

"I'm still a virgin!" I screamed and stomped toward the door.

"Okay, okay." My mom caught me, placing a hand on each shoulder. "There's no need to get upset. We're just concerned. You've got a lot going on, and you just added this rowing thing."

Now trembling, I swatted her hands away. "A lot going on? If it weren't for rowing, I wouldn't be doing anything other than studying and working."

"Well, maybe you should just focus on school for a while," Mom said, her voice barely a whisper.

I looked between Mom and Dad. "You think I can't handle it?"

Dad stood. "You had a big trauma last quarter, so we just want you to take it slow."

"So no rowing, no boyfriend? Fine." I spun and ran up the stairs to my room. I sifted through my clothes, grateful I'd had the last minute thought to include my running gear. Tightening my laces, I popped my earbuds in my ears and turned up the music. I jogged down the stairs to find my mother waiting at the bottom.

"You can't run off like that. We were talking to you."

I took out my earbuds and looked her straight in the eyes. Our faces were barely six inches apart. "I left so that I didn't say anything I'd regret later."

I brushed past her to the door, heaving it open.

"Mass is at eleven."

"I'll be ready."

I put in my earbuds and slammed the door behind me. I checked my watch. It was just after eight. I had plenty of time. I jogged down the street to the city path and stopped to stretch. Running forced me to even out my breathing. My pace was too fast for the length I had planned, but I didn't have the patience to slow down. I needed to not be at home. I did a long loop and by the time I jogged up the driveway to the house, my watch said seven point one miles in sixty-two minutes.

Inside, I jogged up the stairs straight to my room. I showered and washed my hair, taking extra time to dry it out straight. At least I'd be able to see Doug tonight. Maybe I'd ask Tia and Ed to drop me at his fraternity house.

After drying my hair, I found Marissa and relayed the details of the earlier conversation with her.

"I told you Dad is set on getting Doug out of your life. I hear him talking to Mom about it all the time."

"Do these people not have anything else to do?" I complained as I left her room to dress for Mass.

Marissa and I the rest of the family downstairs to leave for Mass at the prescribed time. On the drive and during Mass, I didn't say anything more to them than I had to. Afterward, we had brunch at home. I was polite to Tia, Mom, and Dad, but nothing more.

Halfway through the meal, Dad cleared his throat. "It doesn't seem like you've gained any of the weight you lost from the accident Amanda."

I felt like steam was going to come out of my ears. Taking a calming breath, I placed my utensils on my plate. "Actually, I have. Maybe it doesn't show, but I've gained a lot of muscle tone."

Mom placed a hand on mine. "We just want you to be healthy. It seems like you're really pushing your body hard."

I snapped my hand from underneath hers. "Actually, I'm on a very good nutrition plan and we get weighed for rowing club, so I think someone would have said something to me by now if there was a problem."

Dad pointed a fork at me. "Well, that makes me feel a bit better."

I pushed back from the table and went to my room where I stayed until it was time to drive back to Evanston. When I came down to leave, part of me felt guilty that I hadn't spent the last hour with mom. It was her birthday weekend after all. But she had created this issue, not me.

As I got to Ed's car, Dad dove in and scooped my bag into the trunk. "Good work on those grades. Maybe you can bring that chemistry one up, too."

I stood with my hands on my hips, not responding to him.

Mom placed a hand on my shoulder. "We just want you to be happy." I stepped back from her and noticed tears in her eyes.

"I am happy at school with my friends and Doug." This would have been more of a stretch before the kiss and texts with Doug on Friday and over the weekend. Now happiness seemed like something that might be attainable.

"Sweetie, please..." She reached out to me, but I opened the car door and slid in. I was too hurt to be touched by either one of them.

Tia and Ed got in the front seat, and she turned around to me. "You don't have to be so mean to her. It is her birthday weekend."

"I know." I got out of the car.

I hugged Mom. "I love you." I stepped back from her as she wiped the tears from her eyes. She looked up at Dad.

"Bye, Dad." I waved to him and got right back into the car.

Settling back in, I tapped Tia on the shoulder. "Happy?"

On the drive back to Northwestern, I texted Lila, Elise, Kate, and Doug the whole ride. As I'd expected, Tia refused to drop me at Doug's fraternity house.

"You're being so immature," Tia said as I go out of the car.

I retrieved my bag from Ed and put my head through the open window. "You forget I'm part of the rebellious generation Z or whatever. We text our boyfriends even when we're sitting right beside them." I stuck my tongue out at her. It was official. I was a raging, rebellious teen.

Ed held his arms out and gave me a hug.

"Thanks for the ride. Bye, Ed," I said hugging him back.

He released me. "They're just worried about you, you know."

"Thanks." I waved bye to him and rolled my suitcase up the walk to the dorm. My phone buzzed before I got to the door.

PULLING UP TO YOUR DORM NOW, Doug's text read.

I walked back to the street and saw his car approaching me. As soon as it stopped, he jumped out, wrapped his arms around me, picked me up, and spun me around. "I missed you so much."

He kissed me, and I felt like I was home. The hole that my family was carving in my soul didn't ache so much when I was in his arms.

"Have you eaten? I thought we could go out."

"That'd be great." He grabbed my bag and threw it in the backseat of his car. I hadn't seen myself hosting dinner, so I'd already sent texts making my apologies to Elise and the others on the guest list.

Inching into traffic, he squeezed my hand. "How was it being home? Did you have a good time with your family?"

In our earlier texts, I'd purposely not said anything about the issues with my family. "Fine." I forced a smile.

"Fine? Everything okay?"

I guess I hadn't worked hard enough on my smile or breezy tone. He kissed my hand, and I tried to shoot him a better smile.

He put his hand back on the steering wheel. "I'm not convinced."

"I don't know." I shrugged, unsure of how much I wanted to share with him. We sat there in silence for at least five minutes, and my angst about the experience got the best of me. "Am I irresponsible?"

"What?"

"Am I irresponsible?"

"What? No! Are you crazy? You're like the most responsible person I know. Do you think I'd be dating a slacker?" If he was trying to lighten my mood, I felt bad for him. He had no idea. "Where is this coming from?"

I had to think. Maybe I shouldn't share my problems with my family. I didn't want him to think badly about my parents. On the other hand, I wanted to be honest with him. I looked out the window. "My parents think my grades should be better."

"Your grades are good. You only have one B, right? Most people would kill for those grades."

"Well, they're not good enough for my parents. Oh, and I shouldn't be rowing either."

"Either? What else don't they want you doing?" He rubbed my leg, and I looked away. "Seeing me?"

"They think I'm not eating well."

"You've only gained two pounds back from last quarter. Was it me specifically, or you having a boyfriend in general?"

"In general, I think." I had no way of knowing if that was an honest statement.

"They just worry about you. That's what parents do. But you're not irresponsible. You haven't even had a drink all quarter. I haven't even had a drink all quarter. Maybe that's our problem. Maybe we need to get drunk. You're really cute with a buzz."

We parked in a garage in downtown Evanston. When he stopped the car, he kissed me long and hard. I let myself get lost in the passion. Part of me was thinking I shouldn't be kissing my boyfriend in a parking garage, and the half of my brain said, why the heck not?

Chapter 8

My relationship with my parents was tense at best. My mom still called every day. I was polite and courteous but nothing more. They mailed a case of nutritional energy bars.

For rowing training, the card in the box read.

I guessed it was sort of a peace offering, but I'd never liked bars of any sort. I left them at the fraternity house. They were gone the next day. My parents' disapproval gnawed at the edges of my thoughts, constantly leaving me less confident and more self-critical.

But, with all the preparations for the formal, Doug's demeanor was more relaxed. Distraction, it seemed, was a good thing. He kissed me, he looked me in the eyes, and we even went out with everyone on Thursday night. The next weekend we stayed at his mom's, and she took me shopping. Marissa had given me a couple of dresses when I was home, but in the end, a black dress from Paula's favorite dress shop won out. Cut low in the front, the dark color balanced out my light skin and dark hair.

Lila and I spent the morning of formal day at a salon getting our hair and nails done. Maybe it would've been nice if I hadn't been so anxious about the weekend. As it was, the need for everything to be perfect just heightened my anxiety. Although Doug had seemed more present the past two weeks, I still saw glimpses of his depression lurking in the background.

This weekend was important. Lila, Ross, Mark, and his girlfriend, Holli, had gotten a room, but I had no idea what our room arrangement was. I hadn't asked either, I wasn't sure why, I guess it had just become a habit. It was horribly unhealthy, and I knew it, waiting for someone to be capable of having a relationship with you. But he said he would try, and I saw the effort.

Did I believe he would get through this? Yes. Did I believe he would still want me when he did? I wasn't sure. I didn't think he was using me, but I wondered if he'd processed all his feelings about Zoey and the loss of his child. When he did, I hoped we wouldn't be so far apart in our life experiences that we'd be mismatched. The idea that he cared for me just as much as I did him was the belief I clung to. Without this, I would've surely spiraled into an abyss I wasn't sure I could return from.

After the salon, the guys met Lila and me in the lobby of the hotel, and we rode the elevator up to our rooms. Ross, Lila, Mark, and, Holli got out on the second floor. Doug blocked my exit. "We're going up." He pointed at the ceiling, smiling.

When I stepped back, he pushed the button for the penthouse level. As we rode, he swung our hands between us. Looking at his face, I realized he looked happy, even content. The furrowed brow and creases around his mouth weren't there. When he caught me looking, he squeezed my hand and winked at me.

"This is my dad's treat," he said as we stepped out of the elevator. We found our room, and he opened the double doors into a suite that covered a fourth of the floor. I set down my bag and skipped to the window that overlooked the lake. The left wall was also a window with a view of the north side of the city. There was a master suite as well as a king bed beyond the hot tub and another full and half bath. The Jacuzzi would easily fit six and a bar height counter divided the living area and a kitchen. A dining area held a table that seated eight.

Later this would be party central. At least for now, however, it was only us. I followed him into the master suite where he put away our luggage. We hung our clothes in the closet, and he excused himself to shower. I padded around the suite for a minute and made my way back to the bedroom, sitting on the bed to wait for him. The shower had just cut off when his phone rang. It was sitting a foot from me on the bed. I picked it up to answer it, but noticed it was Zoey. I tapped the screen to dismiss the call.

"Was that my phone?" he called from the bathroom.

The thought of hurling the phone onto the opposite wall flashed through my mind, but I slid it away from me. "It's was no one critical," I called to him, hoping he wouldn't question. Unfortunately his phone buzzed for receipt of a voice message, and he poked his head out of the bathroom.

"Who's that?" I wished more than anything there wasn't this thing between us. He walked towards me, one hand holding the towel around his waist and one hand held out.

I stood up, blocking his path to the phone. My hand was shaking, and I balled it into a fist. When reached around me to pick up the phone, I put my hand on his arm. "It's no one. Leave it." I pressed into his body. "You smell nice."

He forced a laugh. "Seriously?" He leaned down and picked up the phone. He looked at it, down at the floor, and then back to me. "I can't take this anymore. I'm done." He threw the phone on the bed and walked back into the bathroom.

My breath caught in my lungs. I dared not release it, afraid of the pain I might feel upon inhalation of the next one. I don't know how long I stood there frozen, my hands limp by my side. I knew if I moved, even an inch, time would restart, and I never wanted it to.

He barreled through the doorway, half-dressed in his tux this time. His tie hung straight down from his neck, and he slipped his cufflinks into his pocket. "Come on. I need you to call Zack and Bill and tell them to call you if they need anything. Call my mom and tell her we'll be late. I can't take calls on this phone." He turned and grabbed his coat from the closet.

Still in my jeans and bare feet, I trailed behind him, trying to remember all the directions he was giving me.

I just wanted him gone so I could gather my things and leave, but he stopped at the door and looked at me. Whatever he saw in my face made him change course. "Will you be okay here? Shit." He looked at the ceiling and then at his watch. "Can you walk in your dress? How fast can you change?"

Not sure where we were going or why I was complying with his request, I went into the bedroom and threw on my dress and shoes. Hurrying out of the bedroom, I found him in front of the bar talking on his phone. He finished his call. "Do you have a coat and your phone?"

Phone in hand, I ran back into the bedroom and retrieved my coat. He was on the phone again, holding the door to the hall open when I returned. In the elevator he snapped on his cufflinks as he spoke into the phone. He held his hand over the speaker. "Can you make those calls now?"

I placed the calls while he talked and paced the small elevator. I knew Zack and Bill were sharing a room, so I called Zack first. As soon as he answered, I wished I hadn't. Bill would have been much easier to talk to.

"What? Why?"

"I don't know. Doug has to take care of something."

"We have to be at the ballroom in an hour."

"Doug will explain later."

"You okay?"

"Course, I'll see you at the formal." I lied.

Trailing behind Doug, I dialed his mom as we passed through the lobby. Whisking through the turnstile door, he motioned for me to hurry.

His mom picked up on the first ring. "Amanda, we're in the cab. Is everything okay? It sounds like you're outside."

"I don't know." My voice cracked, and I knew if I spoke again I'd cry. I bit my lip and took a deep breath. "Doug says we'll be late."

"Half an hour, in the lobby," he said into my ear.

"Doug says a half hour," I repeated to her. "We'll meet you in the lobby."

Finished with the tasks he'd given me, my thoughts reeled. The cold air shook me from my haze. This was crazy. I was crazy, following him blindly like this. At the corner, I yanked my hand from his grip. "What are we doing?"

He covered his phone with his hand. "Getting rid of Zoey." He kissed me quickly on the lips. Zoey, he was getting rid of Zoey? He didn't talk about her. Although, I knew she called a lot. "It's just three more blocks. Are you okay walking? It'll be faster than a cab."

"Sure," I said, grateful he'd told me to get my coat.

He ended his call and took my hand again as we walked. "I talked to the manager. They can get this taken care of right away. We shouldn't be too late."

I still wasn't sure what the destination was, but knowing the goal, I felt better about following him.

He never talked to me about Zoey or the baby. As for myself, I lit a candle at the altar and said a prayer for them every day. I'd go in the afternoons when I knew he was in class. The priest was there most days, and once he'd stopped me, remembering my connection to Doug. "You're a good friend," he'd told me.

"I want to help, but he doesn't talk to me about it."

"Sometimes helping is letting them have their process." So I'd let him have his process.

We stopped at the corner, and the change in movement brought me back. "Next block, there." He pointed to a store with an apple on the sign. A phone store? He was getting a new phone? No, a new number, I realized, so she couldn't call.

The manager saw him right away. It seemed to take a long time, and I wondered if I should be there, although his arm stayed firmly around my waist. My lips still tingling from the kiss, and I vacillated between panic and euphoria. If he was finally free from Zoey, would I just remind him of her? Was I here because he felt pity or guilt? Was the kiss simply a product of his excitement over finally being rid of Zoey? I wouldn't stay with him because he felt an obligation to me. I'd healed before, and I would heal again.

What was in actuality twenty minutes at the Apple store seemed like an hour. Afterwards, we walked back to the hotel at a pace where I almost had to jog to keep up. He'd gotten a new confidential number that wasn't traceable from another phone. I was glad he explained how it worked, because I'd tuned out during the manager's technical explanation. As we entered the hotel, instead of heading straight to the bar to meet his mom and stepdad, he stopped. "Let's take our coats upstairs, so we can take a minute to breathe."

"Okay," I agreed, letting him lead me to the elevator.

Somehow we managed an elevator to ourselves. He leaned against the back wall. "I'm so sorry." I held my breath, unsure of the direction of the conversation. "I didn't mean for you to have to be along for that. It should have happened weeks ago. Thank you for coming."

I hadn't realized I had a choice, but I was grateful to be included and not left in the dark for once. "Of course." He rocked on his heels and hummed along with the tune from the speakers. But I gripped the railing on the walls, still out of breath from the walk. The walls seemed to be closing in on me as the elevator whirred to the top of the building.

The doors opened, and I stepped out onto the solid hall floor. Inside the room, he threw his keys on the counter. "Oh God."

He slipped out of his coat, and hung it on a chair, laying his tie on top of it. "I am so glad to be done with that." He shook his head and raised his hand above his head, striding to the bank of windows.

Just the site of expansive view had my head spinning. I pointed to the bedroom. "I'm going to freshen up." Halfway across the room, my phone buzzed. It was his mother. He traced back and took the phone from me, and I motioned to the bedroom again. He nodded and walked back to the windows.

Standing in front of the mirror, I took out my lipstick to touch up my makeup. For the first time, I looked at the finished product of the facial, pedicure, manicure, makeup session, and updo. I was glad I'd gone with the less makeup look. Even after our three-block sprint, the cold causing my eyes to tear, my makeup still looked good. Luck bestowed on me a minimally windy day, so my hair was still smooth and neat.

Stepping away from the counter to check that my dress was okay, what I saw in the mirror stunned me. Staring back at me stood an elegant woman. My reflection flipped a switch. I didn't know how he would completely eradicate Zoey from his life, but I did know one thing: I deserved to be in a healthy solid relationship.

When I came out of the bathroom, he was waiting. "Did I tell you how amazing you look?

"I don't remember."

"Well you do, and I'm sorry, again, for this afternoon and the last six weeks. I have something for you." He pulled a small box from his pocket. "It's a late Valentine's present."

I took the box and tilted it back and forth. With the uncertainty of our relationship, I didn't want a gift from him. "Doug, you didn't have to get me anything."

"What do you mean? It's a gift."

"You don't need to give me a present. I didn't get you anything."

"You had the picture from New Year's Eve framed for me." He encircled my hands in his. "I love you. If I could give you the world, I would."

I stared into his face, studying his eyebrows, his eyes, his line of his nose, his lips, and the dimple in his chin, letting the words sink into my brain. Although I knew without a doubt that I loved him, him loving me was an idea I hadn't let myself adopt.

"Is this too little too late? The past six weeks have been horrible, but how I feel about you hasn't changed. I love you."

I looked at our hands and then back into his eyes. "I love you. I've loved you since the day we met."

For the first time in weeks, I could breathe, at least in between kisses. It was as if all my fear vanished in a second. I slid my arms around his waist, and he backed me onto the bed. As he kissed me, he traced from the top of my head, over my hips, and down my leg. But he stopped me when I tried to undo his cummerbund.

Clearing his throat, he pushed himself up. "I am the luckiest guy in the world."

I sat up, kissing him again.

He wrapped his hands around my waist. "Our clothes are going to be wrecked, and your hair and makeup—"

I cut him off putting my lips to his. "I love you."

He smiled, really smiled, and kissed me again, so insistently I didn't want it to end. "Will you please open this now?" He held the box up to me.

Inside the cardboard box was an aqua velvet box. Tucked inside the velvet was the most beautiful piece of jewelry I'd ever seen. A single diamond hung from the top of a silver circle.

"Doug, it's beautiful. Thank you." He helped me put on the necklace. It hung just below the others he'd given me.

"I love you." He kissed me again. I slid my hand down his back, but he grabbed my hand, laughing. "This took me a long time to do, and we should have been downstairs fifteen minutes ago."

I fiddled with his tie. "I know can do ties and cummerbunds."

"I'm sure you can. You probably do this all the time. Really quite shameful, seducing old men in tuxes."

"Okay, I won't help you then." I marched to the bathroom to check my makeup and hair. He grabbed my arm and spun me back into him, kissing me again.

"Okay, now we should make sure we're presentable."

He flattened his shirt and straightened his tie while I touched up my lipstick and eyeliner. He grabbed his jacket and the key from the bar and we headed for the elevator. I wiped my lipstick from his mouth as we waited in the hall.

"Why didn't you want to take the gift?"

I shook my head, sorry that I'd wasted so much time worrying about him leaving me. "You didn't say anything for so long. I couldn't tell how you felt about me."

"I'm sorry again."

He kept his arm around my waist and kissed me when we were alone in the elevator. In the lobby we found Paula and Gary at the bar.

"Oh my goodness," she exclaimed standing to greet us when we were close enough. "You look beautiful." She squeezed my shoulders.

Doug gave her a hug. "Sorry we're late."

"You had me so worried, what happened?"

He squeezed my hand. "I had Dad file the order and the suit, and then we went to get a new phone number."

I put my hand to his arm. "What are you talking about?"

"My dad had a restraining order and a civil harassment suit ready to file. I didn't want to do it, but she left me no choice."

I let the gravity of Doug's actions sink into my brain. She could be arrested if she didn't leave him alone. She had to leave him alone now, right?

We only had enough time for one drink with them. I was glad they'd planned a night out so they didn't have to take a cab all the way to the hotel to see us for fifteen minutes. As we got up, he kissed his mom on the cheek and thanked them for coming. She hugged me and wished us a fun night.

As we approached the ballroom, everything looked like it was running smoothly. Lila, Bill, and Mark were at the reception table, and Zack was standing just to the left of it, giving directions to the band. As soon as we approached, Lila scooted out from behind the table. "You look amazing!" She pried me away from Doug and hugged me. Patting the necklace on my neck, she winked at me. "So things are good?"

"He said he loved me," I whispered in her ear.

"Sex?"

"What, no!" I pushed her away.

Turning back to Doug, I saw Zack approach. "Wow, nice of you to grace us with your presence." He stood chest to chest with Doug. "And so great of you to unload all your crap on us tonight."

Doug didn't move. "What's going on?"

Zack looked at me and then back to Doug. "What's going on is that we we're stuck fielding calls from your crazy ex-girlfriend and doing all your shit." Zack lifted his shoulders and shook out his arms. "And you were hiding in the penthouse. This is not cool anymore. I'm done." He slammed the papers he was holding into Doug's chest and turned to me. "And you should be, too."

Doug dropped my hand and took a step toward Zack. "Fair enough. I've been a jerk."

Their faces were inches apart, but Zack didn't back down. "Are you going to continue being a jerk, or is that your apology? I hope you apologized to her." He pointed a finger at me.

Doug looked at the ceiling, his fingers flexing into a fist. "That is none of your business."

Zack took a half-step closer to Doug so they were nearly nose to nose. I stepped forward, but Bill grabbed my shoulders. The movement was enough to distract Zack's attention away from Doug. Our eyes met, and he immediately took a step back.

Bill released me, and I inserted myself between them, nose to chest with Doug. When I put a hand on his arm, he was shaking.

"Doug, let me talk to Zack."

I spun to face Zack. "Can we talk?" I pointed down the hall.

Doug placed his hands on my shoulders and guided me out from between them. "Zack and I can figure this out."

I pointed to each of them. "Are you guys going to be okay?" They each nodded at me. I walked back to stand beside Bill, trying to ignore Mark, Ross, and Lila who were craning their necks towards us.

"What happened?" I whispered to Bill when I reached him.

"I have no clue. Zack seemed stressed but that came out of nowhere."

"Was he drinking?"

"He pounded down one pretty hard when he came in."

Mark approached. "What did he mean by crazy ex-girlfriend?"

"Doug had an errand, and it ran late," I said, looking between him and Bill.

Bill cocked his head away from Mark. When we were a few feet away he stopped. "Why didn't he call me? If there was a problem, I told him to call me. Where were you anyway?"

I told him about the phone number, the restraining order, and the civil suit.

"I guess that explains all the crazy Zoey calls," he said.

When Doug and Zack came around the corner, they were straightening their jackets and laughing. It was hard to tell if things were really worked out. I knew they were good actors.

They walked straight to me, and Doug slipped one arm around me, giving me a kiss on the temple "You okay?" I nodded. "So, Zack has something to say to you." He looked to Zack.

Zack held out a hand. "Can we?" He motioned away from the group.

"Sure," I told him looking at Doug. Doug rubbed my back and nodded towards Zack. As I followed him down the hall, I was surprised to realize that I was angry. "What's going on?" I demanded when he stopped just around the corner.

"Umm, I thought I was supposed to be apologizing to you."

"What was that about? What happened back there?"

"I don't know." He hung his head, raising it slightly before he spoke. "You just came in looking so amazing, and it flipped me out. Are you guys good? I mean did all of this finally bring him out of his funk? Because you deserve to be happy."

"I'm so sorry, Zack."

"Hey, I'm apologizing to you remember? It's not your fault."

"I'm good. Everything's good. There's a formal to get back to here, right? Are we good? Where's your date?"

"I was about to go meet her."

"Go." I hit his shoulder.

Zack hurried in the direction of the elevators, and I made my way back to the hall. As soon as I turned the corner, Lila accosted me. "What's going on?"

"What?"

"I need details." She gripped my arm.

"Doug was finally able to get that family issue worked out."

She grabbed my other arm and spun me around so we were face to face. "I heard crazy ex-girlfriend. Is there something you're not telling me?"

I scanned the ceiling, trying to figure out what I could say that wasn't a lie. "There were issues that he didn't talk to me about. I'm not sure what they all were. But even the information I do know wasn't mine to share."

Doug approached us, and Lila released me. "Appetizers are starting. Let's get some food," he whispered to me. My stomach churned in response, making a loud gurgling noise I couldn't hide.

"Please tell me you ate since rowing this morning."

"Course." I tried to remember if I was lying or not. I was pretty sure Lila had thrown me a sandwich at some point.

As we finished greeting all the brothers, Mark found me. He stepped between Doug and me, pulling me away from Doug. "Are you okay? Doug isn't talking to Zoey again is he?" His breath was hot on my shoulder and I backed away.

"No, we're good, really good actually."

"Yeah, Lila tells me you have some news."

"Really, like what?"

"New bling? Something about love?"

My face flushed. "Yeah, something like that." I took a sip of my drink.

He leaned into me again. "I don't think your parents will like this, but if you're happy, then I'm happy for you."

"Thanks, that means a lot."

"Well it took a lot, but I can see that he makes you happy. He's a good guy. I wouldn't be in this fraternity if he wasn't."

It was an amazing party. Everything was perfect. From the dinner and the speeches to the band and the music, all flowed seamlessly. We talked to everyone and danced to a ton of songs. The party in the hall went till eleven thirty and then continued into our suite until well past two. Doug's smile didn't leave his face and mine didn't either.

𝙆   𝙆   𝙆

Through my eyelids, I could see light. I smelled coffee. Beside me, papers rustled. Snuggled under the warm blankets, my body fought responding to any of these stimuli. But my mind begged to satisfy its curiosity of the aftermath of last night's party.

I wasn't sure how late or early it was when I fell asleep. I vaguely remembered Doug leading me to the bathroom to brush my teeth and then pulling the covers over me. I opened my eyes to see Doug propped up on pillows beside me, coffee in one hand and a paper in the other.

"What time is it?"

"Day time," he responded, putting down his paper and rubbing my head. "And for the record, you put on your pajamas."

"Okay," I said, closing my eyes again. It was only then that I realized I still had my bra on under my tank top, but my jeans had been replaced with pajama pants. I opened one eye to peek at him.

"What time is it really?"

"Okay, don't freak because it's not a big deal, but you seriously sleep more than anyone I know."

"But you still love me right?"

"Yes, I love you."

My eyes drifted across the room. The curtains were closed, but I could see bright sunlight piercing through the cracks. I smelled food too. Out the open door was a cart with metal-covered plates atop it. I traced circles on Doug's hand.

"How long have you been up?"

"Little over an hour."

I straightened to a sitting position. I needed to use the restroom and brush my teeth. I swung one leg over him and sat on top of his legs. Can I have some water? I pointed at the glass beside him. He handed it to me, and I took a drink, trying to freshen my mouth. I bent forward, brushing his chest, and placed it back on the table. Then I kissed him and jumped away.

"You're a tease." He chased me to the bathroom.

"I'll be right back," I said as I closed the door. As I brushed my teeth, the clock on the counter caught my eye. Eleven eighteen!

I swung the door open, panicked. "Shouldn't we be at brunch?"

"I told you not to freak," Doug said immediately. "Come over here." His tone calmed me, and I obeyed. When I got within arm's reach, he hooked his arm through mine. "I have a question," he continued as I sat beside him.

"Okay…"

"How would you feel about staying with me another night?"

Another night with just Doug sounded like paradise. "Isn't this room really expensive?"

"Compliments of my dad." He set a strand of hair that had fallen into my face on top of my head.

"Really?" I sat up on my knees.

"Yes. So what do you think? I'm not sure your parents would approve."

"No, they won't. But I can't please them no matter what I do."

His answering smile was something I hoped I'd never take for granted. He took my face in his hands and then slid them through my hair and down my neck, tracing them down my back and to my hips. I leaned into him and kissed him gently on the lips. He sat up and pressed his lips into mine, answering my kisses again and again until I had to breathe.

His hands slid down my back finding my waist and then my legs. He picked me up and spun me under him, his lips outlining my collarbone, my shoulder, my neck, my chin, and finally finding my mouth again. He pressed his body against mine, and his heat seemed to saturate me. My fingers trickled over his skin, and I wanted to be closer to him to feel his skin on mine. I sat up tugging at my tank top.

He pushed himself up on his hands and put one of them atop mine as I went to peel off my top. "Are you sure you want to do this?"

I knew this was probably the point of no return. No, I told myself, I could choose at any time. But I knew I didn't want to stop what we'd set in motion. I shed my tank top, and his shirt fell to the floor. I spread my fingers across his chest, marveling at his broad abdomen. My hand didn't even span halfway to the other side.

The world beyond our room disappeared. His smell and touch consumed me. His lips traced down my neck to my chest, and I shivered in response. His gaze met mine briefly. Then he buried his head in my neck and, clutching me tightly, flipped me over so he was staring up at me. My hands floated over his chest, honey colored even in the dead of winter. The difference between us had never been so blaringly obvious. I was amazed at how the length of my hand barely stretched to a quarter of his back while his fingers spanned my whole waist. I marveled that my thin fingers looked like white marble against his bronze chest.

His hand followed the contour of my body, hesitating on my thigh. I brushed my lips along his neck and chest, moving down his abdomen. He gripped my thigh, stopping my motion. He sat up and pulled the sheet over his chest. I stuck out my lip and kissed him. He laughed and bit his lip. "Maybe we should talk about this."

I sat in front of him, just in my bra. I felt exposed, but it was just like a bikini. Or so I told myself. I loved this man, and he loved me. I placed a hand on his cheek. "I want to be with you."

"Are you sure? Maybe you want some time—"

I shook my head. "I love you. I decided two months ago that I wanted to be with you."

"Really?" He got up and unzipped his overnight bag.

"In case you haven't noticed, it takes me a long time to make decisions. I had to be prepared."

"I had noticed that. So you decided this in January?"

"Mmm, hmm." I took a sip from the glass of water that sat on the table. "Give me that." I snatched the package from his hand and tossed it on the bedside table.

"Um, no, we definitely need that," he said, reaching for it.

"We're safe," I said, taking his hand.

"You're taking something? Since when?"

"Thirteen." His brow furrowed. "It allows me to actually walk every day of the month," I said, placing both his hands on my waist. It had only taken my mom and my doctor two months to decide that birth control was a better option than missing a week of school every month.

"Well, we are going to use this." He held up the package and kissed me. "I haven't been with someone who hasn't done this before. You'll tell me if you're uncomfortable, right?"

We were both on our knees and he took my face in both his hands. "I love you."

If I thought it would happen in the middle of the day, maybe I would've been nervous. As it was, I was swept away by my desire to be as close to him as possible. I'd spent the last six weeks longing to be held and be touched by him, for him to show me any affection at all. Nothing could have made me happier than being with him.

We lay facing each other, and he kissed me from head to toe. He traced every inch of my body with his fingers, spreading waves of warmth through me as he went. When he reached my feet, the sensation was almost overwhelming. Chill bumps covered me. I sat up, walked my fingers up his chest and pressed my body into his. His huge arms wrapped around me and warmed me instantly.

I sat on his lower back, massaging the huge muscles of his back and arms. I rubbed my hands through his hair, realizing it was longer than I'd ever seen it. His beard and mustache, normally trimmed to a five o'clock shadow, had grown out during the night. All this suited him. I kissed his back up to his neck and slid down so I was lying beside him.

Before I realized it, I was lying under him and his body stretched out on top of me.

He kissed my shoulder and I shivered. "Too intense?"

"Yes, but that's a good thing," I told him, sliding my hand around the back of his neck and drawing him back to me. He hesitated for a second, meeting my gaze, and then kissed me square on the lips hard. He slid his hand down my back and released my bra. He slid it off my arms and held it in one hand.

"You won't be offended if I tell you that is the smallest bra I've ever seen?"

"Yes, I will," I said with a smile. I took it from him and flung it across the room. I wasn't sure I wanted him staring at my chest, or lack thereof, so I pulled the covers up to my neck. I shivered as his warm body pressed against mine. His hand traced down under my arm to my waist and down to my thigh.

"Tell me if you need me to stop," he said, lifting my chin to look into my eyes.

I nodded. Now I was a little nervous but his kisses removed all my hesitation. My body responded just as it should. I was so happy to share this experience with him, happy that I'd waited for the right person, a guy who loved me and I trusted.

Lying there I couldn't think of a time in my life I'd felt more content. Just being held against his warm body was nirvana. He kissed my head and handed me the glass of water. We lay skin to skin under the covers. I rocked my foot back and forth against his, wondering what he was thinking.

I smoothed the sheet on his torso, and he kissed my head. "I love you. Thank you for letting me be the first person to share that experience with you. Do you feel okay?"

I rolled over and lay on top of him. "I love you." I kissed his chest. "I am so happy to be with you."

He rubbed my head and put a hand around my neck pulling me to him. "You are so beautiful. I am a very lucky guy."

I kissed him. "Yes you are." I yanked the sheet off him and closed it around my body.

"What are you doing?" He tugged on the fabric.

"Get your own."

"I just saw you naked."

"That was in bed. I'm not quite ready to walk naked across the room."

His thumb shot up. "Got it."

I retrieved my clothes from the floor and snuck into the bathroom. I'd intended to be fast but realized I needed to be alone for a bit. I brushed my teeth and ran some detangling product through my hair. I bundled the curls back and secured them into a bun with an elastic band. Curly was going to have to suffice. I showered and toweled off. The cotton felt smooth and fresh on my skin and I stared at myself in the mirror wanting to always remember how I felt today.

I dressed and folded my clothes in my bag. Finding him sitting on the couch reading the paper, I nestled under his arm feeling his warmth and taking in the scent of his soap and shave cream. We ate breakfast in the dining room looking out over the lake. Afterward, we snuggled on the couch together.

"This isn't exactly the way I planned this six weeks ago."

"You had a plan?" I asked, overjoyed that we'd been at least thinking in the same direction before the derailment. "What was it?"

"My mom and Gary were supposed to have a weekend away, so I thought we could have a weekend there. I wanted to make you eggs for breakfast."

"That sounds nice. But this was good."

"So I have two questions," he said, lacing his fingers between mine. "Why did you look so freaked out yesterday when I said I was done with Zoey?"

I cleared my throat. Even though I knew the ending, that moment was hard to relive. "You didn't say you were done with Zoey. You just said you were done."

"You thought I meant us? Why would you think that? Don't you remember what I said to you at the beginning? I said I'd do anything not to lose you. You didn't believe me?"

"I believed you wanted that when you said it."

"But?"

"You didn't talk to me for a long time. I had no clue what you were thinking. I thought I would just remind you..." I couldn't finish the sentence.

He held my face in his hands. "You can't think that way. You were the only reason I pulled through. You are the best thing that's ever happened to me. I figured if you were still with me, then I couldn't be completely evil."

I kissed him. "And the second question?"

"What did Zack say to you yesterday?"

I held my breath. I wouldn't lie to Doug, but there were certain things I thought were best left unsaid. Really only this one, well two if you counted the issues with my parents. I bit my lip, unsure of what to say. When I didn't respond, he continued.

"He threatened to punch me if I hurt you?"

I released my breath and mustered some courage. If we were going to be in this, I needed to be as transparent as possible. "He said I deserved to be happy."

"Does he think you won't be happy with me?"

"He didn't say that. The last six weeks have been really hard."

"I love you, and I don't ever want to hurt you again." He kissed me.

Looking out the window, my life felt surreal. The formal, and after-party, the suite, breakfast at two in the afternoon, having a day with just him—I couldn't have asked for more.

"Did you call anyone?" he asked, ending my mental bliss.

"That makes three questions."

"Granted, but you should at least text Elise, Lila, and your parents. I don't want them to think any worse of me."

I had no problem with Elise and Lila, although I really just wanted to lie in his arms forever. Part of me felt worried that if I connected with the outside world, all of this would disappear.

He stood. "Call them. I'm going to shower."

I looked at my watch. It was just after one. Elise and Lila were easy, as I sent simple texts. My family was a bit trickier. I was standing in front of the windows dialing my home number when Doug came up behind me, placed his hands on my waist, and kissed my hair.

My mom answered. "Hello."

"Hi."

"Manda, how are you? We've been worried. We haven't heard from you since yesterday morning."

"I know. Lila drug me to the salon, and we spent the afternoon getting ready for the formal. We were up late last night, so...."

"Your dad is worried sick. He left early, so you should call him."

"Sure."

"So, did you have a fun time with your friends?"

"Yes, we did. It was a fun party."

"I'm glad, sweetie. What are you and Elise cooking tonight?"

Our weekly dinner was tonight. Elise, being the wonderful friend she was, wasn't upset at all about me missing our tradition.

"Actually, I'm spending the evening with Doug," I said and held my breath.

"But weren't you just with him for the party last night? You can't ditch your friends for your boyfriend, or you won't have any more friends." I slipped out of Doug's arms and crossed the room.

"Mom, we were with the whole fraternity last night. It's one night. I live with Elise." I walked into the bedroom.

"Yeah, but what about all your other friends?"

"I see them all the time."

"Your father and I are still concerned about how much time you spend with Doug."

"Mom, Doug is important. I love him, and he loves me." I hated that she was ruining this for me. I should have called Marissa first. She would've been happy for me. I remembered Tia calling my mom the day after Ed had told her he loved her. Mom was so excited for her. The next weekend Tia phoned Mom to tell her they'd had sex. It wasn't Tia's first experience, but it was her first with Ed. I probably wasn't supposed to be listening, but I'd overheard Mom explain to Tia that when you're with someone you love a lot of good things happen.

"Are you sure?"

"He told me he loved me yesterday. I love him, too."

"This is news. I know you care a lot about him. How is his family situation?"

"They've been able to resolve it."

"I'm not sure what to say, sweetie. I love you, and I want you to be happy. Please make choices carefully."

Would it kill her to pretend to be happy for me? "Of course, Mom, I'll talk to you later." I hung up the phone and stared out the window.

Doug's breath on my neck brought me out of my shock. "Did you tell them where you were?"

"I told Mom I was spending the evening with you."

"I heard that part."

I didn't want to talk anymore about my parents. I walked my fingers up his arm and blew in his ear.

"That's very devious."

"What is?" I opened my eyes as wide as I could and titled my eyebrows up. My phone rang. It was Marissa. I let it go to voice mail.

After I sent a text message to Dad, I turned off my phone. We lounged on the couch and then soaked in the hot tub. We talked about everything. By dinner, there wasn't one thing about the last two months that we hadn't shared. It felt good, really good, for him to be so open and to be able to reciprocate that.

We ate takeout Chinese, compliments of Mrs. Chen, and watched a movie. The night was just as steamy, if not more, than the day had started. I didn't want it to end—ever.

The next morning before class, as I stood kissing him in the courtyard for the millionth time, I felt I'd never been happier in my life.

Chapter 9

Marissa and Lila were beyond ecstatic about my new relationship status. Tia and my parents weren't, but I ignored their criticism as much as possible. All my other friends were supportive, which made life ninety percent perfect. Who was one hundred percent happy anyway? As long as my parents were in Champaign and I was not, life was good. My friends' affirmations helped me feel sane. My family's view of our relationship was irrational. So I'd taken Chinese literature instead of Middle Eastern history because Doug had introduced me to it. I had three more years of school.

I wanted to be with him all the time, and we were nearly inseparable. Even with finals looming, post-Zoey—or Zoey-gate, as Zack called it—life was blissful. We worked out, studied, hung out with friends, went out dancing, hung out at his mom's, and he was present and happy. Even laundry was fun with him. I could have been with him every second of every day.

"Believe me, you'll get sick of me," he said as we drove back to campus the next Sunday afternoon. I didn't think that for a second.

Back in my dorm room, I phoned my parents while Doug studied next to me on my futon. During the week, I'd texted Mom a couple of times but avoided directly talking with her.

Mom had updated Dad on my new relationship status. His first text to me read. Talked to your Mother. Not what I expected from you. Hope you are happy.

What was I supposed to do with that? Doug's a good guy. I replied.

That's not the point. We can discuss when we talk.

That had been Monday. I hadn't replied yet. Breath held, I dialed my parents' number.

Mom answered. "Hi, sweetie. Your dad is just packing for his week. I'll put you on speaker."

I tapped on my computer case, waiting. "Hi pipsqueak, how are you doing?" Okay so that wasn't what I expected.

"I had a good week."

"Well, that's great. Anything new?"

"Nope, just studying, training, and getting ready for finals."

"Yeah, I saw that on the calendar. We were thinking about our spring break trip."

Dang, I'd forgotten about that. Maybe I could get out of it. I needed to be back early for rowing anyway. "Right, the Keys this time? I need to change my flight to be back early for rowing. Am I flying from here or Champaign?"

"Oh, that's fine. I have you flying from Chicago with Tia and Ed," Mom piped up.

I wondered why Tia and Ed were coming. Wouldn't they want to be alone? I know I would have. Of course it was a free trip, and with Tia's law school loans, they probably couldn't afford anything else.

"So, your father and I were thinking you might like to invite Doug. Marissa might invite a girlfriend."

Wow, this was a one-eighty. I jostled the phone in my hand, almost dropping it. "Oh..." I cut my eyes to Doug who was watching me. "Maybe."

"Well, let us know. I'll send you the flight info."

"Okay," I said good-bye and ended the call. I wondered why all of a sudden they wanted to include Doug. They could have asked me to invite Lila.

"What was with the Oh?" Doug asked as I bounced my phone on my leg.

"They invited you to come to the Keys with us."

"Sweet, beaches and bikinis, I can't wait."

"You want to come?" I rested my hands on my legs.

"Are you kidding? Why would I not?"

"It is my parents we're talking about."

"It'll be fine." He'd said the word fine, the kiss of death, I thought.

After Doug left for the evening, I texted Marissa. Doug's invite was just as much of a mystery to her. They'd asked her if she wanted to invite a friend, because they were going to suggest I bring Doug. I hated being paranoid, but I couldn't help but think they had some ulterior motive. Maybe they were going to try and accept our relationship. Maybe they would see how wonderful we were together and stop pestering me, but I doubted it.

꜀ ꜀ ꜀

Our plane left Friday evening after finals, and we would return on Tuesday night. The flight schedule gave us a day to rest up before rowing training started Thursday.

My grades held steady. I'd hoped to be able to get an A in Chemistry, but it just didn't happen. My dad would have to settle for less than perfection. Part of me could see where my parents were coming from. I'd always made above a 4.0 in high school. College was different though. I had the highest GPA of anyone I knew. My grades would just have to be good enough.

I'd had many realizations over the past year: guys could be jerks, parents didn't always know what's best for you, and being in love was the greatest feeling in the world. But my latest was I didn't really want to take any more chemistry. Even Calculus was more interesting to me than my chemistry course. I'd liked it in high school, but I'd also had a really fun teacher. Now I found myself gravitating towards biology. But since chemistry was double major with international studies, I wasn't sure what to do about my feelings. I knew Dad had strong opinions about the chemistry track. He felt it would serve me better than any of the others. He was probably right, which sucked. I wasn't sure if I should switch, or just stick it out and see if things changed.

Not wanting to assume my family was still going to be just as critical as they'd been the last two visits, I decided to start with a fresh slate. I asked Tia about her job and she chatted with Doug and me up until boarding time. They'd just won a big case, and she'd received a lot of recognition for her research. I prompted her to keep talking and asked lots of questions, anything to veer the topic away from me.

During the first two days, we parasailed, rode jet skis, snorkeled, and went boogie boarding and swimming. It was fun and relaxing to be away from the world of school and work. On Monday, the guys headed out early for a round of golf, and the girls planned a day beside the pool.

I'd gotten gun shy since formal about sharing anything with my mom and Tia. They'd become so critical, so I'd stopped telling them anything but mundane facts: how many tutoring sessions I had, what volunteer activities I was doing, what was going on with Lila and my other friends. This week I'd really tried to break that pattern by sharing more about my role on the rowing team and the spring meet schedule, what was going on at the Fraternity for the spring, what intramurals Mark was trying to talk me into, and details about my class schedule.

Mom got up and went to the bar to get herself and Tia daiquiris and Marissa and me virgin piña coladas.

Tia pushed up on her elbows. "So, what about when Doug graduates?"

"I don't know. He's going to start interviewing after spring break. Plus, he's interested in this international training program, so we'll see."

"So, you're staying together?"

"Yes."

She cleared her throat. "We'll see how long that lasts." She rested her head back on the pillow of her lounge chair.

I sat up. "What does that mean?"

She removed her sunglasses. "You've got your head in the clouds if you think your relationship is going to last. I give it three months after he graduates, tops."

I opened my mouth to protest, but she cut me off.

"I don't care how many times he says he loves you, how much jewelry he buys you, or how much sex you have. Long distance is not going to work with a guy like that."

"That's just mean, Tia." Marissa got up, grabbed my hand, and pulled me in the direction of the pool. "We're going to swim."

Marissa and I swam until Tia came into the pool. As soon as she got in, we jumped out. It was immature, but I didn't care.

When we settled back into our lawn chairs, Mom came and sat beside me. She put her hand on my leg. "Tia means well. She doesn't want to see you hurt."

"But why doesn't she say that? She just keeps cutting him down just like you do."

"Things will be different when he graduates and moves away. It was even hard for your father and me, and we were engaged and had been together for two years. I hate that you got yourself so deep into this."

I set my sunglasses on my towel and straightened my spine. "Mom I love him, and he loves me. What part of that do you not get?"

Tia fitted her towel around her middle and sat down next to me. "Did you know Zoey quit her job and checked herself in to a recovery program? How much do you stay with Doug anyway? Are you sure he's stable?"

"Why does Zoey have anything to do with me or Doug? She got crazy on her own time."

Mom rested her hand on my shoulder. "So you're cohabitating now?"

I stood, snatched my towel from under Mom, and walked away. I really had no clue where I was going. Marissa caught up and put her arm around me. We walked to the beach and found some chairs. We stayed on the sand, deciding to be rebellious teens for the day. We paid for reserved chairs on the room tab, ordered lunch and virgin daiquiris from the Cabana waiter, and also charged it to the room. We played our music so loud the people next to us had the waiter ask us to turn it down, and swam in the surf until our fingers looked like prunes.

Finally, just after four, I got a text from Doug that they were back from golfing. Marissa and I packed up our stuff and met them at the bungalow. Doug was in the shower, and I fully intended to hide in my room until I could grab a shower too. Dad caught me stuffing towels into the washing machine. He cocked his head toward their bedroom down the hall where I could see Mom sitting on the bed. I followed him into the room and leaned against the dresser, my arms folded on my chest.

Dad flipped a coin back and forth over his knuckles a few times and then set the coin on the dresser beside me. "All this tension has to stop." Dad pointed at each of us. "Can we come to a resolution of agreeing to disagree?"

"I was being nice."

Mom flung her arms up. "You stomped off like a child."

"I thought you guys were offering an olive branch by inviting Doug."

Mom folded her hands in her lap. "We don't want you to be hurt, especially after last quarter."

Dad sat on the bed beside her. "Are you sure this relationship is in your best interest? I'm not sure it aligns with your goals."

"Goals? What about the goal of being a happy, normal eighteen year old? I'm an adult. I can make my own choices and deal with the outcome. You never treated Tia this way."

Dad stood and adjusted his pants. "You're eighteen, not a fully independent adult. And Tia had a 4.0."

I flipped my ponytail over my shoulder. "So if I get a 4.0, I can have a boyfriend, like for a reward?"

Dad stuck his hands in his pockets and rocked on his feet. "You know that's not what we're saying. We just want you to make smart choices."

I cut through the air with my hand. "If I felt that I wasn't doing my best, then there would be some merit to your concerns. But study wise, I am doing my best. I'm sorry if you don't think it's good enough. I won't talk about grades with you again."

Dad lifted his hands, palms forward. "Okay, but just know that CIA and military agencies are very competitive for the positions you want. And that's the last thing I'll say. You need to be taking Middle Eastern everything, learn Hebrew or Arabic or both, not Japanese or Chinese."

"You know I love learning languages, every one of them are on my list. The chemistry is giving me problems though. I'm not really that interested in it."

He wiped his forehead. "You can't quit something just because you don't like one course. You need to stick with chemistry. It's the best field for that industry."

I slumped my shoulder and rested my hands on my legs. "I'm not saying I'm quitting. I was sharing—" I realized it wasn't worth it. "Are we done?"

I didn't wait for them to reply. Instead, I pushed off the dresser and walked out. Two steps down the hall, I ran into Doug's chest. He caught me by the arms. "Hey, you okay?"

"Sure."

He curved his finger at me and pointed at the end of the hall. I followed him to his room. "Okay, so this is awkward, but I heard the last part of that. Are there more problems between you and your parents?"

"They're just being parents." Overbearing, over-protective parents, I thought.

"They're still concerned about your grades? They do realize you have the highest GPA of anyone I know, don't they?"

I sat down on the bed. "Besides you and Tia. And, yes, I told them. It's okay. It's no big deal."

"I can tell you get stressed about your grades. Is there anything else that you haven't shared with me?"

I bit my lip.

He flipped in front of me and squatted down so we were eye to eye. "Like that they don't approve of us being together."

I covered my eyes with my hands. "Did my dad say something to you?"

"Only in so many words. He was being diplomatic. But then Ed spilled."

I stared at the ceiling and flipped my ponytail over my finger again and again, trying to keep tears from forming. When I thought I could speak without crying, I looked back at him. "They are being irrational. I'm supposed to be a nun or something, I guess." One by one, I put a hand to each cheek. "This, you, mean a lot to me. I feel like what we have is worth fighting for."

He covered my hands with his. "I do too."

I stretched over and kissed him. "I love you."

"I love you, too. Now go shower, because I'm starving." He popped me with the towel hanging over the chair.

Chapter 10

Manda, Manda!" Someone shook my leg. "Hey, you have half an hour before the moving help gets here."

Elise. Grrrr, I thought. Today was graduation day for Elise, Zack, and Doug. It was not a day I wanted to face.

Spring quarter was equally hectic and perfect. With rowing, classes, tutoring, and babysitting, my schedule was full. I loved being on the rowing team. The girls needed an extra rower so I was able to row with them as well serving as a coxswain on Zack and Doug's boat. We had meets almost every weekend. My parents only came up for one, which disappointed me, but I wasn't sure what I expected from them anymore.

Our relationship deteriorated to the point where I only talked to them about my friends, work, and campus clubs, save rowing. It was hard at first. When I was excited or nervous about a meet, when Doug and I did something fun, or I learned something neat in my biology or Chinese literature course, my first thought was to call Mom or Dad. But then I'd remember they didn't want me to like those activities. So I'd call Lila, Marissa, or Mark, or tell Elise.

At first, I held my breath every day when I texted Mom, wondering when she'd bring up Doug again. But she didn't mention him, so I followed suit. It was the same with Dad. With him, even discussions about my classes became hard, as I found myself drawn to biology topics like speech development and language formation. I hoped somewhere deep down in my psyche my interest in biology wasn't stemming from some rebellious streak I'd adopted. That I wasn't interested in biology because Dad said I needed to take chemistry. We even had a new professor in chemistry class this quarter. He was a good teacher. Chemistry just didn't excite me anymore.

Other than the one rowing meet, I saw my family at Easter and Marissa's graduation. On Easter weekend, I waited for the lectures to start, but they didn't. When I mentioned my surprise and relief to Marissa, she rolled her eyes and plopped down on her bed, covering her head with her pillow.

I snatched it away. "What's wrong?"

"They've moved on to new prey." She spun around and stuffed the pillow in her lap.

I sat beside her. "What do you mean, what's going on?"

"They just started again this week. I have to choose where I'm going to college."

"Umm, yeah, weren't you supposed to do that in like January? I thought you were going to UNI."

"That's where I want to go, but they want me to stay in Champaign. They think it's a better school and—"

"Let me guess," I grabbed a pillow and lay back on it. "They can keep an eye on you. You should point out that UNI is cheaper."

"They haven't said that, but I know that's what they're thinking. I already tried the cheaper thing."

"You can't pick a college based on what they think."

She pounded the pillow on the bed and got up. "I know. Remember how we visited UNI like three times. I really liked it there. I just dread making the final decision."

I hugged her. "Maybe they'll stop harping on you when you do. Then it'll be done and there won't be anything they can do about it."

"Yeah, maybe."

The weekend of her graduation was fun. Our aunts, uncles, and cousins came from Iowa. My parents didn't set any rules around Doug being there, so we rode to Champaign with Tia and Ed. With the group being so big and hosting parties there wasn't any time to single me out. Even Tia was nice.

Ending the quarter, my grades were good. I'd finally gotten them up to a 4.0 like my parents expected. I wasn't exactly sure how I'd achieved it. Maybe it had something to do with my adrenaline level. Between rowing, courses, tutoring, babysitting, Greek week, Easter, and Marissa's graduation, I was constantly busy.

I lined up all my tutoring clients for the summer in Champaign. Mostly, they were students who I'd taught before. I'd gotten some referrals and added a couple of new ones. Most weeks my schedule included at least forty hours of work. Not that I would complain. Lila and I signed a lease to share an apartment in the fall. It was more expensive than the dorm, and Dad wouldn't chip in the extra money. That part seemed fair, and the tutoring paid well.

Things were good between Doug and me, really good. We did almost everything together. I wasn't sure how I was going to operate without him. He was such a fixture in my life. I'd tried not to think about it most days, but today I had no choice. The day, the event, I'd been dreading for over six months now, was here. Doug would be leaving tomorrow, off to San Francisco for an eight-week course in international banking for his new job. If he was at the top of his class, he'd get a position in Asia. If not, he would be headed to San Francisco or New York. Doug wasn't ever second best, and I knew he'd be off to Japan in two months.

"Twenty minutes," Elise called from below.

I needed to move. In twenty minutes, Jeremy and Stephen, Elise's family, as well as mine, would descend on our room. After loading my things in our car, my family and I were meeting Doug and his family at the fraternity house. This morning he had a breakfast with his fraternity brothers. The graduation ceremonies started at eleven, and Doug's parents were throwing a graduation party for him that evening at his mom's. Tomorrow I'd drop Doug off at the airport and then drive his car to Champaign.

Everyone had insisted Mark ride with me to Champaign. I suspected they didn't believe I'd be able to operate a car after saying goodbye to him.

"Manda, are you awake?" Elise called again.

"Got it," I responded, heaving myself down from my loft. I showered, did my makeup, fixed my hair, and hurried into shorts and a T-shirt. I'd change into something fancier at the fraternity house. By the time I came out of the bathroom, Jeremy and Stephen were already shuttling boxes down to Elise's and her parents' cars.

"Hey, Avery of the Tavery, you ready for this?" Jeremy called, reaching for my head. I ducked to avoid him. Jeremy, who'd become our local paparazzi, had come up with this 'Tavery' couple name for us last quarter. It only mildly annoyed me, but my psyche was not up for humor of any type today. I stuck my tongue out at him.

I had to get out of this funk. I was happy for Doug. He was graduating summa cum laude and had landed the position he wanted. He'd worked so hard, and I wanted to be able to celebrate with him no matter how bittersweet it felt to me.

Stephen moved his dolly to an upright position, wound around it, and put an arm around my shoulder. "Just ignore him. I usually do."

"That was my plan." I rolled my eyes and loaded a box onto the top of his stack.

I'd miss Elise, too. It seemed incredible how close two people could get in just nine short months. I felt like I'd known her for my whole life and loved her like a sister. After the ceremony, I planned to stop by her sorority house for one last hug goodbye. She'd accepted a position in the DC area, but she was a wildcat through and through. She promised she'd be back for homecoming in the fall if not before.

My parents arrived, and it didn't take our crew long to load their car. We piled in and made our way to the fraternity house.

I was glad I was able to see Doug before he left for the events. He and Zack were all pumped up, and it was hard not to be excited for them.

All the families gathered at the fraternity house, waiting until it was time to go to the ceremonies. After greeting members of Zack's family as well as Paula and Gary, Doug's dad and brothers, and stepsisters, I made my way upstairs to freshen up and change. Sliding my dress over my shoulders in Doug's room, I tried to ignore the flashbacks reeling through my head. Images of first night I met Doug, throwing the Frisbee on the lawn, looking at his trip photos, and the night of the Halloween party, all circled through my thoughts. Other memories like the nights we spent in my room after the accident, our racquetball game, our date at the boathouse, our night in the suite after formal, and the nights we'd spent together at his mom's, played through my mind. All of it was seared into my brain. Ignoring the tightening of my chest, I gathered my things and headed downstairs.

All the families walked the short distance to the ceremony together. The procession to the stadium reminded me of when I'd been Doug's date for the Homecoming game. Before I knew it, we were filing into the stands. Climbing the stairs, Paula sought me out and asked me to sit with her. Lila sat on the other side of me, linking her arm in mine. I should've been happier, but he was leaving tomorrow, and I couldn't disconnect the events in my mind. Excited to share this event with him, I told myself I couldn't cry today. Tomorrow, after he left, I could cry.

I got through the university ceremony and the diploma ceremony that afternoon at the business school without any tears escaping down my cheeks. I watched Doug during the ceremonies and then after, mingling with professors, friends, and his family.

His grin didn't leave his face the whole day, and I was happy for him. We posed for pictures together, but I kept my distance, letting him have time with everyone else. It wasn't where I wanted to be. I wanted to be by his side to soak in every last second I had with him, but that felt selfish.

As soon as we were outside the business school building, he gathered me in his arms, squeezing my shoulders until they almost hurt. "Please do not leave my side until you drop me at the airport tomorrow." He planted a wet kiss on my temple.

"That I can do." I linked my hand with his as we walked to the fraternity house. In his room we retrieved the last of his things and then packed them in his car.

"Let's unload everything later," he said as he parked in his mom's parking garage.

We rode the elevator up with Zack and his family. On his floor, the sweet smell of ham and earthy aroma of beans radiated from his mom's condo. I took in a deep breath, realizing this smelled like home.

A mass of people waited inside, and we moved through the crowd talking with his dad, brothers, and stepsisters. Eventually I had to excuse myself to use the ladies room. When I returned, I searched the front rooms for Doug but couldn't find him. I tracked back to the kitchen and found his mom giving the final orders to the caterers.

"Can you find Doug and tell him it's time to sit down for dinner?" she asked as I approached.

"Course." After searching through the front rooms and not finding him, I walked to the back wing of the house. My heels clinked on the wood floor and the sound echoed off the walls. I rested one hand on the wall and removed my shoes. Hooking the sandal straps on my fingers, I proceeded down the hall towards the bedrooms. As I neared the guest room typically assigned to me, I heard my dad's voice.

"You have to think about what's best for Amanda. What kind of college experience will she have tethered to an absent boyfriend? She won't be happy. Her grades will suffer."

I couldn't believe my ears. Dad was trying to get Doug to break up with me? How cruel was this? Of course all that really mattered to him was that my grades would suffer.

"Sir, with all due respect, I know you have Amanda's best interest in mind—"

"Just think about it some more. It's the right thing to do."

This was my cue. Being as quiet as possible, I slid on my shoes and then walked halfway down the hall and back, the sound of my footsteps echoing from every direction.

"There you are." I forced a smile as they stepped into the hallway. I couldn't look at my dad. How could he even think that Doug ending things with me would be helpful? "Your mom says it's time for dinner." I increased the pitch of my voice in an effort to make the words sound light.

"Of course, I was just congratulating Doug." Dad shook Doug's hand.

Doug's lips formed a thin smile. "Thank you." Doug nodded to my father and stepped toward me, encircling me with his arm. We walked several paces ahead of Dad who followed us into the kitchen.

Paula pointed in our direction. "Round up everyone for dinner."

I walked with Doug through the house, informing everyone that dinner was ready. Back in the dining room, we stood in front of our assigned seats, waiting for everyone to gather.

Paula joined us. She touched my back, and I flinched. "Are you okay sweetie? You look pale, even for you." She squeezed my shoulders with her hands. "You're trembling, darling."

I looked up, and suddenly everyone's eyes were on me.

"I caught a draft from the air conditioning." I pointed at the vent near the ceiling.

Doug put his arm around me and whispered, "You really don't look good. Are you okay?"

"I must have locked my knees." I lifted my chin as I spoke, trying to project my voice. I didn't want any more attention directed at me.

Doug leaned across me and whispered to his mom. "Give us a minute." He placed his hand on my far arm, and I turned into him. He led me to his room.

Stepping inside, he hugged me to him, warming my chilled arms. "Tell me what's wrong. You're still shaking." He titled my chin up and made me look him in the eye.

I shook my head. "It can wait."

"What can wait?"

"It's not a big deal."

"If it's not a big deal, then you can tell me now. It'll take two seconds, and we can get back to the party. If you need to tell me later, then you're making me think it's a big deal."

My leg bounced uncontrollably, and I wriggled away from his embrace. "I overheard your conversation with my dad. I'm so angry I can't even see straight."

He rubbed his hands up and down my biceps. "Your dad is being a dad."

My hands went up. "How—"

He caught them and folded them together between his. "A slightly overbearing and freakishly over-involved dad." I laughed through my tears.

"You know there's no way I would even entertain considering what he proposed, right? If I thought you were just another girl-friend, I might listen to him. But you're not. I know how I feel about you is different, but he can't see that. That wasn't the first time your dad has given me that speech."

I stepped back. "He asked you to break up with me before?" Could this get any more embarrassing?

"At the rowing meet."

I walked away and then back to him. "I would break up with me if I had a dad like that."

He wrapped his arms around me. "Manda, he's right. It doesn't make sense for us to stay together if this is going to end. But I love you, and that's not going to change." He stroked my hair.

"I am really angry with him."

"I know," he cupped my hands to his chest. "It's not much longer. You just have to go out there, smile, and pretend. Just imagine him in his underwear."

"Ewww!"

"Yeah, bad imagery." He shuddered.

"Did I mention that you look beautiful today?" he asked.

"No, but thank you." I kissed him.

"Mmm," he put a finger on my lips. "Save that for tonight."

A knock on the door startled us. "Maybe you should get a room." His brother Michael stood in the doorway.

"In case you haven't noticed, we're in my room." Doug looked around me.

"Mom told me to come find you. Everyone's waiting."

Doug sighed. "Guess that's our cue." Michael hadn't been wrong. Everyone was standing around the long table they'd set to seat everyone. It stretched from the front sitting room, through the dining room, and into the living room.

"You look better," Paula squeezed my arm. We took our seats and his Dad said grace and started the toasts. After the speeches, the traditional Puerto Rican dishes were passed around the table. The champagne helped me relax, and the dinner and energy in the room reinvigorated me. By the end of the meal, I had my emotions back in check.

They served more drinks in the sitting room around the pool table after the meal. I pretended my parents weren't even there until they approached me to say they were leaving. I fully intended to say goodbye to them right there, but Doug suggested I walk with them down to the parking garage.

Mom complimented their house, the food, and the party as we rode the elevator down. As we crossed the parking lot and reached their car, I hugged my mom and Marissa and said goodbye. My dad approached me for a hug, and I hesitated.

"See you tomorrow," I said, keeping the gap between us. I glanced at Mom and Marissa and then back to my dad. My dad nodded at them, and they climbed into the car.

He walked a couple of feet away to an empty space, turned, and put his hands to his hips. "You have something to say to me?"

I thought of Doug's underwear comment and stifled a laugh. "Yes, I do." I squared my shoulders and looked him right in the eyes. "Doug is important to me. How could you ask him to break up with me?"

"It's for the best, munchkin."

The fact that he used such a baby name for me made it even worse. "You know nothing about what Doug and I feel for each other. Can't you open your mind even for a second? What about you and Mom? What about Tia and Ed? You guys all met freshman year, and you're still together. I love Doug, and he loves me. Why is that so hard to accept?"

"You can't compare things like that. Things were different."

"Wow, Tia and Ed were what? Six whole years ago? Times sure have changed since then!" The thought passed my brain that I was being really disrespectful, but I didn't care. He wasn't showing me any respect either.

"You know this is different. You are not your mom, and you are not Tia. This is the first time you've been in love. You have to see the big picture. This isn't the only person that's going to love you, or who you are going to love. I could probably name two or three of them right now. You're eighteen for God's sake, and you're only going to see him like every four months, if that?

Be realistic, it's not going to work. There's no use prolonging the inevitable."

His words cut through me like a knife. I couldn't remember ever being so angry and hurt. I looked at the ground, trying to compose myself. I was on the verge of tears, and I bit my lip to have something else to focus on. When I looked back up, Mom was standing beside him. I'd been so focused on him I didn't see her approach. She reached out as if to console me. I backed away from her.

Dad put his hand out. "I was just trying to protect you, Amanda. That's what dads do."

We were at an impasse. There wasn't anything I could say to make him think differently, and there wasn't anything he could say that would make me believe differently.

"I'll see you tomorrow at home." I took a step back, thinking I couldn't imagine a place I would want to be less.

Mom stepped towards me, but I backed away again. She stopped. "Drive safely."

"Mark will be with me." I turned and walked to the elevator. On the ride up, I concentrated on breathing and letting go of my anger. I wasn't going to spend my last night with Doug thinking about my parents. I'd thought they, of all people, would understand. Tia had met Ed her freshman year, and they'd been together ever since. Mom had been barely twenty-one when she married my dad and moved to the base with him. He was always deployed, except for brief furloughs every couple of months. She'd talked about missing him and how hard it was to be alone. I guessed her career probably suffered. Maybe she'd never achieved the goals she thought she would. She never indicated regretting that choice though.

I wasn't sacrificing anything. No, thanks to the responsible people we both were, I would be in Champaign all summer, earning money for my apartment while Doug was in San Francisco training for his banking position.

When I got back up to the condo, Zack and his family were saying goodbye. Zack grabbed me and spun me around. "I'll see you tomorrow at the house, and we'll drink."

"Zack, I have to drive home tomorrow."

"Seriously?"

"Yes." I shook my head at him.

I said good-bye to his family, and they insisted I come visit. It seemed like an odd invitation, but when I contemplated a summer and school year without Doug, it seemed like a good option.

The rest of his family left just after nine. Doug and I offered to help his mom organize for brunch the next morning, but she wouldn't let us. Quite honestly, I didn't know what we were supposed to do. It'd been such a busy day I didn't feel like doing anything but sleep.

Doug and I walked to his room. "Today was a good day." He rubbed my shoulders. "I'm beat. I think I'll take a shower."

The shower sounded like a nice idea. I hadn't planned on taking long, but I stayed in till I was too hot, letting the warm water and steam calm my nerves. Drying off, I dressed in a tank and jeans and went to find Doug. I found him watching baseball with his family and snuggled up beside him on the couch.

His mom had to be up early to prepare for the brunch, and she and Gary excused themselves for bed. Doug and I played a couple of rounds of pool with Michael, and then we all decided to turn in. When Michael left the room, Doug gathered me in his arms. "I have something for you."

"You haven't opened my gift yet," I told him as we walked down the hall to his room. I had my gifts stashed in my backpack there, and I unzipped the bag and pulled out the two boxes I'd pondered over for a month. When I turned around, he had a box in his hand too.

"Ladies first."

"No, it's your graduation. You first."

He sat on the bed, and I handed him the first box, an engraved pen and pencil set of the brand I knew he liked. The second gift was more sentimental. I bit my lip as he opened the box. I'd wanted to find something that represented our bond. I'd finally decided on a brushed silver bracelet with simple interlocking links.

"You didn't have to get me anything like this." He kissed me, and then fastened the chain on his wrist.

I took the box from him and found the disk drive that I'd saved a slideshow with pictures from the year set to our favorite songs on. He got out his computer, and we lay on the bed looking at them.

"It's kind of ironic," he said, handing me a box after we looked at the pictures.

"Ironic?" I took the package. Inside there was a cardboard box that held a velvet jewelry box. I lifted the lid slowly and realized what he meant. Inside was a silver bracelet formed from interlocking circles. Attached were Chinese symbol charms, the same body, mind, and soul symbols tattooed on his back. Next to it sat a disk drive.

He helped my clasp the bracelet around my wrist and then plugged the drive into my laptop. The pictures he had assembled were amazing. There were images from all the fraternity events, Northwestern football games, intramural games, Homecoming, the formal and rowing meets and socials.

"Where did you get all of these?"

"I do have access to all the fraternity, rowing, and campus pictures." He bragged.

We scrolled through the pictures taken fall and winter quarters, and I couldn't look at any more. I closed the screen on the computer and rolled away from him.

"Too much?" he asked.

"It's beautiful. I love it!" I nestled my head into his shoulder, hiding the tears that were starting to form.

He kissed the top of my head. "I love you! Thanks for making this day great!"

All I could think about was being as close to him as possible and taking in all of him: how he smelled, the smooth skin of his chest, the rough stubble on his cheeks, and his strong callused hands.

I had no idea what time it was when I finally drifted off to sleep, wrapped in his arms. I'd always remember today.

𝄢 𝄢 𝄢

A soft chime was the first thing I heard, then music, and finally a loud beeping noise. Doug, always faster than me, jumped up and ran around the room, shutting them all off.

"You crazy girl." He dove onto the bed. "How many did you set?"

"I didn't want you to let me sleep in." I knew he would, he always did, but I didn't want to miss one second with him.

He rolled his eyes. "Fine, but I get the shower first."

"I'll get the coffee, then."

I slipped on a jacket and made my way to the kitchen. His mom was already chopping fruit. "What was all the ruckus in the bedroom?"

"I set alarms so Doug wouldn't let me sleep."

"Sometimes you have to trick them." She patted the bar stool beside her. "Sit, sit."

"I'm just getting coffee." I stood on my toes to reach the mugs and then went to the coffee pot to fill them.

By the time I got back to his room, he was already shaving. I set the cups down and scooted onto the counter beside him. He had shaved off all the stubble from his cheeks, and I ran my finger across his now smooth face. After a few sips of coffee, I brushed my teeth.

When he was finished shaving, he stood in front of me. "He traced a hand down side to my thigh. "I'm going to miss this." He leaned in and pressed his lips to mine.

It was a long hard kiss that I never wanted to end. When it did, I planted kisses down his neck to his chest.

He pushed back from the counter. "I love you, but we have a brunch to attend and you probably want to do something with your hair."

I spun around to look in the mirror and saw curls spewing from my scalp in every direction. "Wow, yes, okay." I jumped off the counter. "I can't believe I went to the kitchen like this. I'll be quick." I kissed him and placed my hand on his shoulder, backing him out of the bathroom.

"Don't go far." I pointed a finger at him.

"Are you going to stalk me till I leave?"

"Yes."

He put his hands on my waist. "I'll pack while you're showering. After my dad and brothers leave, I'll say good-bye to you, and then my mom. Then, we'll go."

"Okay, now I'm showering." I backed into bathroom. Slipping into the shower, I silently prayed I could get through saying good-bye to him without breaking down. He already felt bad about our separation. I didn't want him to feel worse. Besides, it would only be three weeks till I saw him again. We'd already decided to say good-bye here. I was driving him to the airport, but I would just drop him off at the curb.

I showered as fast as I could and ran some detangling solution through my hair. Doug, Michael, Paula, and Gary were sitting at the bar sipping coffee when I entered the kitchen. Refilling my cup, I went to stand behind Doug.

Brunch with his family was nice, but time seemed to be speeding up. His Dad and two brothers left just after noon, needing to catch flights back to New York and DC. Michael left soon after, and I realized the moment had come.

Doug took my hand and steered me to his room. I reclined against the desk, eyes to the floor. He straddled my legs, kissing the top of my head. Swinging our hands between us, his lips found mine. His finger raked up my neck to my chin, titling it up so I had to look at him. "I love you. I will miss you so much." He kissed me on the top of the head, then again on my forehead, and finally on the lips. I slid my arms under his, around his waist, and then nestled into his chest.

When he released me, I wrapped my fingers around the back of his neck and waited for his gaze to find mine. I repeated his words back to him. "I love you so much. I'm going to miss you." Tears were just behind my words. But his answering kiss begged for a complete response and distracted me from my sadness.

We packed our last few things, and took them down to the car. Back in the condo, I waited in the foyer while he said goodbye to his mom. When they met me at the front door, she was crying. I didn't want to look at her for fear I would cry too.

She hugged me hard. "Come see me soon, and we'll go shopping."

"Of course." I returned her hug.

Gary and Doug shook hands, and we walked into the hall, his mom trailing behind to get in her last good-bye. I bit my lip to keep from tearing up as we stepped into the elevator with her blowing kisses through the closing door. I blinked hard several times and focused on the ceiling. We reclined against the railing. His arm hooked around my waist, and he held me. He nestled his face into my neck and kissed my exposed shoulder. The elevator stopped and he planted a kiss right between my shoulder blades. The wet spot from his kiss mixed with the cool air of the lot as the doors opened and I shivered.

"Three weeks won't be so long." He laced his fingers in mine as we walked.

At the car, he held the driver's door open for me, he let it go and his arms wound round me. I pressed my ear to his chest and listened to his breaths go in and out, his heart beating, let his scent, the feel of his shirt, and the warmth of his body penetrate my senses.

"Okay," he squeezed me to him before releasing me.

In the car, I focused on repositioning the seat and the mirrors, buckling my belt, and finding the keys, anything to abate the tears pooling in my eyelids. On the drive, he gave me directions for the car and showed me where all the paperwork was. I reviewed my to-do list for the rest of the weekend. I'd never been so ill prepared for tutoring jobs. I hadn't even started to outline the lessons.

At the airport, we got out and unloaded his bags from the trunk. His clutched me to him. "I hate leaving you."

"I love you."

His arms tightened around me like vices, and he picked me up and swirled me around. "I love you so much." His released me and turned around for his suitcase. When he turned back, he dropped the handle and pressed his lips to mine.

We kissed until an officer approached. "Hey guys. Is this yours?" He hit the trunk. "You've got to move this car."

He released me, trailing his fingers down my arm and taking my hand. "Work things out with your dad, okay?"

"Okay." I kissed him.

He nodded his head, retrieved the bag, and strode to the terminal doors. I stood and watched him go, unable to move. At the entrance, he turned to look back, waved and then disappeared into the building.

"Miss!" an officer shouted. "This car has to move."

Forced into action, I slammed the trunk closed and jumped into the driver's seat. Tears streamed down my face as I started the engine. I wiped them away and focused. *Drive, Amanda*, I thought. Taking a deep breath, I checked my mirrors and inched into traffic.

Doug called as he waited in the security line. I pulled off the road into a parking lot to talk with him until he had to turn off his phone for takeoff. Restarting the car, I drove on auto-pilot to campus. Passing all the places we'd gone together, we'd hung out, realizing it would never be that way again, put me over the edge. I couldn't stop at the house. Somehow, I reached Zack's apartment complex. The security guard recognized me and opened the gate. By the time I found a space near Zack's unit, I could barely see where I was going from the tears pouring out of my eyes.

Then, the hole that had been waiting to swallow me for the past few weeks opened up and I fell in. I could hardly catch my breath for the sobs emerging from my body. I clutched my chest and willed the pain to stop, but it didn't. Things would never be the same. Who knew when we would live in the same city again?

Even when my breathing finally caught up, the tears still flowed. I surfaced from my grief every once in a while, but never for long enough to think about where I was supposed to be. All I could do was breathe. Eventually, a sound broke through my delirium. A thumping vibrated the car. At first I thought it must be rain or the wind, but then I realized it was coming from the window beside me. I lifted my head enough to see Zack.

"You have to open the door." I deciphered his words through the glass. "It's locked." He knocked on the window again.

"Amanda, you're scaring me. You're going to overheat, unlock the door."

I obeyed. He opened it and ran his arms under me. He lifted me out of the car and carried me to his apartment. After he set me on the couch and I drank the water he placed in my hand, rational thoughts began to return. My head cleared as I sipped on the soda he set in front of me and listened to him talk into his phone.

"I found her. She's okay. Why don't you meet her here? I don't think she can go to the house."

After he ended the call, his eyes focused on mine. "God girl, you scared us to death. It's been three hours since you dropped him off. Where were you?"

I covered my face with my hands. "I'm so sorry. You won't tell Doug, right? I promise it won't happen again." I got up, still trembling, and wiped my cheeks with my arm. "I have to pull it together."

He placed a hand on my shoulder. "Sit down and breathe. You're allowed some mental time."

I couldn't sit still. I stood and paced his living room. I was fine. I would be okay. That had to be the worst of it. I had to get home to Champaign and look together.

Grabbing my bag, I went to the bathroom. I looked in the mirror and splashed water on my face. I patted dry with a towel and dabbed some concealer under my eyes.

"Sorry, and thanks again" I said to Zack when I met him back in the living room.

When Mark, Lila, and Ross got there, I got plenty of sympathy from Lila. I wished I were staying here, with her, instead of going back home.

On the ride to Champaign, I was numb, too tired to feel anything more. Mark insisted on driving, and I could see his eyes cut towards me every once in a while. "So, we're home for the whole summer. Nothing to do but relax and enjoy, right?" He slapped me on the knee.

I dead stared at him. Was he kidding?

"I mean except for the whole Doug...." He cleared his throat.

"It would be good, except my parents hate everything I do."

"That's how parents are."

"I doubt yours are like mine." I'd only made a few references to my issues with my parents and figured it was as good time to talk further with him about it. He listened to my rantings about how insane my parents were for half an hour.

When I finished, he shrugged. "Doesn't he give Marissa a hard time like that?"

"Yes, but she's seventeen. I'm nearly nineteen."

"Your grades were good this quarter, right?

"My grades have always been good: 3.6 fall and 3.8 winter."

"I think it's just the Doug thing."

I slapped the dashboard with both hands. "But it's not fair. They are harassing me. Do you think they're right?"

"Hey, that's what parents are for, right? He's a lot older than you. Dads freak about stuff like that, I hear."

"I guess." I folded my arms over my chest, tucking my hands inside them. He just didn't get it. He didn't get that their constant criticism was penetrating my whole being, threatening to smother me from the inside. Most of the time I could convince myself it didn't matter, that I was okay, except when I talked to them or was with them. How would I keep that at bay when I saw them every day?

We turned on some music, and I texted with Lila and Marissa, trying to clear my head. It wouldn't do to start off the summer with such a negative outlook. After catching up with Mark some more and texting with Doug a bit, I fell asleep and didn't wake until we stopped in my driveway. At the sight of the house, anger bubbled up inside me. Dad came out to meet us. His image repulsed me. I surveyed the yard and our home. There was no comfort here. I took several deep breaths, but as soon as I looked back at him, the feeling resurfaced.

"How was the drive?"

When I didn't respond, Mark answered. "Good."

I stretched my arms over my head and took in a deep breath. "Good, fine."

"So, you and your sister have your own cars now. This looks like it's in pretty good shape."

I slid my hand along the roof, wounding round to the trunk to help Mark unload the bags and boxes. I didn't respond. I felt bad about my behavior. I knew it wasn't right, but I just couldn't help it. One day. I'd given myself one day to be a basket case, and then it would be over.

Mom had dinner waiting, but I told them I'd already eaten and was exhausted. Marissa was out, so I showered and then retreated to my room to unpack and text with Doug.

🖒 🖒 🖒

When I woke the next morning, light was pouring into my window. I'd forgotten to close the shades, and it was just after six. This was not how early I wanted to wake up. I went down to the kitchen and started the coffee maker. Everything was exactly as it had always been, but it was wrong somehow. Then, I figured it out. I was completely different, but everything else was still the same.

Dad came in as I was taking my first sip of coffee. After pouring himself a cup, he asked if I wanted to go for a run. My immediate reaction was a resounding no, but I remembered what Doug had said. I'd try to find a way to feel at peace with him or at least act like I was.

On the run, he asked about my grades and course selection for the fall. He was happy with my expected GPA and approved my course selection. I was happy to be done with calculus, but I had the organic chemistry and physics series to take sophomore year. I was rounding them out with the last Chinese literature class and Middle Eastern history.

I finally made an A in chemistry, but still found it boring. Actually, my interest in the diplomacy protocol and the national security field was waning too. I loved helping the students in the local schools and had started to think that some form of education related field was more my calling, perhaps speech or language. The pay wasn't very good in education, but I didn't need to be rich. I wouldn't have student loans, so it might be possible to live on a teacher's salary. Maybe I'd become a foreign language professor.

"So, home for the summer." Dad brought me out of my thoughts as we neared our house. "It'll be good for you. Maybe give you a chance to reset."

I had actually been enjoying our run, thinking that the summer might not be so bad. "What do I need to reset, Dad?"

"I just meant that you might get some perspective on what's good for you, and how you might want your life to look."

"Dad, my life is good. I like my life." *Except for you being in it,* I thought and then scolded myself. I loved Dad. I just didn't like him right now.

Mom had breakfast ready, and she and Marissa were already at the table eating. I ran upstairs to shower. When I came down, they were ready for Mass, so I grabbed a muffin and picked at it as we drove.

Mom looked back at me from the front seat. "You really need to eat a better breakfast."

"I wanted to shower. I'll get something else later."

"We'd like you to have meals with us."

"Oh, okay. I'm used to my own schedule." I shrugged and looked at Marissa. She waved a scolding finger at me, and I stifled a laugh.

"We'll get back in the groove."

Not with you picking at me every other second, I thought.

In the afternoon, Marissa caught me up on her latest friend, boyfriend, and lifeguard drama while I unpacked and sorted my tutoring supplies. After Dad left and we had dinner with Mom, I finally had to face planning my tutoring sessions the next day. When Doug called that night, I realized not one of them had mentioned him. I'd been texting Doug while Marissa and I hung out, but she never asked how I was or how I felt. That seemed strange, and I wondered if Lila or Mark had told them about my meltdown.

I woke to my alarm Monday, started the coffee pot, went for a run, showered quickly, and was walking out the door when Mom came in dressed for work.

"Aren't you eating?"

"I have to be at my first session in ten minutes." I shook my muffin in the air. "Thanks!"

"What about eating with us?"

"Oh—" I stopped mid-bite. "I forgot."

"Okay, well maybe tomorrow. Have a good day." She hugged me.

On the way to my first appointment, Doug called. It was music to my ears to hear his voice. Lila called me twice that day, even though she was vacationing with her mom in the Caribbean. Talking to her, I had a small epiphany. I couldn't believe I hadn't thought of it before. She'd started school last summer quarter and was enrolled again this summer to be able to graduate with Ross. If I took summer courses, I could graduate early, too.

I berated myself for not having thought of that earlier but decided to begin my research in earnest. It turned out I could still register for summer courses. There were even four that would satisfy my course needs. The only problem was money. The scholarship money couldn't be transferred in time to pay for summer classes. I would have to ask my parents for a loan until I could get the money into my account.

Doug thought it was a great idea, but I was nervous to ask my parents. Doug and I loved each other, and I knew we had something special. Making last minute decisions, assuming we would be together in three years, seemed a little crazy. From a parental view, it probably looked insane. But even if we weren't together, finishing school earlier couldn't hurt.

I waited until Thursday when my dad got home to mention it to my parents. I wasn't sure what to expect. I knew they would assume I was trying to finish school faster to be with Doug, but I convinced myself why I was doing it shouldn't matter. The point was that it was moving me closer to graduation. I waited till Dad had eaten and was relaxing in the den with Mom.

"I've decided I want to do something different this summer," I started.

"Really, like what?" my dad asked, laying his magazine on his legs. "Try out a new gun, maybe?"

I rolled my eyes and shook my head. I was the only one in the family who would go shooting with him. "No, I actually want to go to school this summer."

"Like take a course at Illinois?" my mom asked. "That would be fun for you."

"No, like at Northwestern. I checked into it, and registration doesn't close till tomorrow. There are plenty of courses still open that I need. Lila has the apartment anyway, so I could just move in early."

"What about money?" Dad asked. I knew that would be his first thought.

"I called, and they can switch my scholarship to year round." I bit my lip. "The only problem is that it takes some time to process, so I'd need to go ahead and pay for summer before it would come through."

"Do you have enough money? What about rent for the summer?"

"After my scholarship comes through, I'll have enough. I just need to borrow some till then."

Dad's voice boomed through the room. "Tuition could be expensive. We don't just have that much lying around. Why are you just bringing this up now? Couldn't you have done this a month ago, and the scholarship money would already be there?" His concerns gave me hope. If it was only the money that worried them, we could make it work.

"It didn't really occur to me till this week."

"But you already have commitments to your students," my mom pointed out.

"Yes, I would have to explain to them."

"You should follow through on those commitments," Dad pushed his glasses up his nose. "What's this really about? I'm guessing it might have something to do with Doug."

"Lila's going summers, and she'll graduate a whole year earlier." I knew it wasn't a good argument, but I was losing ground.

Mom twisted her hands around each other in her lap. "We know you miss Doug, but you can't make decisions based on him. Who knows where he'll be, or if you guys will even still be dating a year from now. You have to make decisions that are good for you. You've had a stressful year. I think you might need time to decompress and sort things out."

"Sort things out?" My voice involuntarily rose an octave. "What do you mean?" I narrowed my eyes at her.

"Well, there was fall, with your accident, and then winter with Doug's family issue." She waved her hands in the air. Her voice petered out. She tended to shy away from confrontation, letting Dad be the lead in disciplinary issues.

"Yes, but we got through that, and I'm good."

Dad stood up and adjusted his belt. "Did you get your grades?"

I wanted to scream at him. "I told you I had a 4.0 going into the finals."

"So, how did they come out?"

"Actually, they were supposed to post tonight." I crossed to the computer at the desk. I flung open the computer and punched the keys to retrieve my grades from the college system. I took slow breaths. Didn't they trust that I was being a good student? Did they think I was lying to them? We were back to the same arguments we'd been having since winter. *So much for me making peace with them.* This summer was going to be hell if I couldn't get out of here.

I brought up my grades on the screen. "See, a 4.0." I pointed at the display.

Dad sat back down. "Let your mom and I think about it for a while." I knew what that meant. The answer was going to be no.

Doug called while I was pacing in my bedroom nearly in tears. I was as mad at myself as I was at them. Why hadn't I thought of this plan sooner? The scholarship money could've been there waiting for me.

"You don't know they're going to say no," Doug said.

I didn't detail the whole conversation with him or let on how upset I was. It wasn't his problem. As expected, my parents wouldn't loan me the money for summer tuition. They outlined all the reasons they'd given before but stressed the bottom line: they just didn't have the money. I knew that if they'd agreed with the idea, the funding probably could've been worked out. Friday came and went, and I didn't register for summer quarter.

I'd never felt so ambivalent. Last year, things seemed so laid out and firm, purposeful. Now there just seemed to be emptiness stretched out as far as I could see. There was no reason for me to be here. I was in control of nothing, and I was spinning my wheels working to get nowhere.

Being home was torture. Missing Doug, Lila, Elise, and Kate, I filled my days with activity. I'd run in the morning, be out the door just before eight, get home after dinner, and spend evenings in my room talking to Doug. I didn't interact face to face with many people except my clients. Carter frequented the coffee shop where I had some appointments. The first day he hugged me before I could duck away. He was a harmless ex-boyfriend at this point, and I decided we could be friends.

Mark showed up most evenings, trying to get me to play volleyball with him. Volleyball was not a sport I wanted to be anywhere near ever again. We ended up lifting weights, playing racquetball, or swimming. Mark worked at a fitness center again for the summer. He'd finally decided to major in mechanical engineering. I wasn't sure how that figured into working at the gym, although he claimed the mechanical part was fixing the machines. I was pretty sure the purpose of the job was a free gym membership and hanging out with nice looking girls all day. Marissa wanted me to go out with her every night, but by the time she was ready to go out, I was settled in talking to Doug or listening to Japanese, my new language endeavor.

On Friday night, I opened the front door to find Stephen waiting on the front porch. Then, Mark jumped out from behind a bush. "What are you doing?" He pointed at me. "You're sweaty and gross. Come on, get dressed. We're going out." It occurred to me that my circle of friends was mostly male save Lila. What did that mean about me? I'd made friends with Elise and Kate and sort of with Vivian, but it was mostly the male friends I relied on for companionship. That train of thought would have to wait. Since when was I so into analyzing my psyche anyway?

"Stephen, what are you doing here?" I ushered them in.

"Well, you know that little town, the one in the middle of nowhere, I call home?

"Yes Streator, Illinois."

"Well, it's really boring, and I heard you guys were meeting up, so here I am."

Mark pointed at me. "Zack and Bill will be here in fifteen."

"What? Zack and Bill? They didn't text me." I looked at my phone to see if I'd missed something.

"Well, they texted me." Mark hit his chest. "Are you going to offer us something to eat or what? Stephen's been driving for a while, and I'm starving. Marissa said we had to get here before you started talking to…" He waved his hand in the air. "So here we are."

Half in a fog, I led them into the kitchen. "You can say Doug, you know. I'm not like some psycho that's going to lose it at the mention of his name." I hit him on the shoulder.

"Yeah, well, that's not what Marissa said. What are you listening to anyway?" Mark took the buds out of my ears.

"Oh, nothing. I just came back from running." It was the Japanese courses I'd bought, but I wasn't going to tell him that. Doug might not even end up in Japan.

I pointed Stephen toward the restroom and ran upstairs to shower. Mark knew how to make himself at home. Zack, Bill, Mark, and Stephen were all talking with my dad when I came back down half an hour later. He stood up for me to take his seat when approached the table. "It looks like you have a whole bodyguard squad here to take you out tonight."

"Am I the only girl?"

"Why do you think we came here?" Zack joked, hugging me. "U of I girls are supposed to be hot."

We went to the trendiest spot in town. Their energy and the crowd kept me distracted from obsessing about filling yet another weekend with activities. The drink Zack snagged for me also helped.

I got a text from Doug just after ten. MADE IT HOME WITH TAKEOUT. MISS U.

Zack grabbed my phone as soon as he saw me look at it. He typed into my phone as I was trying to grab it from him. When I got it back, I saw the message he sent: MISS U 2 SWEETIE. SMACK ZACK.

"You look immature stealing people's phones," I whispered in his ear. I read Doug's reply: ZACK MADE IT I SEE.

YES, ALONG WITH BILL AND STEPHEN.

SOUNDS LIKE FUN. WISH I WERE THERE.

NO YOU DON'T, IT'S ILLINOIS. BUT ME 2. CAN I CALL YOU LATER?

I HOPE YOU WILL.

WHAT TIME?

ONE AM CENTRAL TIME?

GOOD, I LOVE YOU! ☺

LOVE YOU TOO. He wrote back.

I closed my phone to see Carter approaching our table with a couple of other guys from our high school.

Zack raised an eyebrow at me. "The wolves are circling." I looked at him confused. "That's what Doug would say, right?" he asked.

"Wolves?"

Zack rolled his hand in the air. "Yeah, remember, like fall quarter? When you guys were just... whatever you were doing?"

"I think they were vultures."

He sidled up next to me. "That's the first time he called you kitten."

"I'm definitely not a kitten anymore."

"Oh yeah, you still are. Just because you fall in love doesn't make you all grown up." He pointed a finger at me. "A broken heart, and then you can graduate to cat-dom."

"Fall and winter quarters don't count for anything?"

Zack took a swig of his beer and set it back on the table. "No."

So much for growing up, it seemed. Somehow I think I'd become his pseudo younger sister. "I think I want to stay a kitten forever."

"Yes, you do, love, and I hope you do. Well, maybe I don't." He winked at me and ran his finger down my nose.

It didn't take long for Carter and Mark to find a group of girls to talk to. It was interesting to watch. Zack and Carter were definitely the most outgoing, trailed by Mark, Bill, and then Stephen.

Stephen chose to hang out with me more than socialize with the group Carter had amassed. After one of the band's sets, we ordered some water and sat at a high top table near the wall. "So, Mark says you're not that happy here."

I shrugged. "That's life sometimes, I guess."

"What's up?"

I didn't really want to detail my issues. "My parents are being overbearing."

"Yeah, I know how that is."

"What's up with you?"

"I got offered a job as a trainer at Northwestern for the summer, but Dad wouldn't let me take it because he needed me on the farm."

"That sucks."

"Yeah, sometimes I hate being the guy who always does the right thing."

"I'll drink to that." I lifted my water glass toward him.

When the bar closed, Mark and Stephen dropped Zack, Bill, and me off at my house. I was pretty sure I still had my old curfew but hoped having company negated my midnight deadline. Otherwise, I was going to have yet another thing on my list of infractions.

Bill and Zack were taking the guest room at my place, and Stephen stayed at Mark's. I called Doug as soon as I got everyone settled. We didn't talk long because we were both exhausted.

When I woke up the next morning, Zack was on my floor. I stepped over him and made my way down to the kitchen. It was after nine, and Dad was at the table reading his paper. I grabbed a cup of coffee and intended to go back up to my room.

Before I could reach the stairs, Dad snapped his paper onto the table. "You could've chosen one of those guys to date, you know."

I wasn't in the mood to fight with him. "I know, Dad," I said as I took the first stair. At least I wasn't in trouble for staying out late.

Zack, Bill, and Stephen decided we needed to play golf, so we spent the day on the course. They were drinking more than playing, but it was fun. After their two rounds, we swam in the club's pool and had drinks at the poolside bar. Back at my house we showered and went out for dinner, hanging out till closing time again.

I hoped they were being paid well to babysit me since they stayed until Sunday afternoon. I only half felt bad, because everyone seemed to be having fun. I wasn't sure what I would have done otherwise, probably just what my previous two weeks had morphed into: running, studying Japanese, and waiting for Doug to call. Instead of getting easier, being away from him just got harder. The only way I was coping was to stay busy.

Chapter 11

I could repeat what I did that week, but I couldn't say I remembered it. Crossing the living room after a run on Thursday evening to grab a water bottle from the kitchen, I stopped short when I heard my name.

"Amanda just runs and listens to this Japanese course all the time." Marissa stood and swiped one of the earbuds from my ear.

"Ow! What's going on?" I narrowed my eyes at her.

"See." She held the earbud up to her ear.

"Does it matter what I listen to?" I snatched it from her.

I scanned their faces, thinking this was part of a conversation I wasn't privy to. Where was this coming from? What had I done to her? "Sorry?" I looked to Marissa, and then Dad and Mom. "Is there something I'm missing?"

Mom stood. "We're concerned about you, sweetie. You exercise all the time, and I never see you eat."

I just stood there. I was toxic, and I knew it. But maybe Marissa was onto something. What was I doing here? In two months there would be no chance I could be with him, but I could until then.

She stood up. "What's the point?"

"To what?"

"Are you just going to do this all summer? I don't get why you're here," she said.

I didn't have an answer to her last question, because I didn't want to be there. Next week we'd be going to San Francisco to visit Doug. Other than the trip, all I really thought about was moving to Evanston in August. Northwestern in the fall without Doug might be hell, but at least I'd be working towards a goal. Being in school would get me quarter by quarter closer to being able to be with him. I'd had plenty of time inside my head to ponder my current environment. There was only one conclusion, it was miserable.

My father stood up. "Your sister is doing exactly what she's supposed to be doing. She has a great education and career opportunity in front of her. She's being responsible and doing what she needs to reach her goals. You might want to take some notes on that."

"But I could go see him for the weekend. Or fly out a couple days before you guys."

There was a moment of silence as my parents looked at each other before turning back to me. Mom spoke for the first time since I'd sat down. "But honey, it's a long flight for two days, and we're flying out next week anyway. Surely that will be enough." She looked to Dad.

Before he could say anything, I wound my earbuds around my phone and crossed the room to the stairs. "I have to shower." I was sweaty from running, but really it was just an excuse to think.

"We'll eat when you're done," Mom called after me as I jogged up the stairs.

They just didn't understand. They kept thinking it would be hard on me when Doug went to Japan or China or wherever they would send him, but living at home was the hard part. Being in Champaign with nothing that reminded me of him, no link to him or what we had, was worse. I guess they knew I loved him, and in their own way, they were trying to help. But eliminating him from my life wasn't the answer.

Of course they had no idea, or chose to pretend they had no idea, of how close we'd been. How we were literally together all the time except for classes and dorm curfew hours. By the end of spring quarter, we were spending three nights a week together at his mom's condo. After the fraternity formal, we'd tried, or I'd tried, to be good, to only spend one night a week there. After the first two weeks, I'd abandoned that idea and just gave into my desire to be with him. Mark hated it and made sure I knew it. Lila was indifferent, since she was with Ross all the time anyway. Marissa knew, and I assumed my parents didn't want to know or turned a blind eye to it.

I finished my shower and bounced down the stairs to the table for dinner. "I think I'll go see Doug this weekend," I said to them as we passed around the food dishes.

Mom put her hand on my arm. "Honey, I know you miss him, but you've got to stay the course here. This is your life, here in Illinois. Doug isn't here and is not going to be, maybe ever again."

A pang shot through me, but I ignored it. I knew they were trying to talk me into realizing and accepting him not being in the picture, but the words had the opposite effect. No, Doug wasn't here, but he was in the country. It was stupid for me to be away from him.

"That's going to be an expensive weekend." Dad put a bite of steak in his mouth.

"Aren't you saving money for rent?" Mom asked.

"I'll have to see how much the fares are. Sometimes they have last minute deals." I was tired of this conversation and the spotlight being on me.

"You're eighteen and you have wheels, so we can't keep you from going. But I don't like it. It doesn't look good. Is he really worth all this?" Mom shook her head and then put her hand on my arm. "In a year, he'll be a distant memory, just another boyfriend."

I could feel it, I was going to blow. Was he worth it? I put my fork down calmly, took the napkin from my lap, put in on the table, pushed my chair back, and walked away.

"Sweetie, you've barely touched your food."

I waved a hand in the air at her. It wasn't worth fighting with them anymore. I took the stairs up to my room and opened my laptop. Searching all the last minute fares, I found nothing. The cheapest ticket was eight hundred dollars, and it had a connecting flight through Denver. I slammed my computer shut but opened it again to check on changing my ticket for next week. With fees, that was going to cost just as much. Eight hundred dollars was just over a month's rent, forty hours of work—fifty if you figured in how much came out for taxes. If I wanted to stay in Evanston next summer, that money was important. Dang, I hated being so responsible and conservative.

There was a knock on the door, and Marissa stuck her head in. "Are you going?"

"No. It's too expensive. Even to move the flight is nearly a month's rent." I shut my laptop.

She sat down on the bed next to me. "That sucks."

"Yeah." Tears pooled in my eyes. She placed her arm around my back.

I slid out from her embrace. "What was that about anyway, before, with the running and eating?"

She tucked her hair behind her ears. "I don't know. I'm sorry. Dad was bugging me about applying for a receptionist position at mom's office, and I got them off topic by talking about you."

"You already have the lifeguard position."

"Didn't you know? That's just hanging out at the pool all day. I could be finding out if I'd like a career in the medical field."

"Well, thanks so much. At least it's not just me they pester. I don't get it, they never did this to Tia."

Marissa lay back on the bed. "Mom says Dad did, but we were just too young to remember."

I lay down beside her. "Maybe, but now she's turned into him. She's just as bad."

She threw a pillow up. I caught it and threw it back. "Yeah, ever since she finished law school. Must be the debt, or the job, or both. Mom says they're trying to get pregnant. Tia had to start taking hormones in February. I think the medicine kind of messes with her emotions."

"Well, she could have said something." I definitely knew about pregnancy hormones.

"I guess," Marissa shrugged. "We should make a pact to be poor and happy."

"I'm all for that."

She flipped over onto her stomach. "But I am worried about you. Mom was telling Dad how she never saw you eat, and I was thinking I didn't either. You do look thin. Although I have to say your arms are way ripped. You have to help me with mine."

"You know how much grief they give me. You just added fuel to their fire."

Her eyes shot from me to her hands and her shoulders slumped. "Sorry." She bounded off the bed. "Hey, we should go shopping and get new clothes for your trip next week."

"Yeah, that might be fun." I turned my phone over in my hands.

She gripped my shoulders. "You should buy something really slutty that annoys the hell out of Mom and Dad."

"Marissa!" I laughed.

"We're totally shopping all day Saturday."

Marissa's rebel shopping trip sounded fun. But I was depressed I couldn't go early to San Francisco, and I didn't even want to talk to Doug. I grabbed my phone, turned on some music, and slipped into bed.

⟨ ⟨ ⟨

The next morning I woke early, prepped for my tutoring session in my room, and went downstairs with just enough time to have some coffee and a bagel. Mom and Dad were at the table as usual.

"You didn't come down to finish your dinner last night," Mom said as I sat down.

"I wasn't hungry."

Dad lowered his paper. "Are you going to California this weekend?"

"No, it's too expensive."

"I knew you'd do the smart thing." He put his glasses on the table.

This infuriated me, but my bagel wasn't finished toasting and I was starving.

When I sat down at the table with my bagel and cream cheese, he put down his paper. "We have some conditions."

I stopped mid-bite. "What?"

"If you want us to pay for the California trip as we arranged and send you back to Northwestern for fall quarter, we have some conditions."

"Why? What are they? You can't keep me from going back to Northwestern."

"You better believe I will." He took out his wallet and held out a credit card. "You can take some classes at U of I. There's still time to sign up for the second session. But you have to see this doctor—" he handed me a business card from his wallet "—once a week till you leave, and your weight has to hold steady."

I looked at the card and threw up my hands. "Who's this? What are you going to do, weigh me?"

"Yes."

I blinked hard as tears threatened to form. Snatching a paper towel, I wrapped the bagel and threw it in my bag.

"Fine." I walked out the door.

I could barely see for the tears filling my eyes. They thought I needed to see a shrink? They could keep me from returning to school? I had just left crazy town.

I made it across town to the library with enough time to eat my bagel in the car. The worst part was I knew their concerns had merit. I'd been filling my days with exercise to avoid being at home. I was probably only getting the equivalent of two meals a day. I was depressed. But who wouldn't be in my situation?

I wasn't sure about the threat about Northwestern. I guessed the most power he had was financial. I had money for my apartment, but if I had to pay for books, gas, and food, even with tutoring, it would be nearly impossible unless I worked like twenty hours a week. That would leave me with no time for anything else. That would majorly suck.

During a break, I contacted the psychiatrist, Dr. Medders, and made an appointment for the next week. When I got home, I went upstairs and brought the digital scale down to the kitchen.

Standing in front of my parents, I got on. The display read nine-ty pounds, two down from when I left Northwestern.

"Ninety." My dad pointed at me. I held up my appointment confirmation on my phone. "Okay." He clapped his hands to-gether. "Did you find some courses to take?"

"Yes." This was one thing I was happy about. "Physics and organic chemistry." I had thought about taking something I re-ally liked. But a few people had told me that courses at U of I were easier, so I decided to try and get some of my dreaded core courses out of the way. I figured misery loved company.

"Great, so we're all set."

I guessed maybe I'd been missing some calories with the schedule I'd been keeping. I'd have to pack myself a lunch so I could eat between tutoring sessions. The appointment with the psychiatrist wasn't until the following Tuesday, so I tried to ignore my anxiety about the meeting.

I was still mad at Marissa for the chain of events she seemed to have set in motion. But I couldn't fully blame her. Our parents were just that type, overbearing and over-involved. Marissa tried to buy my forgiveness, promising to pay for the super slutty outfit she was determined to find me. We spent all day shopping at the outlet stores. Normally I avoided shopping, but her quest for the outfit that would annoy Dad most made it fun. We both came home with three outfits and two bathing suits.

I spent Sunday with Marissa at the pool, wearing the bath-ing suit I'd bought the previous day. She flaunted her suit and flirted with her lifeguard friends while I studied my Japanese. By the end of the summer, I thought I might even be caught up to Doug.

The session with the psychiatrist was humiliating. I had no clue what I was supposed to say to him. Fortunately, unlike Sara who I'd seen after my injury the past fall, he asked tons of questions. Was I happy? Was I sad? Was I depressed? How did I feel about myself? Did I have friends? Did I see my friends? Did I have a boyfriend? How were my relationships with family, friends, and my boyfriend? Was I eating well? I answered all the questions truthfully. I didn't have anything to hide. Yes, I was sad or depressed. I wasn't sure where you the line was between them. Did I think it was a permanent state? No. As soon as I got away from my parents, I expected to feel normal again.

🕊 🕊 🕊

Tia and Ed came in to spend the weekend with Marissa while Mom, Dad, and I were in San Francisco. Marissa had begged Dad to let her have a friend sleep over or stay with someone else, but he wouldn't even entertain the idea.

I was so excited the night before we left it took forever for me to fall asleep, even after staying up past one video chatting with Doug. But it didn't matter. I could sleep on the plane.

"Happy now?" Dad asked as we got on the plane.

"Yes." I smiled at him for the first time probably since I'd moved home.

"Of course." He rolled his eyes.

As soon as we got in our room at the hotel in San Francisco, I changed, excited to meet Doug at his office.

"Whoa Nelly, where are you headed?" Dad asked as I came out of the bathroom. I wore a tight fitting pair of black pants, and my blouse was low cut. Further, I was quite proud of how the new bra made my chest look.

"I'm going to surprise Doug. His office is two blocks down."

"Isn't he meeting us for dinner at seven? It's five o'clock. You're going to show up at his office?"

"Dad, you control almost every bit of my life. You are not controlling my relationship with Doug. We'll meet you back here at seven." I grabbed my bag from the bed and walked out the door.

Dodging everyone leaving the building, I dialed Doug's number. He answered on the first ring.

"Hey, are you just landing? Sorry I didn't get a chance to check your flight."

"Nope."

"No, how are you calling then? Was there a problem with the flight?"

"Are you still in your office?"

"Yeah, the social doesn't start for fifteen minutes. Why?"

"Could you come down to the lobby?"

"You're here, already? You said your flight didn't come in till five."

"I wanted to surprise you."

"This is awesome! Now you can meet everyone." I could tell he was walking now, and I heard the elevator tone.

The anticipation of seeing him had me tapping my heel. Watching the women exiting the building, I saw that Marissa and I had guessed right on my outfit. It was a great match to the other women's attire.

My phone buzzed. "Where are you? At the security desk?"

"Yes," I said, scanning the room. Then I saw him. Within seconds he'd closed the distance between us and I was in his arms. I buried my face in his shirt and took in his smell. He picked me up and spun me around.

"You're here," he whispered into my ear as he set me down.

"Yes," I smiled, our faces barely inches apart.

He kissed me.

"I love long weekends," came a low, rough voice from behind us. We turned to see a security guard, arms crossed in front of his chest, looking down his nose at us. "Well, are you taking her home or what?" He waved his hand at the exit doors.

Doug squinted his eyes. "You okay with coming up for the barbecue? Are we still joining your parents at seven?"

"Of course, and yes." I signed in, the guard handed me a visitor's badge, and we headed upstairs.

"This is good. The guys were starting to say I made you up," he told me when we got on the elevator. We inched back to the back wall as the elevator filled with people. The elevator stopped, and we got out on the twenty-sixth of thirty-four floors.

"You can see my cubicle, and then we'll go up to the roof."

We walked hand in hand in silence past rows of desks, many empty now. We zigzagged around the temporary barriers. Just about in the center, we stopped in front of one that read: DOUGLAS TAYLOR and TRAVIS EDGINGTON.

He waved his arm toward his desk. "Not very exciting." He had one picture of us at graduation pinned to the cubicle above his laptop. I sat down at his desk.

A guy ducked his head into the cubicle. "There you are, mate. I thought you'd jumped. But this must be Amanda. Nice to meet you." He held out his hand to me, and I shook it. "Wow, so it's true you're not gay. All the girls will be crushed."

"Amanda, this is my cubemate, Travis."

"So, are you guys headed up to the party? The piranhas are already circling. Maybe one of them will need consoling after realizing her loss to Amanda."

Doug slapped his hand on Travis's shoulder. "Maybe you'll get lucky, but I think that's enough. You're going to make Amanda nervous."

"Excuse me, but you have nothing to worry about. Doug here is the pinnacle of virtue, much to the dismay of our female colleagues."

"Thanks." I looked to Doug, and he motioned for me to follow Travis. He didn't stop talking the whole elevator ride. I wondered if he always talked that much. Doug had never mentioned it, so I didn't think so.

The elevators opened into a glass-enclosed room. Outside, there was a sidewalk lined grass area, with a sand volleyball court in the middle. There were a few people playing on the court, and the rest seem to be huddled around a bar.

"I'm going to get another drink." Travis motioned to the bar as we exited the elevator.

"Nice to meet you," I said.

He winked at me. "I'll see you again." He tipped his drink at Doug.

"Does he always talk that much?"

"Only when he's drinking." We followed behind Travis to the crowd gathered near the bar. "This is really impressive, isn't it?" I nodded in agreement. "I'm really happy you're here." He kissed me, but we were interrupted. *Torture, pure torture*, I thought.

"Hey Doug, who you got there?" came a male voice.

Doug introduced me to his colleagues who were gathered around. I tried really hard to focus on their names, but it had been a long day and they all looked similar. Doug ordered a Diet Coke for me. I realized I was probably the only under aged person there. Most of the others seemed even older than Doug. He'd said many of them already had their MBAs. If Doug didn't get the position he wanted this summer, he planned on getting his MBA. He'd already been accepted at Wharton in Philadelphia, Carnegie Mellon in Pittsburgh, and at Stanford.

We moved over to the crowd gathered around the food area for more introductions. I instantly recognized the women Travis had spoken of. They were both tall, nicely built, and oozed confidence. They were Zoey, minus the crazy part, or so I hoped. Doug introduced me to the manager of the group, Brad, and his wife, Courtney. They both seemed very nice. Next he introduced me to the Zoey twins, Monica and Alexis. They smiled and shook my hand, nodding their heads, but said nothing.

Conversation topics varied from recapping the day's world markets, to guessing what the trend might be for the following week, to plans for the weekend, which generally seemed to be lots of studying mixed in with a short trip to a nearby sightseeing destination. I hoped I wouldn't put Doug too far behind.

He really wanted to stay on top in this program. I figured I could study my Japanese while he studied his banking.

To my delight, I found I was able to keep up with and have some intelligent comments on whatever conversation that was presented to me. I was grateful for my dad's daily recap of the economic situation, and that I'd really paid attention each evening when Doug told me about what they'd been doing. Finally my soda caught up with me, and I had to excuse myself to the restroom. I ended up walking there behind Courtney, the manager's wife, who slowed down to talk to me.

As we entered the restroom, the sound of heels on the hard floor was hard to ignore. Monica and Alexis stood in front of the mirror talking. I used the bathroom and went to wash my hands. As I reached the lavatory, they switched to speaking in Japanese.

"Do you believe she's really his girlfriend?" one asked.

"She barely looks sixteen. She can't be a day over eighteen."

"She must do something for him."

"Wish I knew what it was." The other smiled and laughed, finishing the application of her lipstick.

I swallowed hard and caught Courtney's eye. Did she know Japanese?

They left the restroom, and Courtney and I walked out just after them. She leaned into me. "Doug tells me you're sort of a language buff. Which ones do you know?"

"The usual." I shrugged, not wanting to brag. "I've taken up Japanese most recently." My hunch had been right, she knew Japanese and understood perfectly the Zoey twins' conversation.

"Well, I'll leave this ball in your court then." She winked at me.

We rejoined the group and someone suggested playing volleyball. Not the outcome I'd hoped for, but at least it was a sand court.

"You up for this?" Doug whispered to me as we walked.

Suddenly Monica and Alexis were right behind us. "Hey, can we get in on this?"

Doug turned to them and smiled. "Sure." Travis, Monica, Alexis, and a guy I couldn't remember the name of formed a team opposite Brad, Courtney, Doug, and me.

"Perfect stage," Courtney whispered to me as she passed me the ball to serve. "Those girls have been bugging me for weeks. They deserve to be moved down a notch."

Really? I thought to myself. Are we in fourth grade again? From across the court I heard them speaking, again in Japanese.

"Hey," Brad called, pointing at them. "English please, for our guests." He motioned to me.

It was the perfect setup. I couldn't have asked for a better one. I took a deep breath in and cast my voice so that I would be sure everyone on the court would hear.

"It's okay if they speak in Japanese. I have only been working for four weeks, but already understand a lot." I said trying to copy the pronunciation from the podcasts perfectly. Judging by their blank stares first at me then each other, I had achieved the goal of letting them know I'd understood what they said in the restroom. Just as I finished my sentence, I served the ball over the net. It landed on the ground right between them. Amanda, I and Zoey twins, 0.

As we rotated, Doug tapped me on the arm. "You know Japanese now?"

"Can't be unprepared to visit my man in Japan," I whispered back in Japanese.

"You're amazing." He kissed me on the cheek.

After the game, we needed to leave to meet my parents. Courtney congratulated me on my win with the Zoey twins as we said good-bye.

As soon as we were alone in the elevator, Doug planted a long slow kiss on my lips. "I am so happy to see you. You're amazing. How did you learn that much so fast? Did you understand what they were saying or just know it was Japanese?"

I came clean on the whole Zoey twin story, leaving out that I thought of them as the Zoey twins. "It was pretty grade school, but Courtney seemed happy."

"Believe me, that's their level. How such intelligent people can act so immature I have no clue."

We walked to the hotel and met my parents in the lobby. Dad had a reservation for dinner, so we caught a cab to the restaurant. I was worried about how the conversation would flow. Dad ordered champagne for all of us. After drinks, the discussion came easier. As dinner ended, I dreaded returning to the hotel with my parents. It would be beyond uncomfortable for me to go back to Doug's apartment with him, so I didn't even mention it. Besides, the next day my parents were driving up to Napa, so Doug and I would have the whole day alone.

In the morning my parents dropped me at Doug's apartment. He'd rented a room on the top floor of a row house. As we

strolled up the walk to the apartment, we were stopped short by
a loud coughing sound.

"Craig, hi," Doug began as a man leaned out the window.

He waved and pointed to me. "This must be Amanda."

"Yes, hi." I waved back.

Doug pointed between me and Craig. "Craig, Amanda, Craig,
my landlord."

He hesitated, looking back inside and out at us again. "Madison is really into figuring out what girlfriends are and what
married people do. Maybe Amanda could just be a friend." I remembered that Madison was their five-year-old daughter who'd
become very fond of Doug.

"Of course," Doug told him. "Just one friend—" he dropped
my hand "—visiting another."

"That should work. You guys have a good day."

"You too." Doug waved at him and took my hand again.
Upstairs, the door had barely shut when his lips found mine. I
dropped my bag near the door as he picked me up and spun me
around. I curled my legs around his waist, answering his insistent
kiss with my own. His hands raked through my hair and down
my back as he carried me through the apartment. It was small,
and we didn't go far before he lowered me down on the bed.

"God," he said, kissing my neck. "I thought we'd never be
alone. Last night was pure torture."

I held his face between my two hands and looked directly in
his eyes. I hadn't imagined the last nine months. What we had
was special, and this was where I belonged. He kissed me more
insistently, and we became seamlessly intertwined. I couldn't

touch him enough or be close enough to him. I peeled his shirt up from his torso and over his head. He smiled, pressing himself to me as I became lost in him.

This is perfect, I thought as we lay stretched out beside each other, him stroking my hair while I traced circles on his chest. "What do you want to do? We probably shouldn't stay in bed all day."

"Probably not." I stood, grabbed the sheet from him, wrapped it around myself, and padded across the room. Opening the closet, I slipped one of his shirts off a hanger and put it on.

"Did you have breakfast?"

"Nope."

He got up and pulled on his jeans. "Me either. He started some coffee and got some eggs from the fridge. "So what do you want to do?"

"What do you usually do?'

"Run, laundry, study. My life is quite mundane really."

"Sounds fine with me." I shrugged. I didn't care what we did as long as we were together.

"They say the fog might lift this afternoon, so maybe we could go to the park for a picnic."

"I like picnics."

"I know." He kissed my forehead.

I excused myself to use the bathroom, and then we dressed for running. After breakfast we walked down the stairs to the street for our run.

I heard a high-pitched squeal come from inside the house. "Doug!" The door flew open and a girl, of about five, bounded up to us. Doug dropped my hand, bent down, and scooped her up.

"*Hola. Buenos días.*"

"*Buenos días,*" she replied back.

"*Cómo estás?*"

She hesitated. "Daddy wouldn't let me come up for eggs." She stuck out her lower lip.

"Sorry, I have a friend visiting today."

"That's what Daddy said." She peered around him to look at me.

"He turned to face me, lowering her to the ground. This is Amanda. She came to visit from Chicago."

"Your friend?"

"Yes."

"Hi, Madison." I bent down and held my hand out to her. She took a step toward me and shook my hand. Her eyes traced from my feet to my head.

"You have princess hair, dark like Belle's. But your eyes are green like Rapunzel, and your skin is white like Snow White." She reached out and touched my hair. "It's soft."

"Thank you. You have pretty hair, too."

"Mommy won't let me have princess hair."

"It's a lot of work to wash and brush."

"She says when I'm eight I can have princess hair."

"Eight is a good age."

Just then Craig came over from plant bed he'd been weeding in. "Did you meet Amanda, Madison?"

"Yes, she's Doug's friend from Chicago." She looked up at Doug. "Can I come up later to learn more Spanish?"

"Yes, later. Amanda speaks Spanish, so you can talk to her too."

"Okay." She shrugged and skipped away.

On the sidewalk, we stretched and started to run. The hills in San Francisco were challenging, and I was breathing hard after just one mile. I was determined to make it the three miles, though, and did it at a much slower pace than I was used to. The weathermen had been right, and the fog started lifting as we walked back to Doug's apartment.

"I know it's not very fun, but I'm on my last pair of shorts. I have to do laundry."

"I don't care what we do. I just love being with you."

Back at his house, we grabbed his clothes and walked to the laundry mat. There weren't many people there, so we were able to get two washers at once. He dropped off his work shirts and slacks to be dry-cleaned, and we were finished with that task in just over an hour. Afterward, we picked up sandwiches at the market and headed to the park. Finishing the sandwiches, he studied and I lay with my head on his chest. Every once in a while, he would comment to me about his reading and I would nod. He caught me one time.

"I just said this president was the best president ever."

"Oh, well obviously not."

"Are you bored?"

"No, I'm perfectly content." And I was. I lay there thinking that this was my real life, where I belonged. My life in Champaign was just a bad dream. One I had to get through six more weeks of.

It got chilly in the evening, and we walked back to his apartment. On the way, we stopped at the local mart to get food for dinner. Not long after being at his apartment, we heard a knock at the door. I opened the door.

"I'm sorry," a young woman started. "Madison has this habit." Madison peaked around the woman's legs.

"It's fine, I told you, she's a princess and princesses are always nice," Madison said.

"I tried to reel her in," she said to me apologetically.

"No worries," I said.

Doug motioned Madison in.

"You can help us with dinner," I said.

"My mom likes it when I'm gone when she's making dinner so she can concentrate better," Madison said.

"My mom always used to tell me that, too."

She smiled at me and ran over to Doug.

"Hi, I'm Rebecca." The woman held her hand out to me.

"Hi, nice to meet you."

"You guys don't have to entertain her."

"It's fine. Amanda loves kids," Doug called from the kitchen.

"I'm making a simple dinner, so it won't be long," she said. "I'll come fetch Madison in a few minutes."

"No worries, whenever."

"Hey, we're having a barbecue tomorrow evening. You guys should come, if you're around."

"Thanks, but we're sightseeing with her parents."

After Madison left, we made dinner and sat on the floor in front of the bay window, watching the people go by.

He started tracing lines on my arm as we rested on the couch. "So, how long do we have before your parents get here?"

I retrieved my phone. "Ooh, they're just starting dinner. At least two hours."

"Perfect." He kissed me, stood, picked me up, and flung me over his shoulder. He crossed the room and dumped me on the bed. He lay down beside me, planting kisses one by one up my arm to my face. He walked his fingers down to the bottom of my shirt, lifting it up over my head.

Today was our only day alone and not a second of it had been wasted. As I lay nuzzled in his arms, my phone beeped. I picked it up.

"Half an hour. I should shower."

"Come here." He circled me in his arms. "I love you."

I could've listen to him say those words a hundred thousand times. "I love you, too." We kissed for a few more minutes before I had to pry myself away from him.

We spent the rest of the weekend with my parents. It wasn't as much fun as when it'd just been us, but we were together and that made me happy. Monday came too soon, and when I woke, all I could think of was not seeing him for six more weeks. I didn't want to waste my last few hours with him being sad, but it was hard to hide. My parents were nice enough to give us the afternoon alone. After a couple of hours in his apartment together, we walked to the park and played Frisbee, ate lunch, and napped on a blanket until it was time for me to go.

Chapter 12

The next day my courses at U of I began. I had tutoring sessions for eight hours, a half hour break to grab some dinner, and then three hours of lecture in the evening. I decided to get up early so I could run in the morning before work. I had to schedule my psychiatrist appointment during the day, but I fit it in between sessions. My mood was better at the beginning of the week, but by the end, I missed Doug like crazy. It was hard because I had no social time. My morning run was really the only thing I enjoyed.

On these runs, I'd fantasize about how it could've been if I stayed in San Francisco with Doug. I pictured us making breakfasts together, taking runs, and having picnics in a park on the weekends. I pictured coloring with Madison and teaching her Spanish. Yes, I was certifiable. But imagining how our days would've been, and how great our two weeks in August together would be, got me through.

On Friday evening after my class, all I wanted to do was sleep. I took a long hot shower and was drying my hair when the doorbell rang. My dad yelled up to me that Stephen and Mark were waiting. I dressed quickly and ran down the stairs, thinking I'd rather just crawl into bed.

"Hey guys, you could text, you know." I hugged each of them. "Are Zack and Bill coming too?"

"No, just us. Disappointed your boy Zack's not here?" Mark hit me on the butt.

"No, just trying to figure out if I had time to dry my hair."

"You should hurry." He pushed me toward the stairs. "We're supposed to meet Carter."

I motioned them up, and they sat on my bed while I dried my hair. "Since when are you and Carter friends?" I bumped Mark's leg while I ran the brush down the length of my hair, blowing it as I went.

"Since that weekend we all went out."

Stephen shrugged. "I'm just along for the ride." I ducked into the bathroom and finished my hair and makeup.

I wasn't really keen on Carter being added to our little party, but I appreciated the distraction. Mark didn't seem to notice my mood, which was way too heavy for a Friday night. But really what did I have to look forward to? The weekend spanned out like an abyss in front of me. Unstructured time just meant more time to think about being miserable. At least I had plenty of studying to do. Maybe I'd pick up some babysitting hours.

Stephen tapped me on the shoulder after we were settled at a table at the local pub. "So things not any better? Are you going to sulk all night?"

"Is it that obvious? I'm just tired. I signed up for two courses, which is good, but now I have twelve-hour days."

"That's rough."

"You probably work just as much."

"Yeah, look at these arms." He lifted his sleeve and flexed his bicep. I put my fingers on his arm, and they didn't even reach halfway round it."

"Wow, you got major buff. But where's your farmer's tan?" I joked with him.

He opened up his collar to show me the tan line from his tanks. "Sexy." I laughed.

He pushed me out of my seat and pointed at Mark. "I win. I got her to smile first."

Somehow I got roped into being designated driver for this party Carter and Mark wanted to go to. Even Stephen was drinking, which was uncharacteristic of him, or so I thought. I realized I hadn't ever been to a party with him, not a real party off school grounds. He wasn't drunk by any account, but he had a pretty good buzz going. Carter and Mark on the other hand were drunk, very drunk. By the end of the party, it was two in the morning. I'd missed my talk with Doug, and I just wanted to climb into my warm bed.

Mark's house was the closest, so I took him and Stephen there first. It was late, and Stephen wasn't especially keen on me driving Carter across town alone. At least the drive seemed to sober him a bit. When we got to his house, he wanted to talk. I humored him for a while. When I stood to leave, he grabbed my arm. "Hey, just stay here, we have an extra room, or I have a king bed."

I placed his hand back on his chair. "Goodnight, Carter." I waved his keys at him.

"Seriously, I have to come get my car?"

When I got home, Dad was waiting up for me. "It's after two. You could have texted or something."

It hadn't even occurred to me. "Oh, sorry."

"We'll talk tomorrow."

I said him goodnight to him, washed my face, and brushed my teeth, nearly asleep before I got in bed.

In the morning, Marissa shook me awake. "Hey, head's up. Dad's coming."

I shot out of bed, grabbing my phone to check the time. Ten, another hour of sleep would've been nice. He wasn't happy I'd gotten in so late without calling or with Carter's car in driveway.

I was done fighting with him. He was mad. I got it. But, I couldn't do anything right anyway.

The weeks started to tick away. My tutoring sessions and organic chemistry and physics kept me distracted from missing Doug. I got on the scale each week, my weight holding steady, and went to the psychiatrist appointments as Dad demanded.

I got nothing out of the meetings. He'd ask a question, and I'd answer. Then he'd wait. When I said nothing, he'd ask another question. It was uncomfortable enough for me to start relaying to him my year and why my parents felt I needed to be there. It didn't really change anything. I didn't like where I was in my life. There wasn't much to do about it except wait for it to change. August sixteenth, the day I would meet Doug in Chicago, could not come soon enough.

Doug got his job offer two weeks before the end of his internship. They wanted him in a position in Japan. It was an entry-level analyzer's position, but he had expected that, no one started out in management.

"I am so excited for you!" I said into the phone.

"Are you sure you think I should take it?"

In my mind there wasn't a decision to be made. It was his dream job. "What? Are you kidding? Of course you should take it!"

"I have forty-eight hours, so we could think about it."

"Is it not a good position?"

"Well..." He was hedging, and I could hear it in his voice.

"What? It's what you worked for. You earned it. It's what you've wanted for a whole year."

"What about us?"

"What do you mean? We talked about this already. You go to Japan, I go back to school, you come back at Christmas, and I visit you for spring break."

"I know that's what we talked about. But I really miss being with you..." Again with the hedging. "Are you really okay with this? Will you really be okay?"

I looked straight into his eyes the best I could on a webcam. "I love you, and I'll miss you, but I will be fine. Where is this coming from anyway?"

"I just know how hard this summer has been."

"Yeah, I'm sorry about that, but it wasn't you. It was my parents and being home."

"Your dad thinks it's just me. He thinks you'd be happy if you didn't miss me, if you would move on." There it was, the bombshell. My dad.

"When did you talk to my dad?'

"He called yesterday."

I paused the call and hurled a pillow from my bed across the room. Taking a breath, I looked back into the camera and restarted the connection. "Doug, I love you. I'm so happy that you have this opportunity I can't even put it into words. I wouldn't dream of taking that away from you. Do you think we should break up? I mean, is this not worth it to you?"

"Oh my God, Amanda, please never think that. You are the most important thing in the world to me, and that's why I'm asking this. I want there to be an us next year, and the year after that. I could always get an MBA at the University of Chicago or take a job with a bank there."

My whole body melted. "I love you. I'm not going anywhere Doug."

"I know and that could be a problem."

"It would be a problem if I felt like I was the reason you didn't take your dream job. I can't live with that. I knew what I was getting myself into from the beginning. I chose you because of who you are, and this is part of it."

"Okay, well, I want you to think about it, and we can talk again tomorrow."

"Okay, fine. But I'm not changing my mind."

"Just promise me you'll think about it, and really imagine what the rest of your college experience will look like."

It was the closest we'd come to a fight since last fall. But it felt like the opposite of how a fight would make someone feel. Instead of creating a problem, it had solidified our relationship in my mind. We had the same goal: staying together. Whatever my dad had said to Doug, it seemed to backfire. The more Dad tried to pry Doug and me apart, the closer we got. And I wasn't just trying to be a rebellious teen. When push came to shove, I loved Doug. Maybe it wasn't reasonable, but when was love ever reasonable?

I smiled to myself when my phone played his ringtone at seven the next morning. "Checking to see if I'm still in?" I asked right off.

"Something like that."

"I'm still in." I could see him relax.

"Okay, well, I have a meeting with my boss at ten, so I'll call you just before then." That was noon our time and perfect for my lunch break.

"I'm not changing my mind."

"I love you."

"I love you, too."

I ended the call and took the stairs two at a time. In the kitchen, I got some coffee and grabbed a muffin. As I was headed back upstairs for a shower, Mom came into the room.

"You're humming. Haven't heard you hum in a while."

"I'm happy today. Doug got the job in Japan."

"Wow, well, how do you feel about that?"

"Are you kidding? It's great! I'm so happy for him."

"But what about you? Are you okay staying behind? Being away from him? Okay that he didn't choose to stay with you? Will you be happy?"

I didn't have time to sling at her all the thoughts that went through my head. What about me? What about her and dad? Did she regret leaving school and marrying him, was that it? Was that why she never sided with me on this? But if she did, would she have ever admitted it? Could any parent admit to their children that they wished they'd chosen a different path? I doubted it. And she was happy, right? With dad? With Us? She'd always seemed to be.

It wasn't like I was going to leave Northwestern. I loved it. At least I loved my language, biology, and history courses. The chemistry I just had to trudge through. And I had a scholarship. I wasn't about to give that up. I couldn't afford to.

I looked her straight in her green eyes. "I love him. I knew from the beginning that he wanted to go overseas. I'm happy for him. It's part of who he is, and I wouldn't ask him to change."

"Okay, sweetie. You know I just want you to be happy." She crossed the room and wrapped her arms around me. I stiffened at her touch, and she backed away.

"It breaks my heart to see you this way."

I squinted my eyes, trying to decide how to react. I hated that I was angry with her. But I didn't trust her. I didn't trust that she just loved me and wanted to support me. Each of our interactions seemed laced with judgment.

She picked up a towel and folded it, setting it on the counter. "I'm not going to say that all of your dad's tactics are the best route. But I see you spiraling. As parents, we just can't sit back and watch you harm yourself. We had to do something to stop your cycle."

She picked up the towel and set it down again. "I love you."

"I love you, too," I forced and left.

I called Doug just before ten California time. I was almost giddy, being truly happy for him. Maybe I was just glad that this phase of our lives, waiting for a definite plan, was over. Whatever the reason, I was happy. This time he didn't hesitate or ask me again.

"Okay, let's do it," he said. The let's in the sentence was probably the second best word I'd ever heard.

"I love you. Text me after your meeting."

That week the psychiatrist suggested a joint session with my parents. It made sense because my only issues were with them. I only agreed to include them because he knew Dad. Even with doctor-patient confidentiality, I didn't trust that the doctor wasn't sharing our sessions with my dad.

It was an intense week with two finals, the last tutoring sessions with clients, and planning for the move to my apartment. The last thing I wanted to do was sit in a room with my parents. My plan for resolution with them was giving them the receipts for the psychiatrist visits, showing them my weight, and walking out the door. I didn't feel there was anything left to say.

The session was even worse than I could have imagined. I thought Dad would at least pretend to be open-minded for Dr. Medders, but he didn't hold anything back. He wasn't happy that I was moving back to Evanston a month before school started. He thought I was giving up a month's wages, and it was totally inappropriate for me to spend those weeks with Doug. Yes, we'd gone past pretending that we wouldn't be cohabitating, as Mom called it.

He didn't like the courses I was taking. I'd rearranged my schedule to include the second organic chemistry, inorganic chemistry, second physics, last Chinese literature course, Middle Eastern studies, and Japanese II. I'd hated the organic chemistry course at U of I but decided to give it another chance at Northwestern. CIA or FBI jobs were really good, and I did have the best shot at those agencies with a chemistry background. Thankfully, I'd tested out of Japanese I since that would've been a big waste of time and money. All the classes he thought I should have were there, but now I was being too ambitious.

Mom didn't like that I wasn't spending my birthday at home. She believed I wasn't taking care of myself and eating healthy. I listened and cried. It hurt beyond words to hear them pick apart my life and my passions. I was doing everything they wanted me to do, and they still didn't approve.

My parents took forty-five minutes going through their opinion of my mental state, but it really all traced back to Doug. In their eyes, Doug was the source of all my problems. At quarter till, Dr. Medders spoke for the first time. "Amanda is an adult."

Dad shifted in his chair, rubbing his hands down his legs to his knees. "She is an adult but an adult child. We as parents have an obligation to help our children choose good paths and keep them from harming themselves."

Dr. Medders nodded his head politely at Dad. "Yes, I hear your concerns, Mr. Avery." He turned to me. "Do you mind me giving your parents my assessment of our talks together?"

I hadn't told him anything my parents didn't know. "No." I folded my arms across my chest.

"As I was saying, Amanda is of legal age. I don't believe she's depressed. Certainly she's not happy with her current situation, but we all know that's temporary. Her weight is about ten percent below normal. But she has a small frame, and I believe, if my memory serves me correctly, her current weight is only five pounds below her top weight."

Dad straightened his back. The psychiatrist held his hand up. "Amanda, you were crying. Can you tell us how you're feeling about your parents' concerns?"

Was he kidding? I took a deep breath and tried to think about moving towards a better relationship with them. "I love them."

The psychiatrist raised his hand to stop me. "Amanda, please talk to them." He pointed to my parents.

I didn't want to, but I looked at them as he instructed. "I love you, but I can't give you anything else. I'm eating three meals a day. I'm taking the courses you think I need, and I'm paying for my apartment. I don't like being with you because you constantly tell me I'm doing everything wrong."

Mom was in tears, but Dad had his arms folded over his chest.

We were a broken unit. But there seemed to be no solution.

Chapter 13

Mom invited Tia and Ed up for the weekend before my birthday and made my favorite spinach lasagna. Dad wouldn't let her buy anything for the apartment, so they got me gift cards from my favorite clothing store. That was fine because I didn't really need that much since Lila had already stocked the kitchen and gotten furniture with her Dad's funds. I had my futon from my dorm to sleep on and was taking hangers for most of my clothes. Doug was loaning me a desk and small chest.

It was Marissa's last weekend at home too. Mom and I were driving her up to UNI on Monday. I didn't really care about celebrating my birthday with my family and tried to push the spotlight off myself as much as possible. It wasn't that hard since the house was in such a state of flux with both of us packing.

What I cared about was Doug being back from California and being free of Champaign and my parents. Lila had a huge party planned at our apartment for my birthday anyway. Big parties weren't really my thing, but Lila loved them. She'd invited all our friends, and I was looking forward to seeing everyone.

Before Dad left Sunday, he asked Mom and me to join him in his office. He leaned against the desk, drumming his fingers. "You've met all of our requirements, and we are allowing you to return to Evanston."

Anger boiled through my veins, but I held my tongue. This is what I'd worked for, to be officially released from this house. He lifted the scale from behind his desk and sat it in front of me. The read-out indicated ninety point two.

He held up the scale. "I'm going to bring this up when we come up for the games." My hands automatically went to my hips. He pointed his finger at me. "Your weight will stay at or above ninety, or we will bring you home."

I threw up my hands. "Didn't you hear Dr. Medders? I am healthy and not depressed. It's only you and Mom who are making things bad for me. We weigh in for rowing anyway. They'd kick me off the team if I didn't stay at a good weight. Why did you have to ruin this weekend? I'm leaving Thursday morning, and I won't see you again till September."

He stood up, crossing his arms over his chest. "I'm just making things clear."

"Thank you for that." Wow, the man was taking tough love to a whole new level. I stormed out of the office and up to my room. Mom didn't even try to get me to come down to say good-bye to him.

It was fun driving up to school with Marissa and helping her move in. I was sad that I hadn't spent more time with her. I'd lived right beside her all summer and could only count on one hand the number of times we'd hung out. Between our jobs and my course work, there was little time. But I knew my home avoidance strategy was mainly to blame.

When we got home from dropping Marissa off, it was just Mom and me in the house. I was glad we'd stayed up there two days so we only had one night together. Mainly I wished we could go back to being like we were before. A year ago, I would have named one of my favorite things as snuggling on the couch, watching a movie with Mom. Now, I could hardly be in the same room with her. Our relationship was so different from what it used to be, so far from what I would've expected.

That night I went through my room again, making sure I didn't leave anything behind. I had five boxes for pictures, books, movies, clothes, linens, and toiletries. Doug had my futon at his mom's, and we were going to use Zack's SUV to take it, the dresser, and desk to my apartment.

I was so excited I could barely sleep. As soon as it was light out, I was up. With nothing else to do than kill time, I went for a run. Mom was in the kitchen when I returned, dressed for work. She stood. "I have to get to work. Have a safe drive. Text me when you get there so I'll know you made it okay."

She spoke as if this were just another good-bye, one of many too come. Perhaps she hadn't been in my room, hadn't noticed that I packed all my clothes. Not just ones for the season, but all of them, except a couple of old formal dresses. I cleaned out my dresser, desk, and closet. Everything that I wanted to keep was packed in the car. This good-bye was more to me. This good-bye was my break from them—me becoming a separate entity with a separate household.

I had no clue what to say to her. "I'll text you when I get to the airport."

She wrung her hands. "We love you."

"I know Mom. I love you, too."

She stepped forward, arms open, but I didn't move. Then she put each of her hands on my shoulders but didn't speak. She turned and retrieved her bag from the table and walked toward the garage.

Wow, that was weird. I shook off the funky energy as I jogged up the steps. I had an hour before I needed to leave, so I ducked in the shower. I dressed and finished packing the car. Doug called me from the airport in San Francisco as I started the drive. It was an easy route I'd taken a hundred times, so the time passed quickly.

Lila and I talked as I drove. We planned out the weekend, and she detailed my party plans. I wasn't moving in till Saturday, so Doug and I could spend my birthday alone. After I picked him up from the airport, we were meeting his Mom, Gary, and Michael for dinner.

At the airport, I parked in the deck and nearly skipped up to the terminal. I bought some flowers and checked his flight on the board. Arrived, the board indicated. It wasn't five minutes until I saw him walking towards me with a huge smile on his face. He ran the last couple of feet, taking one of my hands in his and sliding his other hand around my neck. He kissed me and all the things that happened with my parents were forgotten. He was my home.

His phone buzzed, and he backed away, clearing his throat and answering the phone. I studied him, thinking I'd never forget his smile.

He dropped my hand and lifted a finger towards me. Turning around, he spoke only a few phrases into the phone. "Okay, we're good." We retrieved his bag, and I started to walk to the exit leading to the parking garage. He tugged me the other way. "Let's get some lunch. I'm starving."

I didn't care what we did, so I followed him up the escalator and to a bistro. Just inside, I spotted Dad. I stopped, dropping his hand.

He turned around. "What?"

"My dad is here."

He stooped down so that we were eye level. "Yeah, he wants to have a birthday lunch with you."

"My birthday's tomorrow. He called you?"

"I guess he didn't think you would agree to meet him."

"He was right."

"We don't have time for you to fill me in on what's going on. Let's just have lunch with the man. This is a good restaurant, and I'm starving. That wasn't a lie."

"Okay, but I don't like it."

I put on my best smile, walked into the restaurant, and greeted Dad. "Hi, this was a little unnecessary don't you think?"

"Hey, I just wanted to buy my girl a birthday lunch."

Okay, this was a complete one-eighty from Sunday.

We sat down and ordered. Dad had a flight, so he wasn't drinking, but Doug got a beer. I ordered a chicken salad, but my stomach churned just being near Dad. To my astonishment, he wasn't mean at all. He asked Doug about his job and me about my apartment. He was being the normal Dad I'd grown up with. It was almost nice, except I knew how he felt, how he disapproved of everything I was doing with my life.

As we left the restaurant, he gave me a hug. "Thanks for having lunch with me. Happy birthday, and we'll see you in September."

"Thanks." I half returned his hug.

He shook Doug's hand. "Best of luck. Don't be a stranger."

Doug's eyes cut to me and then back to Dad. "Wouldn't hear of it."

"Okay," my dad said, squeezing my shoulder. He turned and walked away. I wanted to believe that he was trying to be nice and mend our relationship, but it just didn't fit with the rest of the summer.

Doug's mom was at the condo when we got there. She was so excited to see him and gathered him into a hug right off. Like me, she'd only been out once to visit.

He showered and unpacked, and it wasn't long before we were intertwined with nothing between us. Being with Doug was complete contentment. I could have lain there with him the rest of my life. He got up, and I reached out, catching his arm and pulling him down to me.

"Hey, tomorrow we will do anything you want. Well, mostly." He rolled his eyes. "I do sort of have a birthday plan."

I sat up. "Do I get to know what it is?"

"No, it's a surprise. But now we should shower. Puerto Rican moms can get very mean."

"Got it." I jumped up, wrapped a sheet around me, and went to shower.

His mom had appetizers prepared in the kitchen. We talked, waiting for Gary and Michael to get there. After some drinks, we left for Mrs. Chen's. It was a great dinner and fun company and well after nine by the time we got back to his Mom's building.

In the lobby, I tugged on Doug's arm. "Can we go up to the roof? Even though it's not my birthday yet?"

"Course," he replied. We said goodnight to his family and took the elevator up to the top. When we got there, we walked hand in hand around the edge.

"So, I don't have your present yet. It's not ready."

"I don't need a present. I have two weeks with you."

"Well I got you one anyway."

"Do I get a clue?"

"Nope."

"Okay." I shrugged. Really he could have told me he got me wet spaghetti and I would've been happy.

Falling asleep beside him was pure bliss. The next morning, he woke me by stroking my back, kissing my neck, and waving coffee in front of my nose. I peeked up at the clock.

"Eight, why are we waking at eight? I thought it was my birthday." I rolled over, smiling in spite of my complaint. I took the coffee, sniffed it, and took a sip.

He kissed me. "Happy birthday, and eight because we have things to do."

His phone buzzed, and he picked it up. It was his mom. "Mom, why are you calling me from down the hall?" He ended the call and I got out of bed.

We walked down the hall to the kitchen. She had a wonderful breakfast laid out for us.

"*Feliz cumpleaños, querida*." She kissed each cheek and hugged me. "I have to get to work but have a wonderful day." She kissed me again and asked Doug to pick up some parts at the hardware store that morning. She looked at her watch. "They open at nine, so you can go first thing and then have the rest of the day to yourselves." She patted my cheek, retrieved her bags, and left to catch the train.

After breakfast, Doug insisted on showering and going to the hardware store right away. "You could take a long bath or something while I'm gone." I stuck my lips out in a pout, and he kissed me. I'd sort of made a pact with myself not to leave his side for the next two weeks.

"How should I dress after my bath, and do I need to do my hair and makeup for today?"

"Shorts, and don't worry about hair or makeup."

That gave me no clues. "Not just one hint?" I begged as he walked out the door on his errand.

"Nope." He ran back and kissed me.

It was an hour before he returned, and I'd showered, dressed, and was answering birthday texts when he got back.

As soon as I heard the door open, I jumped up to meet him.

"Hi, do I get to know the plan yet?"

He opened one of the bags he was carrying and took out a hat. He put it on my head. "Yes, I'm taking you sailing."

"Like on a sailboat."

He laughed, took out another hat, and put it on his own head. "Yes, you do sail on a sailboat."

"Where?"

He headed towards the kitchen, and I followed him like a puppy. "On the lake. There are two bags in my closet if you could go get them."

I ran to his room and found the bags as instructed. I set them on the counter in front of him. He pulled a picnic basket from the cabinet below. "Our lunch."

"Wow, can I open my bag?"

He nodded. Inside I found a bathing suit, cover up, towel, sunglasses, sunblock, and lip balm.

"Where's the boat? Who's taking us?"

"What do you mean? It's just us. I'm the captain."

"Really? You can sail?"

"Are you kidding? I've taken lessons since I was six."

"Okay, make that two things I learned about you in the past twelve hours."

"What was the other?"

"That you know plumbing parts."

"I am a guy with a single mom, or used-to-be single mom."

"So when's this happening?"

"Now."

"Really?" Part of me was so excited because it sounded so amazing, the rest of me was nervous. "And you're sure you remember how to sail? Because I haven't known you to sail since we met."

"It's like riding a bike. We've owned a boat forever. Are you nervous? I would never do anything dangerous. Besides, you weren't anxious about rowing."

I tapped my hat against my leg. "We were on a river with banks nearby."

By noon, we were properly attired and had the cooler, picnic basket, and rest of the equipment at the marina. It was a beautiful day, sunny and warm with just a slight breeze and no storms forecasted.

The boat was big, which, in my mind could be good and bad. On one hand, I figured it was less likely to turn over, but on the other, it seemed that it may be harder to maneuver.

I tapped my finger on the railing as I sat and waited for him to get all the sails right. As he worked, he reviewed what he was doing and why. Once he finished, his eyes landed on my face. "You're nervous. You don't trust me?"

"No, I trust you. I just don't trust the elements." I pointed at the water and sky.

"It's not too windy, just windy enough, and there's not a cloud in the sky. It's going to be awesome."

"Okay, let's do it then," I said a little more confidently than I felt.

He kissed me. "Off we go."

He hadn't lied. He was a good sailor and a good teacher. It wasn't hard, except I could never remember my left from my right. Starboard and port were lost on me. Otherwise, I was comfortable on the boat in no time.

It was a hot day, and there was a mild breeze, perfect weather. We'd worn our suits, and we lay in the sun just soaking in the day. We talked about my apartment, courses, and all his plans for the move to Japan.

"Did you go to the hardware store?"

"No, it was all just an excuse to get out of the house and get some last minute items."

"I love you." I sat up and kissed him. The kisses lasted until we got a honk from a passing boat.

"How long do we have the boat?" I asked.

"All day."

"All day? Really?"

"We can stay out here as long as you want." I smiled, and he kissed me again. I didn't want this day to ever end. We lay in the sun till my stomach grumbled, and he anchored the boat so we could eat lunch.

After lunch, we sailed to Evanston and anchored just off the Northwestern campus. I was lying nestled in his arms, almost asleep, when he roused me with a kiss on my forehead. He sat up and took my hands in his. He pushed back a strand of hair that had blown in my face and kissed me on the lips. "I love you."

"I love you, too." I placed my hands on each side of his face. It was what I'd missed most when he was away, and what I'd miss most when he was gone again—his face, his amazing sweet face.

"If you'd told me a year or even eight months ago that I'd be happy, I wouldn't have believed it." He took my hands into his, and I kept my eyes glued on his eyes. "It's because of you."

"You have a lot of things to be happy about."

His smile was infectious. "This job, although exciting, wouldn't make me happy. Maybe I would've been happy enough, but knowing you, loving you, being with you, it's the best thing that's ever happened to me."

Tears began to pool in my eyes, and he wiped away one that escaped. He dropped his gaze and cleared his throat. He let go of one hand and moved his hand to his pocket.

"This isn't your birthday present. As I said yesterday, it isn't ready yet." He took a box from his pocket and looked at me. "I love you. I want you to have something that symbolizes our bond. So, I have this ring that I hope you'll want to wear."

He opened the box and held it up so I could see inside. In the middle of the white velvet sat the most beautiful ring I had ever seen, a green amethyst flanked by two blue sapphires set on a brushed silver band.

"It's beautiful." I was so stunned I couldn't form any other words. It was such a sweet and perfect gesture, and all I could think was that I loved this person more than anything.

"So, do you want to take it?" He held the ring up to me.

I realized I hadn't answered his question. I nodded. "I love you and I'd love to wear it. It's beautiful."

He laughed. "Yes, you said that."

My hands were shaking as I took the ring from him and slid it on the ring finger of my right hand. It was a perfect fit.

"It looks good on you. Do you think your dad will freak out?"

"I am beyond caring what my dad thinks. I love you, and nothing is going to change that."

He kissed me. "Good, because I feel the same way."

All I could do was stare at the ring or at him for the rest of the afternoon. After we returned the boat we checked into a suite at a hotel downtown. He'd even already packed suitcases for us. We had sushi at a restaurant on the lakefront and soaked in the hot tub in the suite afterwards. It couldn't have been a more perfect day.

He held my hand up, and ran his finger over my ring as we sat in the bubbly water. "So, what are you going to tell your parents about the ring?"

"It doesn't change anything." I shrugged and kissed him.

"I think you're going to get a lot of push back."

"I told you. What they think doesn't matter to me, you do."

"You should at least return their calls from earlier."

"I talked to Marissa this morning, but fine." I stood up, wrapped a towel around myself and retrieved my phone from the desk.

I phoned Dad and left a message and then dialed our home number. "Amanda," Mom answered on the first ring, "happy birthday, did you have a fun day?"

I described my day with Doug omitting the ring story and that we were staying a night in a suite. Afterwards, I called Tia and recited the same story. Slipping back into the hot tub beside Doug, I kissed him on the cheek. "Happy now?"

"Why didn't you tell them about the ring?"

"I sent a picture to Marissa and Lila. I don't want any negativity on my birthday. Can you just allow me that?"

He smiled and kissed me. "Yes."

The next morning we slept in and had brunch at a restaurant beside the marina. We walked along the lakefront, watching the boats and the birds. I was exhausted by the time when we returned to his mom's apartment. We turned on a movie, and I was asleep within half an hour. The next thing I knew he was waking me.

"Hey sleeping beauty, it's five. My mom will be home soon, and we're meeting for dinner at seven.

"What dinner?"

"Bill, Zack, and a few more brothers. We're going to a club after, so you may want to wear something fun."

I crinkled my eyes at him. "Why didn't you tell me before?"

"Because I knew you wouldn't sleep." He kissed me on the forehead.

That much was true. If I knew I had to be all dolled up, I would've never taken that nap, and I'd need it if we were going to be out late.

"You really want me to come? I won't be offended if you want to just go with your friends."

"Yes, I want you to come." He handed me a cup of coffee and I finished half of it before showering. His mom came home and drooled over the ring. He looked happy and proud, and I realized he might want to show it to his friends.

We had a good night out with Zack, Bill, and a slew of other fraternity brothers and friends. Some of them had dates, and we had a big group on the dance floor when the band started. We were having so much fun dancing. It shocked us when the house lights came on at the end of the night.

The next morning, I slept in, and then we went for a long run. In the afternoon, Zack met us to pack my futon and boxes in his truck. We drove to my apartment, where Lila, Ross, and Mark help us unload and carry all my things inside. The apartment was in the same complex as Zack's. He'd be moving in a couple of weeks, but Kate had rented a place with Jeremy and some other friends a few units down. I loved that most of my friends would be as close as they'd been in the dorms.

Lila had planned a huge combination birthday-welcome back party for me that night. I was frustrated my boxes were sitting in my room waiting to be emptied, but I reminded myself that un-packing could wait. Stephen had come up for the weekend, and Kate, Jeremy, Zack, and Bill were there. She'd even invited some friends from the rowing team. I didn't love being the center of attention but after a toast, people stopped wishing me a happy birthday and the conversations drifted to other subjects.

Halfway through the evening, Mark found me. "Hey, how long has it been since you talked to your folks?"

I finished a swallow of beer and rolled my eyes at him. "I talked to them on my birthday."

"That was two days ago."

"How long do you go without talking to your parents?"

"Okay, point taken, but they're texting me."

"Fine." I pulled out my phone and sent texts to Mom and Dad. "Happy?" I held up my phone to him.

He shook his head and walked away. I knew my avoidance strategy wasn't a solution to the problems in our relationship but I couldn't bear their condemnation anymore. If I didn't hear it then I could pretend I was fine.

The next week Lila visited her family in Champaign, and Doug and I stayed at the apartment. It was fun to get my boxes unpacked and room put together. Lila had already decorated the living room and had the kitchen organized, so there wasn't much work to do. I reached out to prior tutoring clients and began lining up my schedule for fall. Doug had some bank and phone details to iron out for his move, so we kept busy.

On Wednesday morning, Doug announced my birthday present was ready. He drove me to a house in Evanston. In the front yard there was a pen that housed seven lab puppies. Three had blue ribbons around their necks and four had pink. A woman came out of the house and introduced herself.

Doug took my hand. "Happy birthday, you get first pick."

"Really!"

The breeder opened the gate, and we walked in. I kneeled down on the grass.

Doug squatted down beside me. "I did some research. Supposedly the males are generally more mellow, but it's up to you."

"If you play with them a while, you can get a better sense of their personalities," the breeder said.

I looked at Doug. "A boy then?"

"If you want."

"Yeah, a boy."

The breeder turned and yelled toward the house. "Madelyn."
A girl of about twelve walked out. They rounded up all the female puppies and took them inside.

One yellow lab, so light it was almost white, bounded over
to us right away. He sat on Doug's feet. A black lab approached
but backed away when I moved towards him. The third puppy,
another yellow one, sat a few feet away. He yawned and lay down
on his belly.

I picked up the puppy on Doug's feet. "This one." I held it
up to his face.

"Okay." He took the dog and studied it. "Looks good to me."
He handed it back to me. "Happy birthday."

"Thank you. This is the best present ever."

We finished the paperwork with the breeder and drove to a
pet store. There was a vet right there, so we were able to make an
appointment for the next day.

"What are you going to name him?" Doug asked as we got
back in the car.

"I think it should be our puppy, not just mine."

"Well, it's your present."

"What do you think?" I held the puppy up to him.

"Michi for Lake Michigan?"

I crinkled my nose. "Michi? It sounds like mushy!"

"Okay, better ideas?"

"Northie for Northwestern."

"That's way better."

"Northie it is." I held the dog up to my face. "Hi, Northie."

Back at my apartment, we got his collar on and the leash attached, and took him for a short walk. Afterwards, we got his crate assembled and his water and food bowls set up.

The doorbell rang and Zack bounded in, not even waiting for us to open the door. "I have to see this puppy. I've been waiting for weeks." I picked Northie up and handed him to Zack. "Okay, so you may see me a lot for the next week. This little guy is adorable."

Zack hung out with us, and we grilled some burgers out on the patio. Somehow we ended up with ten people at the apartment. It was a fun evening and I was glad to be making so many good memories of time with Doug.

That weekend, Doug's dad and brothers came in from New York, DC, and Milwaukee. We spent the weekend at his mom's with everyone. She made Doug promise that he'd see her every night till he left, so we did. We spent our nights and most of the day at my apartment with Northie, and then in the evening, we'd take him over to her apartment.

The Friday of his departure came way too fast, but I didn't feel like we'd wasted a single second of our time together. We slept at his mom's the night before so she could say goodbye to him in the morning. He had an early flight, so we were up at three thirty to get him to the airport in time.

I felt both sad and happy. Sad that we'd be apart, but happy he had the opportunity to do exactly what he wanted.

At the airport, he set his bags on the curb and hugged me. "Are you going to be okay?"

"Yes," I said with as much conviction as I could muster. I could feel the tears just behind my words.

He wiped a tear from his cheek. "I'm not."

I kissed him. "I love you, and I'll see you every day on my phone." I shook the device in front of him.

He'd bought us the newest and best video devices, including phones and tablets, and set up and synced them all. He'd spent hours making sure they all worked perfectly and I knew how to use them.

"I love you so much." He kissed me again.

"I love you, too."

He gave me a tight squeeze and backed away.

I blew a kiss at him, and he turned and walked into the terminal.

I watched till I couldn't see him anymore. Circling to the driver's side, I opened the door and slid into the seat. The car felt empty. I shook my head. *Of course it feels empty*, I told myself. I took a deep breath and started the car. Checking for oncoming traffic, I pushed the accelerator and pulled away from the curb. On the highway, my phone buzzed and I tapped the screen to answer the call.

"Hi there," came Doug's voice.

"Hi, did you make it past security?"

"Yes, it was fast. Now I just have to wait an hour for boarding."

"You can talk to me." We continued the conversation as I got off the highway and snaked through the streets to my apartment. I parked, and when I got to the door, I unlocked it quietly, trying not to wake anyone. Whispering to Doug, I went to my room and retrieved Northie from his kennel. He stretched and wagged his tail. I hooked his leash on his collar and quietly crossed back through the living room and out the door. As I walked, Doug and I chatted until he had to turn off his phone for takeoff.

"I love you." His voice cracked.

Tears welled up in my eyes. "I love you, too."

"Bye."

"Bye." I ended the call and squinted my eyes, cutting off the tears.

Northie tugged at the leash, and I bent down to pet him. We wound back to the apartment on the path, and I tiptoed to the pantry to fill his food and water bowls. I picked them up and took them into my room, and he followed. Setting the bowls down, I sat next to Northie, petting him while he ate. When he finished he laid beside me, his snout resting on his paws. Realizing I was exhausted, I shed my shoes and climbed onto my futon, covering myself with the comforter. Northie placed his paws on the mattress, trying to jump up. I put my hands around his middle and lifted him up beside me. I hadn't planned on letting him on the furniture, but that seemed like a pointless endeavor. I lay down, and Northie snuggled in beside me. His breathing evened out quickly, and I fell asleep.

I woke to the sound of pounding footsteps and slamming doors. Hearing voices, I got up, splashed some water on my face, brushed my teeth, and smoothed my hair into a ponytail. When I opened my bedroom door, Zack and Bill were lugging a keg through our living room.

"Where are you going with that?"

"To your deck." Zack said.

"What time is it?"

"Eleven." Bill pumped a single finger in the air twice.

I skipped ahead of them, sliding the glass door open so they could get through. There was already a trashcan half filled with ice water beside the railing. They lowered the keg into the ice.

"Why is there a keg at our apartment?"

Zack stood up from his task of screwing on the tap. "I have to move out of mine, so I can't have it trashed."

"Yes, you're moving today, remember boxes need to be packed and loaded into your truck. You guys can't start drinking now."

He bumped his fist on the railing. "Guess you haven't heard the good news yet."

"Really? What?"

He started dancing in a circle around the deck. "I got into my physical therapy program. I'm going to Northwestern Medical PT school."

My hands clapped to my mouth. "Oh wow! That's awesome." I lifted my palm, and he slapped his against mine.

"I know, right?"

"What about your apartment? Do you still have to move out?"

"Yeah, but hey listen, you won't believe my luck. One of the fraternity alums at the med school needs a roommate. He lives on other side of the complex. We'll still be neighbors."

Bill already had drained the foam from the keg and held two cups out to us. "Sweet, right?"

"Yeah, sweet." I took the drink. Bill drew another beer for himself and dodging the foam spilling over the edges, we downed the first sips. We held up our cups, and tapped them together. This was going to be a good year.

About the Author:

TRICIA COPELAND grew up and attended college in Georgia. After graduating from a master's program, she moved to Pennsylvania where she worked as a research scientist. After nine years, she and her husband moved their family—one daughter, twin boys, and dog Jake—to Colorado. Her first published title Is This Me? was released in May 2015. This manuscript, If I Could Fly, is the sequel and second book of the Being Me Series. If she's not on a trail, you can find Tricia at triciacopeland. com, on Facebook, Instagram, Google+, Pinterest, or Twitter.

Connect with Tricia and other readers!

Facebook: facebook.com/TriciaCopelandAuthor

Instagram: instagram.com/tricia_copeland_brzostowicz

Twitter: @tcbrzostowicz

Pinterest: pinterest.com/triciacopelanda

Website: triciacopeland.com

Is This Me?
Book One of the Being Me Series
by Tricia Copeland

Have you ever chosen a path that led you astray?

Amanda has no trouble choosing a college or picking a major. What she does have a problem with is what she would have least expected, a guy. Smart and sexy, Doug is focused on school responsibilities and post-graduation plans. Their paths intersect and Amanda must accept his help or risk losing her scholarship. Determined to maintain appearances, Amanda begins to lie to family and friends. The ease at which she repeatedly deceives those closest becomes disturbing and leaves her questioning: "Is this me?"

Can Amanda find her way out of her contrived world?

Available Now!